Rebecca

Volume 4

Another Dimension

A Novel by Stephen M Davis

AUTHORS NOTE

Once I'd finished volume 3, I genuinely believed Rebecca's story was complete. The thing was, after a few months, once I'd finished my angling book, her next chronicle started rumbling around in my head. Several times I put pen to paper, but for some reason wasn't ready to take the next step.

Then one day, Rebecca shouted so loud, I couldn't ignore her any longer. Opening up my laptop, unlike previous attempts, the words flowed naturally. Once more, I was hearing Rebecca's every word. I've said it before, I hear her voice so loud in my head when writing, I would recognise her in a crowded room.

So, we were once more off and running. I must say, while writing this volume, there were so many unexpected twists and turns, it often made the hairs stand up on my arms.

I hope this unexpected journey does the same for you.

Rebecca – Another Dimension – Volume 4 in the award-winning series. The Rebecca Chronicles, Winner of Book Talk Radio Club's "Book of the Year 2019."

Setting: Tomorrow

After Rebecca had affectively brought a stop to global warming, she was certain her jaunts into the past or future were over and her destiny fulfilled.

Now happily married and with two young girls, her focus was on family life.

Then one cold February morning, the disappearance of her six-year-old daughter, sent her life spiralling down a path of anguish.

Her intrepid, fearless nature immediately took over, suggesting she could journey back through time and prevent this painful event ever happening.

Stepping into the unknown, she soon established for every good time-fixer of her making, there was an evil antagonist.

She'd always felt her destiny was to prevent history taking a negative direction. By contrast, she learnt, her malicious counterparts had the opposite purpose.

Establishing a genetic link between a malevolent 12th-century time-twister and an unscrupulous gang in her own period, sets her on a mission back through the corridors of time.

Can she once more change the pages of history?

Copyright © Stephen M Davis 2021

The rights of Stephen M Davis to be identified as the author of this work has been asserted by him in accordance with the Copywrite, Design, and Patents act 1988

All rights reserved. No part of this publication may be reproduced, distributed, or transmitted in any form or by any means, including photocopying, recording, or other electronic or mechanical methods, without the prior written permission of the publisher, except in the case of brief quotations embodied in critical reviews and certain other noncommercial uses permitted by copyright law. For permission requests, contact the author via stevedauthor@gmail.com

First Published 2021

Typeset Stephen M Davis

Cover Design Stephen M Davis

Published by DMS Literary Publications

Author's website stevedauthor.com

Previous volumes:

Volume 1 in the series:
Rebecca & the Spiral Staircase

Setting: Modern Day

Free-spirited, fearless, and independent, Rebecca is far from your average twenty-first-century 15-year-old girl.
She'd rather leave her mobile phone indoors and being a dreamer, sit in the woods, sketching imaginary worlds.
When her parents move to a Gothic mansion in the north of England, she sets off exploring their 26-acres.
On one of these jaunts, she finds a Victorian key that opens the door to a ramshackle summerhouse.
Inside, she finds an old spiral staircase, which is the start of her adventures through time.
Each door leading from the staircase takes her back to a different point in the history of the old house.
Join Rebecca as she uncovers the secrets beyond the staircase. She may help change the way you see the world around you.

Volume 2 in the series:
Rebecca – A Way Back

Setting – Modern Day

Rebecca is a little older now, and after her first year at University, common sense rears its ugly head a little too often for her liking.

She finds herself applying rational thinking to all that life offers, and this includes her previous meetings with Meredith and the information within the three boxes.

What university could not teach her was how to prepare herself for what was about to happen.

Again, all balanced thinking was going to tumble into a world beyond common sense.

Volume 3 in the series:
Rebecca – Beyond all Reason

Setting – 2014

Follow Rebecca as she travels into the future and witnesses our planet devoid of human life.

She learns that mankind has been wiped out by its own relentless destruction of the environment.

Mother Nature though is thriving, albeit without mankind.

Rebecca now faces an epic voyage of discovery, which takes her right back to the "cradle of civilisation" where her story unfolds.

On her journey through the ages, she meets other time travellers of her making.

All though have failed to stop the unrelenting greed-clock from derailing humanity.

It now falls to Rebecca.

Also available

Rebecca's Book of Fairies, Pixies, Elves & other Amazing Things

This novel is an illustrated storybook. A full colour chronicle, which is available in paperback and EBook versions.

This book takes a tactile look at Rebecca world of Fairies, Pixies, and Elves.

All books are available through Amazon.co.uk or Amazon.com.

A brief look at Rebecca & the Spiral Staircase, volume 1

Here is an insight into Rebecca's world, just in case you haven't read Volume 1. This introduction is a synopsis of *Rebecca & the Spiral Staircase*.

Rebecca's relationship with her 11-year-old brother, Tommy – who was forever kicking his football in her direction - was typical of most teenage brother and sister interactions. Rebecca shared a delightful, close bond with her mother, Elizabeth. Often though, she felt troubled by her mother's passive relationship with Rebecca's father, James. In particular, Elizabeth's inert response to James' Victorian marital attitude maddened Rebecca. On occasions, she would escape her frustration, and find solace in an imaginary world beside the Whispering Pond, which nestled in the grounds of the family home in Cheshire.

Just before Christmas, James announced he had bought a big old Gothic mansion up by the lakes for a bargain price. Outwardly oblivious to sentiments and feelings towards their present home, he informed everyone they should be ready to move soon.

Although Rebecca missed her old house, she quickly delighted in her new surroundings and set about exploring the vast grounds. Unbeknown to her, she had in fact arrived at her real home. Her imagination really kicked in when she found an ancient key and discovered it unlocked the door to a derelict summerhouse down by a lake. One day, when alone inside the summerhouse, a previously locked door opened, leading to a spiral staircase.

Taking to these stairs, she embarked on a series of journeys into the history of their old family house. Her first encounter was with a woman named Meredith in 1853. She was a troubled woman whose husband had a lover named Millicent, an unsavoury character, with a chequered past.

Rebecca challenged Millicent's unpleasant behaviour. She then set about showing Meredith an alternative approach to her marital situation, which helped Meredith resolve her issues.

Once back in her own time, Rebecca discovered by way of an old newspaper article Millicent had been shot to death. The report went on to say Meredith had been indicted for Millicent's murder.

Reading this article troubled Rebecca feeling powerless to do anything about Meredith's predicament. Having established a strong mother-daughter bond with this woman, Rebecca was certain Meredith was incapable of a murderous act.

Months passed without the door opening again, but when it did, she found herself in 1943. Here the mansion was being used as an orphanage for children evacuated from war-torn London. She soon learnt Judith, the lady of the house, was an outcast in her own home. Instantly aware of the bizarre similarities between Judith's life and Meredith's, she set about untangling this woman's relationship. Observing Judith's complicated plight, she drew upon her experiences from her previous trip and helped her towards an amicable resolution.

Back in her own time and with school finished for the summer holidays, Rebecca sat on her balcony sketching. For a couple of days, she felt an overwhelming pull towards the summerhouse. Having not been able to get Meredith's predicament from her consciousness, she wondered if this was the reason for this tangible, physical sensation. One particular day, unable to resist the call, she headed down to the summerhouse, and once again took to the stairs. This time, she found herself in 1911, where the family relationship was the complete opposite of her previous experiences. This time, the woman was a passive-aggressive who controlled all around her. With little to do here other than observe, she headed back to the summerhouse, wondering why she'd ended up in this era. Upon entering the summerhouse, she found a sixty-year-old suicide note written by Millicent. Armed with this note, she now knew why she'd arrived in 1911, and her next mission was to find her way back to Meredith.

Although her next journey seemed complicated and fraught with difficulties, she drew solace, now convinced Meredith's troubled spirit was leading her way. Assured by this belief, and going on a hunch, she followed her instinct. Armed with the suicide note, Rebecca found her way back to 1853 and thereby proved Meredith's innocence.

Attempting to return home, Rebecca found she'd travelled three months ahead of her own time. Here, she witnessed the aftermath of a tragic accident involving her mother. This time, unlike her previous adventures, she was invisible to all. Only able to stand, watch, and listen, she heard her sobbing father wishing he had taken notice of Elizabeth and fixed the heating boiler. Before returning to her own time, she concocted a plan that would convince her father to take action, and in so doing, prevent her mother's death.

The plan worked, and unwittingly she'd opened the door for her parents to re-establish their forgotten love, something Rebecca had always known was there. Reflecting on all that had happened over the last year, Rebecca believed Meredith had exposed this impending disaster as recompense for Rebecca clearing her name by uncovering the suicide note. She now felt confident Meredith had been her guardian angel throughout her journeys and believed her mission in all of this was to help Meredith's tormented spirit, which in turn led to her parent's rediscovered love. Sitting on her balcony, she again considered everything, and believing Meredith's spirit had at last found a resting place, Rebecca was certain her jaunts into the past were now over.

That indeed seemed to be the last of her journeys, as she suspected, and now entering her eighteenth year, Rebecca left home to take up residence at Warwick University. Returning home for the summer break at the end of her first year at university, she learnt her father had commissioned the rebuilding of the summerhouse. If there were any doubts before, with the old spiral staircase now gone, replaced with a new shiny one, she was sure her journeys were over for good.

During supper, her mother told her they had found four boxes in the summerhouse's loft during its restoration. With an element of apprehension, she set about exploring the contents of the boxes. To her amazement, the first box contained sepia photos of Rebecca with Meredith in the 1850s. With the nagging time-travel dream notion dismissed, she opened the next box with eagerness, only to find little other than some history relating to the house and its occupants. The third box, however, contained a letter from Meredith addressed to Rebecca. It stated that Rebecca's soul and spirit had always been present in this house. It also proposed Rebecca could manifest herself into previous eras, thereby seeing those worlds through her own eyes. Not only had this letter turned rational thinking on its head, but it had also conceivably opened a permanent doorway back.

Rebecca left box four unopened...

A glance at Rebecca – A Way Back, Volume 2

Following on from the Spiral Staircase, Rebecca, having finished university tried to apply some logical thinking to her journeys into the past. Whichever way she looked at the events that led up to meeting Meredith and beyond, there was no reasonable explanation for the phenomenon she'd experienced. With those around her now outwardly accepting her stories, abandoning their previous dream or fanciful story notions, Rebecca felt at ease talking of her time in the past.

After a few weeks at home, and annoyed with the rational, sensible thought process, which kept showing itself, she decided to go for a walk in the woods.

As she wandered down towards the area where her adventures had started, she kept thinking about the unopened fourth box. As much as her curiosity wanted to look inside, some odd emotion tucked away in her subconscious was telling her to wait. Meredith had suggested to Rebecca she would, in time, find a way to control her movements into the past and this was at the forefront of her thoughts right now.

As she arrived by the summerhouse, a tingling sensation ran up and down her spine, seeing her father had instigated a complete renovation. Gone were the old decaying veranda, the creaky door, and rather spooky spiral stairs. In fact, the spiral staircase, which served as her doorway through time, had been replaced with a sparkling new flight.

Well, that's the end of my time with Meredith and co she thought.

As she walked around outside, something was amiss, but for the life of her, she couldn't put her finger on anything. Unbeknown to Rebecca, as she had exited the shiny new summerhouse, she had somehow jumped through a time loop and was once again in the past.

This was the beginning of a new set of adventures for Rebecca. Amongst others, she helped Queen Matilda, a 12th-century Scottish-Queen escape the tyrants who wanted rid of her. She also journeys to 1623 when the old manor house she lives in was being built. Her mission was to stop plague-infested workers arriving at Liverpool docks, with a pestilence that would change her mother's existence. Indeed, every jaunt she ventured on would have a significant impact on her life or those dear to her. That was unless she could find a way to interrupt time and stop it taking an alternative direction.

Rebecca – Beyond All Reason – a short synopsis

In Rebecca Beyond All Reason, she has one destiny, to save humanity. Having seen way into the future and discovered humankind is heading towards a sad and dramatic end, she faces a number of potential pitfalls. How will she ever make the world listen when they've ignored so many warnings. Travelling back to the 'Cradle of Civilisation,' she sets her mission in stone. Although she fully understands the implications of her meeting with the original Rebekah, she could never conceive the way her actions would change the future.

Subsequently, she meets a youthful Princess Elizabeth in 1945, just before Elizabeth becomes Queen of the United Kingdom and ultimately, the Commonwealth. This meeting opens the door, allowing her the opportunity to make the world listen and effectively bring a halt to global warming, thus saving us all from this damnation road we pursue endlessly.

Contents

Chapter 1 - Waking up 18

Chapter 2 – Something's Stirring 24

Chapter 3 – Football, and that phone call.......................................29

Chapter 4 – The Letter 37

Chapter 5 – The Unexpected Door 42

Chapter 6 – Days into Weeks 46

Chapter 7 – The Police 53

Chapter 7 – Interpole..58

Chapter 8 – Christmas Day and...63

Chapter 9 – Page 138..74

Chapter 10 – What Next 80

Chapter 11 – That Door Again 87

Chapter 12 – Focussed..99

Chapter 13 – Where next?..109

Chapter 14 - Locked 119

Chapter 15 – Unlocked 130

Chapter 16 – The Journey 140

Chapter 17 – The Clans 157

Chapter 18 – Just a chat..164

Chapter 19 – Daughter from Another Life 172

Chapter 20 – Two Days 185

Chapter 21 – Back home...200

Chapter 22 – A Football Twist...215

Chapter 23 – Time Will Tell the Truth...223

Chapter 24 – Visionaries, or not 237

Chapter 25 - The Move 254

Chapter 26 – The Door Opens 266

Chapter 27 – The Door Back 273

Chapter 1 - Waking up

Rebecca woke up in the Summerhouse on the eve of her 31st birthday to the sound of her 2nd daughter, Gabrielle murmuring. She lay there for a couple of minutes, seeing Duncan, as always, taking his turn with their newly-born. Seconds later in burst their 6-year-old, Faith, ear phones in, listening to some music on her phone. She launched herself on the bed, which was fine when she was 3 or 4, now though, she was getting a little heavy.

'Morning, Mumsy. Kiss, kiss. When's breakfast ready?'

'Morning, Darling Heart.' Rebecca eased her legs from under Faith, and asked, 'what are you listening to this early in the morning?' She'd known right from the minute Faith was born, she had Tommy's genes, and was always going to live life full on.

'Oh, that new band from Liverpool, "The Boyz". Gonna marry the lead singer one day. Mum, when's breakfast ready, I have my football training at eleven this morning.'

Running her fingers through Faith's sunset auburn hair, Rebecca said, 'in good time, it is only...' she then glanced at the clock and shook her head, 'five a m.' And again, shook her head. 'Duncan, are you okay there? There some fresh milk in the fridge.'

'Yes, we are just fine here, I have already been down to get the milk. You were sound-oh and I didn't want to disturb you. Madam here has been up a while. A sleeper she is not.' He then grinned. 'Bit like you, I suspect, eyes everywhere, wakes up totally alert. Hey, wouldn't have either of you any other way. Are you okay, Bex? Thirty-one tomorrow.' He then chuckled, 'a couple more years and you'll catch me up.'

'Thank you so much for getting up this morning, what with that business meeting today.'

'No need to thank me. I am just finished with Gabri's milk and am going to sort some breakfast. Anything you fancy? I know what Bouncy will want, as always, eggs-n-bacon.'

'I am happy with anything, Duncan, thank you. Actually, I'll have some toast, please. Be good for your father, Faith.' She then blew the two of them a kiss.

'Come on Faith, let's go cook some breakfast for your mother.'

Rebecca laid there listening to Gabrielle's oh so quiet gurgle, wondering how two girls could be so different. Faith, who they named Faith Matilda, was full-on tomboyish, although at times, she was really quite feminine and had been like that since day one. Gabrielle Meredith, who was now 7-months-old, was an eyes wide thinker. Right from the moment she graced this world, Rebecca knew her daughters were chalk and cheese, and wouldn't wish for either of them to be any other way. For certain, Faith, who they'd nicknamed Bouncy, was going to be a sportsperson of some description. Gabrielle, who they just simply called Gabri, was destined to be a writer, thinker or explorer. Rebecca had known within seconds of her being born, she had her genes.

Once breakfast was finished, Duncan helped Rebecca tidy up and then headed off to work. After she'd waved him goodbye, Rebecca started to get the girls ready for football training.

'Make sure you pack your boots this time, Faith,' she called out and then finished dressing Gabri.

Moments later, Faith appeared, seemingly ready to take on the world. As always with football training, she was just like Tommy, eager to get going.

'Come on, Mum, don't want to be late.'

'Two ticks,' Rebecca said tucking Gabri into her car seat.

On the way to football, Rebecca's focus was on stopping Faith from juggling her ball in the back seat. As soon as they arrived, and before Rebecca had a chance to speak, Faith was heading over to the other girls in her team. Standing watching Faith, and remembering the way Tommy was with a football, Rebecca's mind started to drift. *Where have all the years gone*, she thought, bending down and checking on Gabrielle.

With Faith being born soon after Rebecca's trailblazing meeting with the Global Summit hierarchy, she'd focussed all her attention on her new born. Even though the family had distanced themselves, there was a smattering of background noise from the media. For sure, there were a few meetings with various scientists. Largely though, at the express wishes of the British Government, the press had left the family alone to live a normal life. Well, as normal as it could be, considering the world knew Rebecca was humanity's first confirmed time traveller. Occasionally, there were times in the early days when Rebecca often thought of Meredith, and in particular, the other dimension quoted so often. Over the last six years, those thoughts had drifted further away and there were times when the whole experience had felt like offcuts from a favourite film. There were occasions when she considered her many in-depth conversations with various scientists who wanted to know about her time jumping. Their prying questions had left her wondering if this had somehow affected her ability to travel through time. It had been four years since Meredith and the spiral stairs had played a noteworthy part in her thoughts. For some reason, Meredith had come to mind over the last couple of days. She was sure this was because her mum had brought the subject up, suggesting James was considering having the paintings of Meredith and Millicent reframed. Rebecca had been horrified by this idea and suggested it could and probably would change things. She hadn't been able to express what might change, although her dad had accepted her fears, as he always did.

Driving home from training, with Faith still full of beans on the back seat, Meredith once more came into Rebecca's thoughts. She pulled up in front of the manor house, and rather than drive down to the summerhouse, where she now lived with Duncan and the girls, she decided to stop off and have a chat with her mum.

'Hello, Mother,' she called out, beckoning Faith to follow her inside.

'Hello, Sweetie. To what do I owe this pleasure,' Elizabeth asked, bending down to Gabrielle. She lifted Gabri out from her car seat come pram affair, 'Hello, Darling,' she said, tickling Gabri's cheeks.

'I thought I'd pop in with the girls and catch up. Faith, outside if you're going to bounce that ball please, and no climbing up the wicker fence, there's a good girl.' 'Turning back to her mum, she said, 'Was Tommy and I this different?'

'Well, kind of yes, but you were a girl and boy, so it was to be expected. Anyways, how are you?'

'All good, Mum. Been thinking about Meredith over the last couple of days, and not sure if it's because of dad's idea.'

'Well, no disappearing up the spiral stairs with either of the girls in tow,' she chuckled. 'In all seriousness, not as if you can go anywhere with these two so close by. Oh, hang on, I'll be back in thirty years. Perhaps that is why Meredith has been so far from your thoughts.'

'Yeah, I thought that. Also, I can't imagine there is anything else for me.' She then called out the window to Faith. 'Faith, get down and behave. That girl, need eyes in the back of your head with her. She was trying to work out how she could get on the roof of the summerhouse the other day.' Again, she shook her head and grinned. 'Going back to Meredith. There is one thing that has constantly left me a little puzzled. In fact, it comes to mind whenever I so much as consider my time jaunts.'

Narrow eyed, Elizabeth asked, 'So what is that then?'

'Well, I am not sure if you recall me mentioning the other dimension. Towards the end of my journeys, it was often talked about by Meredith, Matilda, Rebekah, all of them.'

'What about it?' her mum asked, again narrowing her eyes clearly uncomfortable speaking about this subject.

'I guess because I never really found out exactly what the other dimension was all about, it left a space in my thoughts. To be honest, with the girls, I had kinda moved on. Of late though, especially the last couple of days, it's been nudging me, for want of a better term.'

'Hey, thirty-one tomorrow, young lady.'

'I know, Mum, don't remind me. Where have the last sixteen years gone? It was like yesterday we sat here talking about my sixteenth birthday.' Suddenly her mind drifted the way it hadn't for a long time. Her minds-eye was right back at the bottom of the spiral staircase, staring into the darkness. She shivered and rubbed the goose bumps on her arm. Then aware her mum was looking at her, she smiled.

'Bex, you've gone all goosy. I saw your eyes drift away, where were you, need I ask,' she said and grinned almost as if she had seen what Rebecca had seen.

Rebecca shook her head, a little surprised by her own emotions. 'I was right back at the bottom of the staircase, all those years ago. It actually felt as if I was there for the first time, fifteen-years-old and all, not having a clue what was about to unfold. Then, in the blink of an eye, I was back to being me with all my knowledge. It was as if I stepped from my thirty-year-old body into my fifteen-year-old body and back again. It was so weird.' She glanced at her mum, then out of the window. 'That was such a strange feeling. It was as if, just for a second, I had travelled back in time to that first episode.'

'Ooh, how weird. Especially with you saying you hadn't had anything for so long.'

'I know, very odd,' she said. In the back of her thoughts, she couldn't help wonder if this bizarre experience was leading somewhere.

She continued to chat to her mum for the next hour or two, until it was time for Gabri's nap. Over the next few weeks, occasionally, Meredith and co came to mind, although life ticked along just fine. Those weeks turned to months, and before Rebecca could blink, she was getting Gabrielle ready for her first day at school. What with Faith's tenth birthday, and sadly, Duncan losing his father, weeks seemed to last about fifteen minutes for Rebecca. Strangely for her, although she had occasions when Meredith had popped into her thoughts, there was nothing other than passing memories. This pattern continued over the next few years.

Chapter 2 – Something's Stirring

'Duncan, bring Faith's school bag down with you please,' Rebecca called out.

After a couple of minutes, he called out, 'it's not in her room, or anywhere upstairs, Bex.'

'Faith,' Rebecca hollered to her out the front where she was kicking a ball around, 'where's your school bag?'

'I gave it to Gab; I have a new one. My old one was becoming a bit young for me, what with the fairies all over the back, especially now I am getting ready for my O-Levels.'

Rebecca turned to Duncan. 'Where have the last ten years gone? I can recall asking mum where the years had gone as if it were yesterday, and that was on the eve of my thirty-first birthday. Here I am staring at forty-one, and our babies are sixteen and ten.'

'I know, I was thinking exactly that the other day when I was looking at Faith's homework. There I was one day teaching her how to spell, and here I am with her teaching me.' He shook his head, kissed Rebecca on the forehead. 'Right, I'm off to work, do you need anything bringing home?'

'No, I'm fine thanks. Got a food delivery today from the farm. Have a lovely day. I love you.'

'Love you too. Have a great day,' he called out, 'do your best, Faith, Gabri, and that will always be good enough.'

On the way to school, with Faith listening to some music on her phone, Gabrielle asked, 'Mum, who is Meredith?'

Caught off guard, and more than a little surprised, Rebecca wasn't sure what to say. She glanced in the mirror at Gabrielle. 'Why do you ask, Gabri? Have you seen the painting of her in Gran and Grandpa's house?'

'No, Mum. I just keep dreaming about a very beautiful woman and her name is Meredith.'

A little taken aback, she asked, 'does she speak to you in your dream, darling?' Again, she glanced in the mirror. She really didn't know what to make of Gab's comment and wondered where this might be going.

'It is always the same dream and we are in Gran and Grandpa's house but it is only Meredith and I. She always says she knows you and asks if you are okay.' She paused briefly and then continued, 'it's all a bit odd, it is as if we are not in the old house. The carpet is different, the wallpaper, lots of things. I can't explain really. It is as if I am in an old-fashioned film set.'

Dumbfounded by Gabrielle's comments, Rebecca thought for a moment. 'I did know a Meredith a long time ago, before you were born. I haven't seen her for many years.' She again thought for a moment, and asked, 'in your dream, and I know dreams can seem distant, what clothes does she wear.' The instant she asked, she wasn't altogether sure if she should have. 'It doesn't matter if you cannot remember.' She pulled the car up outside the school, and turned around to Gabrielle. In the back of her mind, she was wondering if Gabri perhaps shared more of her genes than she'd originally thought and it was now manifesting through her dreams.

Smiling, Gabri said, 'she always wears a white dress and says she will come to see me soon.'

Leaning over, and touching Gabri gently on the hand, Rebecca said, 'Meredith lives a long way from here.' In the back of her mind, she knew only too well something was stirring. She then dropped the girls off at school. On the way home, she kept going over her brief chat with Gabrielle. As she drove the car down the bumpy track leading to the summerhouse, she wondered if and when she would see Meredith again. Standing on the veranda, she glanced across the lake while going over so many scenarios in her head. The one thing that was right at the front of her thoughts, was why Meredith would visit Gabrielle in a dream. The niggling question nudging at her consciousness was what Meredith could have meant by saying she'd come to see Gabrielle soon. This then led her on to thinking again about the other dimension. The more she thought about it, the more anxious she felt, remembering Princess Rebekah telling her the good live in the other dimension. This then led her to wonder if Gabrielle was in any danger. 'Wash your thoughts out with carbolic soap,' she mumbled to herself, not having a clue why she would even consider that notion. She shook her head, realising she'd been standing there for over an hour. As she went inside and made herself a cup of coffee, she once more went over all the possible scenario's in her head. Just as she was about to call the school, just to check, the phone rang. Not expecting a call from anyone, she stood staring at the phone for a few seconds. She then grabbed it and a little out of breath answered, 'hello, Rebecca Fergusson.'

'Hello, Rebecca. This is Ms. Black at the school.'

Immediately, Rebecca's brain went into overdrive and made her feel a little anxious, even though she'd told herself she was overanalysing the Meredith dream. To compound her tangled emotions, she was thinking Millicent Black by any chance. 'Hello, Ms. Black. How can I help, nothing to worry about is there?'

'Oh no, sorry. I was just calling about Faith. She has been put forward to play football for the Ladies County side this coming weekend. We were wondering if you would like to come along and if perhaps your brother, Tommy could come along too, what with him coaching Ladies football now. The game kicks off at noon over on the Liverpool Ladies training ground.'

Taking a deep breath, Rebecca answered, 'That would be fantastic, although I will have to check with Tommy first. Let me give him a call and I'll get right back to you.' Rebecca came off the phone, annoyed with herself for turning Gabrielle's dream into such a ridiculous paranoid notion. 'Just a dream,' she mumbled, realising she'd known right from her birth Gabrielle was of her making and it should be no surprise she'd dreamt about Meredith. She then called Tommy, who suggested he wouldn't miss this game for anything. He also added he was going to adopt Faith soon, and laughed, saying, "that's my girl," asking if Faith uses Rebecca as a moving target.

'Once a twit, always a twit. Be here at nine and not in the blinking Ferrari.' She then called the school and made arrangements.

As it was a nice September day, she took her coffee outside on the veranda. Staring across the lake, although she'd kind of dismissed the notion that Gabri might be in danger, she couldn't help wondering why Meredith had said she'd visit Gabri. To compound her feelings, she had this tiny nagging notion at the back of her thoughts that just wouldn't go away. Thinking about her time with Meredith and realising she'd never dreamt about her, she drifted off completely. Suddenly, something nudged her attention, and rubbing her eyes as if she been asleep, she noticed what appeared to be a rowing boat. Immediately, the hairs on her arm stood up. Once more, just as she had twenty-six years earlier, felt certain she'd seen a woman, standing in a boat, shrouded in mist. As with the first time, when she focussed, the vision had vanished.

She sat there going through everything in her head, jumping from one idea to the next. She recalled Rebekah telling her there was only ever one of her kind around at any one time. Adamant Gabrielle was of her making, alarm bells once more started ringing. Confused by her mixed emotions, she was going between feeling anxious to allowing her common-sense to tell her she was being paranoid. Nevertheless, everything Rebekah ever told her, had subsequently proved to be precise. So, if this trusted woman was right, how could her and Gabri be of the same making and here at the same time. Realising she was taking her emotions in circles, she went inside and started preparing supper.

Chapter 3 – Football, and that phone call…

Just as Rebecca expected, Tommy arrived, wheel-spinning his red Ferrari across the gravel of the main house. 'Thirty-seven going on seventeen,' she mumbled. Having not seen the twit for a couple of months, she hurried across the drive to greet Tommy. Before she could say hello, Faith was out the front door, had cuddled Tommy and was sitting in the front seat of his car, complete with her football boots hanging around her neck.

'Hello, dear brother. I so knew you'd bring this car, then again, someone's happy you did,' she said indicating toward Faith. 'How did a daughter of mine end up being a mirror of my brother.' She then shook her head and kissed Tom on the cheek. 'At least she doesn't use me as target practice.'

Tommy kissed her back. 'Hey, Gab is a mirror of you. Every time I see her, I see you. The only difference, I wouldn't kick my ball at her. She is like one of your Fairies, so petite and feminine. Kaitie is always saying how much Gab is like you. By the way, she couldn't make it today, what with her mother being poorly and all.'

'She rang me this morning. Thanks for letting me know though. Mum, Dad, along with Duncan and Gabri are all coming today. Be quite a few of us. Roxy is driving over also.'

Moments later, Elizabeth and James joined them outside.

'Mum and I will go in our new red Mazda MXFive and see you guys there. Nice broom-broom, Tommy,' James said, and patted Tom on the back.

'Apple doesn't fall far from the tree,' Rebecca said and shook her head.

'Except with you, Sweetie. The apple fell and still hasn't landed yet,' Elizabeth said, and grinned, kissing Rebecca on the cheek.

As Duncan pulled up in the family car, Faith called out of the window of Tom's car, 'Mum, Dad, going with TommyHawk.'

'Okay, Faith, be good, although I know you will with Tom.' She then shook her head, remembering when Tommy got that nick-name. It was the first time he played a game for Stevenage FC in his last two years as a pro-footballer, before his knee gave up on him. It turned out to be a club he loved and it was still his favourite nick-name, often saying they were the best fans ever, win lose or draw, they bounced.

They all met up at the training ground and were greeted by the sports teacher from Faith's school, along with a couple of county representatives. Tommy headed off with Faith to meet up with the other players, while the rest of the family joined Roxy in the small covered stand beside the pitch.

'Hey, Roxy. So nice of you to pop over,' Rebecca said, greeting her with a kiss on the cheek.

'Wouldn't miss ya bruvver's daughter play for anything,' Roxy said and chuckled in a way which sounded cockney, if that was even possible.

Watching the game took Rebecca back many years, reminding her of the first time she watched Tommy play an important game. Just before half time, Faith, who was playing central defence, went up for a corner. As the ball swung across the goal-area, she leapt at the back post and met the ball full-on with a header. Rebecca was sure it was going in the goal, and hollered, 'Go, Faith.' Only to see the ball cannon back off the post. The second half was a niggly affair, with not a lot of goal mouth action, finishing nil - nil.

After the game, they headed over to the changing rooms to wait for Faith. As they passed some high metal sheet fencing, Rebecca called out to Duncan to wait for them. Just as she did, she turned to hurry Gabrielle along. There was no sign of her anywhere. Anxiously, Rebecca shouted, 'Gabri, where are you?' A little way back, Rebecca could see a gap in the fence and reckoning Gabrielle may be the other side, she scrambled through the narrow opening, calling the rest of the family as she did. There was no sign of her anywhere. Now alarmed, again, she called out to the others. Frantically, she then hollered for Gabrielle several times. Suddenly, all those horrid thoughts she'd dismissed weeks before seemed so real.

Tommy was the first on the scene. 'What on earth is the matter, Sis?'

'Gab has vanished, one minute she was just behind me, singing quietly, the next, gone. I thought she may have slipped through the gap in this fence, but there's no sign of her anywhere.

Joined by the others, including a couple of the school representatives, they searched for several minutes.

Now beside herself with fear, Rebecca turned to Duncan, 'how could she have vanished?'

Cuddling Rebecca, he said, 'we best call the police.'

Tommy, James and Roxy carried on looking, all heading in a different direction, calling as they went.

A moment later, another school official joined them along with Faith.

With a look of anxiety that Rebecca had never seen before on Faith's face, she asked, 'Mum, mum, what's going on?'

'Gabri has gone missing.'

'Mum, want do you mean?'

As Rebecca explained what had happened to Gabri, for some reason Meredith came into her thoughts. Before she had time to consider why, the Police arrived.

A police officer walked over to Rebecca. 'Hello, Madam. I am WPC Unwin. Would you please explain what happened?'

Rebecca went through the story step by step making sure she didn't miss anything out. Although still distressed, she felt pleased with herself for being so focussed.

'Rebecca, do you have a photo of Gabrielle, ideally on your phone?'

Rebecca took out her phone and showed the police officer a few photos.

'Would you send this photo to my phone,' she said pointing. 'I can then send this out to the other police officers in the area. Please do not worry Madam, we will do our best to find your daughter.'

After around thirty minutes with still no sign of Gabrielle, and on the advice of the Police, they all headed back home.

'Bex, you're understandably quiet. Even so, you've not said a word. I can feel you thinking though.' At some traffic lights, Duncan turned and touched Rebecca on the shoulder.

She turned to Duncan. 'I am not sure how I feel. For sure, I am beside myself with anxiety. Bizarrely though, I don't feel as panicked as I should.'

'Have you any ideas why you feel like this?' he asked as they drove along the gravel road leading to the main house.

Rebecca didn't answer, unsure what she was feeling and why she felt the way she did. As she got out of the car everyone was there, including two Police officers. She greeted everybody, but her mind was drifting. For some reason, in the middle of her concerns for Gabrielle, she kept thinking about Meredith.

Elizabeth came over to her, gave her a cuddle, and said, 'Bex, understandably you're distant. However, the look on your face says an awful lot more. I know you, where are you?'

Rebecca squeezed her mother's arm. She then looked her straight in the eyes. 'It's not what it seems. Something is going on here. She can't have vanished, unless…'

Rebecca, even by your standards, that statement doesn't make sense. You'll have to explain what you mean.'

Just as she was thinking what she should say to her mother, a bizarre idea filled Rebecca's thoughts, almost as if she'd just watched something on TV. 'Mum, bear with me, I need to check something.' She then called out to Duncan, who was talking to the Police officers. 'Duncan, I am just going to check something down by the summerhouse.'

He immediately came over. 'What ever do you mean, you're going to check something, What exactly?'

Rebecca could tell by the look on his face and Elizabeth's face that they both needed an explanation. The thing was, she didn't have one. 'I don't know. Mum, you know my hunches,' she said nodding. 'This is one of those hunches, although this time, I have no idea what it means. I'll be back in a moment.' As she turned to head down to the summerhouse, they both offered to come with her. 'No, I need to do this on my own. I can't explain.' She then hurried down towards the lake, somewhat spooked, but nonetheless, strangely settled. As she turned to walk along the path by the side of the lake, she could see Gabrielle sitting on the veranda outside the summerhouse.

She hurried over, knelt down, and with her hands on both of Gabri's shoulders. 'Where have you been, Gabri?'

'Mum, I am confused. One minute I was with you, the next I was with Meredith and two other women.' She squinted in an odd way. 'I was with them and felt safe, but I don't know where I was.'

'What do you mean, you've been with Meredith? What happened?' In the back of her mind, Rebecca now knew why she'd felt oddly calm and why Meredith had jumped into her thoughts so many times. Although completely calm, she shivered. At the back of her thoughts were so many questions, mostly though, she wondered where this was leading.

'Well, there I was walking along behind you, the next minute, I was standing here by the lake. The thing was, our house was white, not blue like it is now, and I was with Meredith, and a woman named Matilda and another very pretty woman who spoke a foreign language. She was dressed very strangely. She had a red and orange thing on, kind of like a dress, but not.'

Going on Gabrielle's description, Rebecca reckoned this could have perhaps been Rebekah. 'Did Meredith say anything to you?'

'She did, Mum although I am not sure I knew what she meant. She did say I would understand in time and then she gave me this letter for you.'

Focussed on Gabri, Rebecca took the letter and put it in her bag.

'Mum, are you going to read the letter?'

'In good time, Gabri. First, we need to go and see your father.

As the pair headed up the hill, everyone started hurrying towards them both, meeting them half way.

With his voice shaking and appearing totally bemused, Duncan asked, 'Whatever has happened, Rebecca, Gabri?'

'Mum, Dad, Duncan, I will explain in a moment. I need to speak to the Police first. There's just something in the back of my thoughts, and well...'

As she walked over to the Police officers, she could see from the look on their faces, they needed an explanation. Thinking carefully, she said, 'Hello, I am not sure where to start here, suffice to say my daughter is safe, as you can see.' She then shook her head. 'Do either of you know about our family?'

'Madam, I know of your history and your abilities,' the female WPC said through narrowed eyes. 'Looking at your daughter, I suspect something has happened here, something only you and your family would fully understand or comprehend. Leave it with us, I will speak with my senior officer and we will delete all records of this event. I must say, we were alarmed because a number of young blond-haired girls have gone missing over the last few months.'

'Oh dear, that is so sad. How those parents must feel.' She shook her head inwardly, having had a brief moment in their shoes, giving her an insight and understanding of how they must feel. 'That must be terrible for them. To live with the pain of losing a child is, well, beyond most of our comprehension. Sadly, you hear of it all too often through the media, never expecting it to happen to you. My girl is back now, safely. However, those poor families and their torture.' With her eyes filled with tears, she shook her head, unsure what to say.

'Mum.'

'Sorry, not right now Gabri, there's a good girl. I will speak with you in a moment, my lovely.' She then turned to the Police officers, thanked them for their time and said her goodbyes. After they had left, she turned to Gabri. 'Sorry I stopped you, what did you want to say?'

'Mum, what the police lady told you is what Meredith was talking to me about.'

'What do you mean?'

'Meredith told me about the blond girls going missing, and told me some names.'

Completely caught unawares and unsure what to think or make of this, Rebecca asked, 'Can you remember any of the names?' She was wondering if Gabrielle could recall the names, this might just help the police in some way.

'Yes, Mum,' she said and then rattled off half-a-dozen names.

Chapter 4 – The Letter

Seeing everyone half listening to Gabrielle, Rebecca suggested they all headed back indoors.

As they entered the kitchen, Elizabeth said, 'I'll put the coffee on and listen from here.' She then glanced at Rebecca and nodded.

Rebecca knew, as always, her mum needed a back seat when anything like this occurred. Turning to the others, and picking her words carefully, she explained what she believed had occurred with Gabri.

'Seems the apple really doesn't fall far from the tree,' Tommy said, squeezing Rebecca's hand.

Pulling on Rebecca's sleeve, Gabri said, 'Mum, what about the letter?'

'Yes, lets open that now.' Rebecca then explained to the others about the letter Gabrielle had brought back with her.

With narrowed eyes, James said, 'that's unusual in itself. I thought in the past, letters appeared in places like the bureau, seemingly on their own. I don't recall you being handed one before, certainly not like this. I think also, it being via Gabrielle is, well, unexpected.' He then seemed to think briefly. 'Also, Gab going missing in Liverpool and then turning up back here, via Meredith or not, that's very, let's say, peculiar.'

Rebecca nodded, considering her father's words. 'I must say, this whole situation caught me a little off guard, although I am sure there is a good reason. As you say, the letter is one thing, but Gab seemingly disappearing and then reappearing, well…'

Elizabeth placed the coffee on the table and sat down. Staring straight at Rebecca, she said, 'it's been several years since Meredith and co have shown their faces. I genuinely thought this was behind you.'

'Me too, Mother, maybe it is Gabri's turn. I must say, I am somewhat concerned, she may be a little young to understand what is going on. I mean, I was fifteen when I started down this road and I remember struggling with all that was happening.' She then squeezed Gabri's arm gently. 'It may have appeared as if I was taking it in my stride. Hmm, not sure I did inside.'

'Mum, I understand. Meredith told me in my dreams I was the same as you.'

Wide eyed, Rebecca said, Gabri, you never told me that before.

'Mum, read the letter.'

'Yeah, that I will do,' Rebecca said, taking the letter from her bag and glancing at the others. She read it through once in her head, and glancing at the others, said, 'I'll read it aloud.'

Dear Rebecca,

It has been many years. There is a threateningly dreadful situation we need your help with.

Rebekah, Matilda and I are all now in the other dimension you heard me speak of many times. For that reason, the only way we could contact you at this stage was through Gabrielle. Uniquely, Gabrielle has an open door to our world. She is the first of her kind to have this ability.

As we have with this letter, we will send you further guidance, although this may not always be in your time, in the form of a letter, or through Gabrielle. You must follow your intuition and find your way back to speak with us alone. As in the past, we may step briefly into your world.

You will know, as you always do, when the door has opened for you.

My love is with you and your daughter, delightful Gabrielle.

Rebecca glanced around the room, unsure what to say. She'd suspected for some time Gab was of her making. This letter not only confirmed this, it took it to another level.

'Well, as much as we thought your time with Meredith was over, clearly there is more for you,' Roxy said. She then glanced at Elizabeth.

'Mum, how do you feel?' Rebecca asked.

'Oddly fine. Although, like us all, I thought your jumping through time was over, it seems not, and somewhere in my brain, I knew this day would come. Gabri seemingly has your ability, although I would not want to go through that emotional roller-coaster this morning or any time soon, at least until we have a clearer picture. The idea of dear Gabrielle jumping not only through time, but also in and out of the other dimension is, well, a tad scary.'

'Not Scary for me,' Gabrielle said.

'Faith, you're very quiet, are you okay?' Rebecca asked, touching her gently on the arm.

'Gab told me many times about Meredith and although I obviously know your story, Mum, I only ever thought she was kind of mimicking you. I never believed she was actually meeting up with Meredith, albeit through her dreams. Although now she has actually met her for real. What is truly odd, is when she went missing, I knew inside my tummy, she was okay.'

'Me too, Tommy said, shaking his head. 'I don't know how, I just did.' Again, he shook his head.

'I did as well,' Rebecca added. 'I can't explain it, I just knew.'

'I couldn't understand why you were so calm,' Duncan said, touching Rebecca's arm. 'Now I comprehend, if that is the right word, a little more of your world. Although, I don't think I will ever truly appreciate what has happened in the past,' he nodded, 'or the future.'

'I guess it's just a waiting game now, Rebecca,' Roxy said.

'It always is. There's been times in the past when I've had to wait months. This time though, I suspect I will not have to wait too long. Seems rather urgent. Suddenly a weird notion came into her head. She picked up the letter and read it again.

'What are you thinking, Rebecca?'

'Not sure, Dad. Just a hunch.'

Shaking her head, Elizabeth said narrowed eyed, 'I know your hunches. Do we get a glimpse into your thoughts?'

The WPC said to me about a number of young girls going missing. Gabri said that Meredith had said something similar.'

'She did, Mum.' She then rattled off a number of names again.

'Gabri, slow a little,' Rebecca said, scribbling the names down. 'I think I need to speak to a Police officer about this.' She then thought for a moment. 'One that understands my ability.'

So, you're thinking this is about these girls going missing?' Roxy asked, appearing animated. 'How exciting if you can somehow fix this. After all, you stopped global warming, why not this?'

'Wow, yeah. How brilliant would that be, Muvva,' Faith said.

Nodding, and glancing at Roxy, Rebecca said, 'Muvva indeed, as if I don't know who that came from.' Glancing at Roxy, she chuckled and called loudly, 'Muvva.' This instantly relaxed the mood of everyone.

That evening, James ordered an Indian take-away, which went down well. Over dinner, they continued to discuss what may lay ahead for Rebecca. Having decided to stay in the main house, once Gabri and Faith had gone to bed, they chatted about what might be around the corner for Gabrielle.

'I have gone over this in my head so many times. You know what though, I must trust she is in safe hands. Over the years, whenever I fell, Meredith was always there to pick me up and point me in the right direction. I can't explain it, but I just always knew she watched over me. I have no doubts, she will look over Gabrielle. She has today.'

Chapter 5 – The Unexpected Door

Over the next few days, Rebecca tried to focus her attention on Faith, Gabrielle and Duncan. She'd made a decision to push any thoughts of what might lay ahead to the back of her mind and wait for something to nudge her subconscious.

It was now a week since Gabri's disappearance. After preparing breakfast for the girls and Duncan, she waved them off. Duncan was going to drop the girls off at school on his way to work.

Sitting outside on a lovely late September morning, Rebecca decided to give the WPC a call. Within a few minutes of chatting the police officer asked if she could pop over for an informal chat.

Around 11am, Rebecca met the WPC and a rather senior looking female officer in front of the main house.

'Hello, Rebecca. This is Chief Inspector Mary Simmonds. I'm not sure I introduced myself fully. I am WPC Jan Unwin, but please call us Mary and Jan.'

Rebecca made them all a coffee and sat at the kitchen table. 'Well, I am not sure how to explain this. Something has come up with Gabrielle that is both intriguing and could prove advantageous to you two.'

'Can I please say,' Mary said, 'we are open to anything you have to say. We know of your strengths and realise nothing is impossible.'

Okay, so you mentioned a number of girls going missing.'

'Yes, I did,' Jan said.

'May I intervene here?' Mary asked.

Rebecca nodded, intrigued to hear her viewpoint.

'Well, over the last few days, we have made some alarming discoveries. Initially, we believed twelve girls, all around Gabrielle's age had gone missing over the last four months in the district of Liverpool. We have now discovered this pattern has shown up across the whole of the UK. Alarmingly, it has been happening for at least twenty years. The reason we hadn't drawn a pattern before was because the girls went missing as individuals. By this I mean, one in such and such a town, then one somewhere else. It was always small towns and there was no correlation. The perpetrators had acted with incredible stealth. It was only because of an insightful PC we noticed the age and blond correlation. In total, we believe two girls a year have been taken. There would be one in Scotland, and then maybe six months later, another one in the South West of England. Hence little connection. That was until now, where twelve have gone missing in four months. We now believe this is a huge operation.' She hesitated for a moment. 'Only the Police know what is happening. We now believe the girls may have been pushed into some international child abuse circle. Possibly running abroad. As it stands, we have little to go on. The only defining factors are their age and the colour of their hair.'

Rebecca pulled a note from her bag. 'So, Gabri brought back a mental list of girl names from her brief time with Meredith. Do you have a list of the girls who have gone missing recently?'

'I can get the list up on my laptop. Give me a moment,' Jan said. Opening up her laptop, after a few seconds, she said,' Okay.'

Over the next few moments, they compared the names and all were the same, with the exception of one.

Something suddenly occurred to Rebecca. She looked directly at Jan and Mary. 'Okay, this may sound a little bizarre, but you have to go with me on this. Clearly, Meredith knows what is going on and will undoubtedly have some answers and a possible solution. I just have to wait until the door opens to get her input.'

Appearing somewhat perplexed, Jan asked, 'door opens, what does that mean?'

Rebecca then showed the two of them the letter from Meredith. 'So, you see, I am waiting for my intuition to lead me in the right direction.'

'Does it always happen like this?' Mary asked.

'In essence, yes. Happen, it always does though. It can take minutes or months. Only though when the time is right.'

Jan shook her head. 'How do you deal with not knowing what is going to happen and importantly when?'

'In the early days, it was exasperating to say the least. Over the years, I've learnt to accept it for what it is.' Thinking for a moment, Rebecca nodded. 'As alarming as this situation is, one thing is for sure, there will be a solution. Something I am concerned about is the name on Gabri's list that isn't on your list. Just a hunch here, I'm wondering if this is the name of a girl who hasn't been taken yet.'

Squinting, Mary asked, 'can it work like that, because that's predicting something that hasn't happened yet.'

'Well, as inexplicable as this sounds, it's all happened, just in the future. I don't expect you to understand this, I know I don't. We just have to trust. What I suspect though, is I will be able to stop Millicent from being snatched. I must say it's just intuition here though.' She shook her head. 'Ironic name though, but that's a long story.'

Again, appearing quizzical, Jan asked, 'so, how do you think you'll be able to stop Millicent from being taken. If that is the situation.'

'Well, I don't know, but one thing I do know Gabri's list was accurate and complete. I guess, I am just joining up the dots, so to speak. If she is yet to be taken, then the only reason Meredith gave Gabri the name is because we can do something about it, which is how it always works.'

Mary lent over and touched Rebecca's hand. 'Well, you saved the planet, so in you we trust. I just wish I could come with you on one of your adventures, if that's the right word.'

Rebecca smiled and nodded. Noticing Mary had glanced at her watch a couple of times, she said, 'Well, I feel I am closer to understanding what might lay ahead for me. Ever since I received the names and letter, my curiosity has been running away with me. Perhaps we can meet up again soon.'

The three chatted a little while longer and then Mary suggested she really must go. They all said their goodbyes, making plans to speak again soon.

After they'd left, Rebecca headed back down to the Summerhouse, made herself a coffee and sat on her rocking chair on the Veranda. Staring across the lake, she wondered what tomorrow would bring. Considering all that had been said between her and the two police officers, she at least had an idea of what to expect. Her emotions were quite mixed by the time she headed off to school to pick up the girls. Part of her was distressed for the plight of the girls that had gone missing over the years. She settled her emotions a little, convincing herself she would be able to stop Millicent from being snatched. All the way to school though, she kept stressing about all the girls and their families over the years. Her sentiments kept focussing on what they may have gone through, that was if they weren't dead. Suddenly a penny dropped. 'I can stop any of this ever happening,' she mumbled to herself. *I just need to find a way back twenty years* she thought, *not as if that's a bridge too far.*

On the way home, she focussed her attention on Faith and Gabrielle, pushing her emotions to the back of her thoughts.

Chapter 6 – Days into Weeks

It was now late November and unusually cold. Rebecca had just arrived back having dropped the girls off at school. In spite of the chill in the air, Rebecca decided to go for a walk. It was one of those beautiful autumnal frosty mornings. The grass was a patchwork of green and white. With a crystal blue sky and a big buttery yellow sun dodging the odd sheep like cloud, the grass was still frosty white in the shadows of the huge pines. Without a breath of wind, the lake was like a sheet of glass. Deciding to head down towards the old cottages, Rebecca hadn't a care in the world. As she headed through the woods, trying to follow the path she'd trodden many years before, an odd surge of nostalgia rippled through her thoughts. Bizarrely, the further she went into the woods, the clearer the path became. *This is odd* she thought, knowing twenty years had passed since she trod these nettles and brambles down. She shook her head, unsure what to make of it. As she entered the clearing, she could see an elderly man standing outside one of the cottages. As she approached him a chill of anticipation shook her body. Noticing the cottages were in pristine condition, she thought, *here we go*. She approached the elderly man, who was now looking directly at her. Somewhere in her deepest memory his face was strangely familiar.

'Good day, Miss. I 'ave waited here every day at this exact time since Miss Meredith came ta' see me.' He then delved into his rugged old brown coat pocket and produced a letter. 'Miss Meredith said you'd 'da be here, Miss. She gave me this letter for ya' Miss.' He then handed her the letter. 'We met many years ago when I was working on the roof of this cottage as a youngan'. You gave us food, Miss, which I thank ye' for.' He then nodded and turned to head off.

'Sir, may I ask, are you well? And Thank you for this letter.'

'Miss, thank ya for calling me Sir. No one has ever called me that. I am well, although my life's journey is vanishing with every sunset.' He nodded, bent down and seemingly picked something out of the long grass. Then in a flash, before Rebecca could say anymore, he'd disappeared into the woods behind the cottage.

Rebecca stood there for a moment looking around. As she turned back to the cottages, she realised, in a breath, she was back home. 'Few years since that's happened,' she mumbled. She stood staring aimlessly for a moment considering her emotions. She looked at the letter, thinking about all that's happened since the last time she was here. *Somethings never change,* she thought, feeling as if it was only yesterday.

Heading back through the woods, she decided to wait until she was indoors before she read the letter. On the way back, she had to stop a few times to regain her direction. The path she had followed into the woods had vanished and in its place were twisted knee high brambles and decaying nettles. After a few wrong turns, which surprised her, she arrived back beside the lake. She made her way along the path and entered the summerhouse. In an odd way, as she opened the door, she wasn't sure what to expect. Part of her subconscious was telling her there was more to come.

She pushed the front door open, half expecting to see the old spiral staircase. 'Hmm,' she mumbled, finding everything as it should be. She sat at the kitchen table, poured a coffee and opened the letter.

My dearest Rebecca.

I hope this letter finds you well. Once more you have trusted your instincts.

The thirteenth name, Millicent.

Yes, she is a descendant of our Millicent. We now have an opportunity to give back to her family.

On the seventh day of December, she will be taken. To prevent this horrid occurrence, you must arrange for your Police to be in attendance at Liverpool Train Station. In your time, it will be directly in front of the entrance to platform eleven at 11.38 in the morning. Millicent and her mother will be standing eleven foot away from the barrier, slightly to the left. She will be wearing a red tartan school dress, a grey school jacket. She will be with her mother. Her appearance is as such. Four-foot five-inches. Shoulder length white-blond hair. Blue eyes. Her mother will be five-foot six-inches tall. Short blond hair. She will be wearing a long black coat. She will be holding a white paper cup and a red shoulder bag. The mother's name is Diedre.

They will be approached by four dark haired men. I have given a full description of their appearance in a separate note with this envelope. As the mother drops her coffee, they will pounce, push the mother to the ground and run in a northerly direction with Millicent. They will head to the large staircase under the broken green shop sign. One of the four men is the leader of this group and will be a key to stop this from happening further. At this juncture, we can only ensure Millicent's safety. If your police act with furtiveness and industry they should be able to prevent any further incidents.

At a point, I expect to see you back in 2010 when we can confidently make inroads toward extinguishing this horrid sequence of events. Thereby prevent all that has happened subsequently. The path is complicated and our actions in 2010 will have either a positive or a dramatically negative affect upon future events. At this time, there is no more we can do.

Be assured, we are occupied toward a conclusion. Our conundrum is, do we stop the main criminal at birth, or on *the day he first treads this awful road? He is a nature, not nurture and his life was destined to take a horridly insalubrious path.*

We will reach the right conclusions, and we will do this together. For now, all you can do with success, is prevent the horrid future events impacting upon Millicent.

Trust your instincts and follow your heart.

My love is always with you through every turn.

Rebecca sat there reading the letter over and again. Sipping her coffee, she knew she had to contact the police, sooner rather than later. While considering how she'd explain her story to the police, a story that would sound outlandish at best, her phone rang. It was Duncan.

'Rebecca, where is your phone. The school rang me as you hadn't turned up to pick up the girls. Fortunately, I was just around the corner.'

Horrified, she blurted, 'oh my goodness. I am so sorry, Duncan.'

Please do not worry, Gabrielle was playing quite happily and Faith was teasing the boys with her football tricks. I know you will have a good reason. I'll be home in ten minutes. I love you and please do not stress.'

Dismayed and perplexed, Rebecca searched everywhere for her phone. Frustrated, she got out Duncan's old phone and tried to call hers. It beeped a few times and then a message came through… "This phone is disconnected from the network, check with your provider."

Perplexed, and trying to work out what was going on, the door opened and in came the girls with Duncan close behind. She greeted the girls and kissed Duncan on the cheek. 'I don't have a clue what has happened to my phone. I went for a walk in the woods this morning and…' Suddenly, as if she was watching herself on CCTV, she saw her phone fall from her pocket and the elderly man pick it up. 'Blast, that could change things,' she blurted.

Narrow eyed, Duncan asked with an element of curiosity in his voice, 'what could change things? Where have you been, need I ask? And, by your expression, I am guessing you lost your phone somewhere you shouldn't.'

'Well, it's all rather confusing. I went up near the old cottages and ended up back when they were first built.' She shook her head. 'Sometime in the sixteen-hundreds. Anyways, I met an elderly man who gave me this,' she said, waving the letter. 'So, I lost my phone there, at least I think I did. The problem is, I reckon the elderly man might have it, which could pose a...' She paused, considering what he might do with her phone. 'No, he wasn't from an educated background and it's unlikely he'd know what to do with it. Besides, he was, is, part of Meredith's broader circle, and was actually waiting for me to give me the letter, which is from Meredith. What I don't get is me being gone for a few minutes, literally, and when I got back here, which was a little while ago, I just thought it was still morning, hence missing the girls.' Having then gone through the letter with Duncan, she said, 'Right, I think it's best if I call the police now.'

'Definitely, because that's, what in?' he said, checking his phone, 'ten days' time.'

Rebecca then called Mary Simmonds. After a brief chat, Mary made arrangements to visit at 10am the following day.

After supper, Rebecca and Duncan sat around chatting about the implications of the letter.

'I think the sticking point with me is the letter suggesting the path being complicated and the actions in 2010 dramatically affecting future events either positively or negatively. I've been going over in my head what that could possibly mean. I keep coming back to the same notion.'

'What do you mean, the same notion?'

'Well, this is difficult to explain.' She thought for a moment. 'Simply put, perhaps one of the girls we save from being taken ends up… I don't know. I keep focussing on the word negative. What if she gives birth to someone who will change the future in a bad way?'

'You know, I often think about your time in the past and how it can, will, or has changed events. I can't get my head around the space-time-continuum thing. Obviously stopping global warming was… well, it saved humankind.'

'I know, I struggle with this often, even when I stopped Meredith being accused of murder. Imagine if she was a murderer, I mean. The thing is, she wasn't. I think also, I trust my instinct and I do so because I trust Meredith.'

Eventually, the subject turned to Rebecca's phone.

'Potentially very dangerous leaving something like that in the… When was it, sixteen something? It could, in the wrong hands, completely change history.'

Rebecca shook her head. 'I've been thinking about that. I had like ten percent battery, which the way that blinking phone runs down will last a few minutes at best. Besides, I doubt that man would have a clue how to turn it on, let alone do anything with it. To be fair, and it was rude of me to suggest he wouldn't know what to do with it just because he hadn't got an education. Hmm, nothing to do with it, because I don't suppose anyone would know what it was, let alone work out how to use it. Might have been different in say, the nineteen-sixties. I dare say, at some point Meredith will get it back to me. Well, I hope so,' she said and raised her eyebrows.

'In the wrong hands, it could, well, change things. Although as you say perhaps not in the sixteen-hundreds. On your journeys into the past, have you ever considered the impact of what you take with you, as opposed to your actions?'

'All the time. In particular when I was with Matilda and I used penicillin. That was eleven-twenty-three, eight-hundred years before it was discovered. I covered my tracks.' She thought for a moment. 'I often think about my kind and how they could have changed the past and I don't mean by their actions. In effect, sped up man's journey. Back in the nineteen-eighties we seemingly went overnight from computers the size of a house, to ones that would fit in the palm of your hand. How did that happen, unless one of my kind from the future, intentionally, or carelessly brought something back with them. Imagine a scientist getting his hands on my phone in say, nineteen-seventy.' She thought for a moment. 'You know, I often think about things like the electric light. How anyone sat there beside a candle and thought, I know, I'll invent an electric light. He then told his mate who asked, "what's electric?" I mean, really. That's beyond clever. Same for the phone. How can you dream up that your voice could pass down a wire, especially when they'd barely invented wire?' She then thought for a moment. 'Tommy was speaking to his football pal in Vancouver the other day. Ten-thousand miles and they might as well have been in the same room. How does that work?'

They spent the rest of the evening chatting about historical events that seemingly happened out of sequence. In the end, they couldn't decide if it was intervention, or invention.

Duncan said, 'I was chatting to my uncle the other day about the Knights Templar. So, history would have you believe they were all murdered by order of King Philip of France in the early thirteen-hundreds. There is a strong path which suggests many escaped and colonised Canada well before Columbus. There is much to suggest they left Scotland and headed west across the Atlantic. In Nova Scotia, there is tentative evidence they hid their vast treasures. Never found I might add. Importantly, imagine how they would have changed history if they'd spread across Canada in great numbers.'

Chapter 7 – The Police

Duncan had taken the girls to school, and Rebecca sat drinking her coffee, trying to work out how she was going to explain the letter to Mary, someone who was largely unaware of how her time-travel works. Just as she made her mind up to tell her the whole scenario, she heard a car pull up outside the summerhouse. Still a little curious how this was going to pan out, she opened the door to Mary.

'Good morning, Rebecca. What a beautiful place to live. I believe this is where your story started, what with the magical Spiral Staircase and all.'

Relieved Mary had obviously done her homework, Rebecca realised why this woman was so senior. 'Good morning, Mary. I must say, I had a bit of a conundrum working out how I was going to explain to you about the letter.'

'I knew about your abilities anyway, but nonetheless, I decided to do some extensive research last evening. I must say, it's all a little elaborate the things you can read on the internet. I came across an old article in the daily telegraph that dated back a few years ago.'

Rebecca shook her head. 'I recall doing that interview. It was before the world had changed direction.' She raised her eyebrows. 'Things changed quickly soon after. Anyways, it would seem you're open to what I might have to tell you.'

'Indeed, I am.'

The two then spent the next few minutes going over the letter. Mary decided that their first port must be dealing with events on December 7th.

'Yeah, perfect, we can come back to what we may or may not be able to do in two-thousand and ten.' Although

Rebecca's focus was on Millicent, she knew at some point there would be more for her.

'I'm curious though, how will that work?'

'Well, here's the thing. Because it's in the past and has effectively already happened there is no time restrictions. By that, I mean, it wouldn't matter if I went back today, tomorrow or next month.' She nodded. 'It could even be in a year.' Having thought about this extensively since receiving the letter, she had found comfort from her previous jaunts into the past where she'd been able to effectively change history for the better. In particular, she'd focussed on the Meredith incident where she'd been wrongly charged of murdering Millicent Black.

'That's complicated, but I kind of get it. It must be frustrating for you knowing something is afoot and then you're in limbo.'

'It has occasionally driven me to distraction, wandering around aimlessly, especially when I was younger. Now though, I just know it's going to happen, so just shrug my shoulders and well...'

They sat around chatting for a while longer. Just as Mary was about to leave, she said, 'I think I am going to play this carefully. I will just involve senior officers in events of the seventh, including any arrests and so on. That way, we can apply some stealth and importantly know that the press won't get hold of this story. Not that I think any police officer will leak it, but if one inadvertently mentioned it to a loved one, the next thing, well. If it got out that you had instigated this, people will be saying, "can't you fix this or stop that plane crash, or change that.'

'That is so true. You know, in the early days there was an agreed embargo on the press and my family. That was nearly twenty years ago. Now, well... Thank you for being considered in your approach.'

After Mary had left, Rebecca decided to get the Christmas decorations down from the loft. Her mother had always been one for putting the decorations up at the earliest opportunity and this was something Rebecca had carried on. As she pulled the loft ladder down, Rebecca felt an odd chill. It was the kind of chill she hadn't felt for a long time and kind of spooked her. As she climbed the ladder, sticking her head up into the darkness added to her mood. It was a strange feeling, because she was sure nothing was going to happen today, but even so. She lent inside the loft hatch and flicked the light switch on. With the loft lit, which had been boarded out, she could still visualise the first time she climbed up here. She was in her mid-twenties then and unlike now, the place was dust laden, covered in cobwebs and really quite spooky. She stood on the ladder for a moment glancing around. In her mind, it was if she was there all those years ago. She had been certain she'd find something significant, perhaps a message from Meredith, something, but it had been empty, barring a few ludicrously big house spiders.

She shook her head and climbed into the loft. Gradually, box by box she took all the decorations down. Just as she was trying to work out how she was going to lift the large Christmas tree box down, she noticed a panel in the corner that looked like it was coming away from its fixings. Some years back, Duncan and her father had completely insulated the loft and that included some wood panelling in the eaves. Looking closely at the loose panel, she could see all the screws were missing.

That's odd she thought and leaned forward to see if the screws had somehow fallen out. With no sign of the screws anywhere, she sat there staring, her mind now going in circles. 'Hmm,' she mumbled, 'only one way to find out,' and pulled at the panel. It didn't take much convincing, coming away very easily. Peering behind the panel, she was sure there'd be something there, having convinced herself Meredith had somehow taken the screws out.

She shook her head, thinking *this isn't what I expected. Maybe Duncan and Dad just missed this one.* She again shook her head, knowing they hadn't because the panel had screw holes. She sat there for a few seconds and decided to investigate a little more. Now on her knees, she leant forward to peer around the side and into the eave struts. On the left, she could just see something but couldn't quite reach whatever it was. Then she remembered her litter picker downstairs. *That'll do it*, she thought heading down.

Returning a few seconds later, she reached in and clasped hold of what now looked like a book, a heavy one at that. Clicking the lock in place on the picker, she thought *I'm so glad I bought the expensive one*, knowing without the lock, she wouldn't have been able to hold onto this object. Twice, she nearly dropped it, but after a few seconds she sat staring at what appeared to be a very old book. Carefully, she brushed the dust away to reveal the title, "The Witch Register." A cold shiver run up and down her body, almost as if she'd just opened the freezer door. It was a long time since she'd had this type of emotion. Mixed between the memories of the past was a recollection of something she'd seen in the mysterious book shop in town. Suddenly, recollections cascaded through her consciousness, remembering the old man who worked there and how the shop had seemingly disappeared. Something very odd was tapping at the back of her brain. She closed her eyes and tried to focus. In a flash, she was sitting with the old book keeper, looking over his shoulder at a book that was on the shelf behind him.

She opened her eyes and took a deep breath through her nose. The book in her lap, was the one on the shelf. She recalled asking the old man about the book as if it were yesterday and she also recalled him saying, "that ones for another day."

She placed the book by the hatch and finished taking the tree down bit by bit. 'I should have left this for Duncan,' she mumbled, but had decided she wanted to surprise the girls.

After closing the loft hatch, she took the book downstairs. For some strange reason, even though her intrigue was animated by the possible contents, she wasn't quite ready to open the book just yet. Instead, she focussed her attention on setting up the Christmas Tree and decorations, even though it was only November 29th.

It was around 2pm when she finished and although she'd glanced at the book several times, still wasn't ready to look inside. Looking at the clock, and knowing she had to go and get the girls, Rebecca decided to put the book in her bureau and leave it until she felt the time was right. Right from the first time anything like this had occurred, Rebecca had always known there would be a right time and now wasn't right.

Arriving home with the girls, she pulled up outside and having already decided not to tell them, she thought it would be nice if they found the Christmas decorations on their own. She did though have a trick up her sleeve and as it was just getting dark, the timing was perfect.

As always, Faith was the first out of the car while Gabri hung back with Rebecca. Before Faith opened the front door, Rebecca pressed the remote for the lights, something Duncan had set up last year. The entire front of the Summerhouse lit up with sparkling lights. Faith turned to her mum, looking like the cat with the cream.

'Gabri' come look see what Muvva has done,' she hollered.

Job well done, Rebecca thought as she watched the girl's excitement. She was particularly delighted by Faiths reaction. Of late, she'd become a little too grown up for her liking.

Shortly after, Duncan arrived home and the family had a lovely, early Christmas evening, they deciding to watch Mary Poppins, again.

Chapter 7 – Interpole

The next few days passed quickly for Rebecca as she spent a lot of time helping Faith with her mock exams. This in itself took Rebecca back and she could recall how bored she used to get revising for her maths exams. Several times, the book had come to mind, but once again, she just wasn't ready to look inside. She questioned this numerous times and was unable to come up with an answer.

It was now the evening of the 6th December and after chatting with Mary Simmonds about tomorrow's events, she decided on an early night. As she lay in bed she wondered how tomorrow would pan out. She was also certain she may feel more inclined to look at the book after tomorrow's events.

The following morning, after dropping the girls off, she decided to give Mary a quick call. For some reason, she'd previously suggested she didn't want to attend today's events. For some reason, she'd woken up wanting to go and watch events unfold, especially as it was her concept. It was 11:00 am when she was greeted by Mary at Liverpool Train Station. Although, Rebecca wanted to be nearby, she felt uncomfortable being too close. Adjacent to the platforms was a raised shopping walkway that directly overlooked platform 11. Rebecca felt comfortable here and with her coffee, watched the minute hand on the big clock.

Although Mary had offered to have a police officer stand with her, she wanted to be on her own. As the minutes ticked by, she felt a mixture of anxiety and anticipation, wondering how this would unfold.

At 11:36, she spotted the mother, complete with red bag and coffee stand with her daughter exactly where the letter suggested. Mary, who was standing nearby the woman and girl glanced up at Rebecca and nodded. At exactly 11:38, Rebecca watched as four men approached. Just as one of the men leant forward to push the woman over, the nearby police officers moved in. In what seemed like a second, the men were apprehended. Without barely a scuffle, the four men were led away. Mary was speaking with the woman for several minutes, and then looked up at Rebecca and beckoned her down. Rebecca wasn't sure how she felt, but decided to go down anyway. It was an odd emotion. All the way through, she had wanted to keep her distance from events, now though, her feelings had changed a little.

'Rebecca, thank you,' the woman said, holding her hand out.

'You're are so very welcome,' Rebecca said, shaking the woman's hand.

Mary intervened, 'I must explain Rebecca. This woman's husband is a senior Police officer in London. I have explained who you are and how we learnt of today's events.'

The woman then said she had followed Rebecca's story as a child. 'I never thought for one minute, I'd meet you, let alone this. I don't know what…' She then paused, and appearing tearful, touched Rebecca on the arm. 'Thank you.'

They continued to chat for a while. Rebecca exchanged numbers with the woman, reckoning her husband may be a helpful contact. Once the woman had headed off, Rebecca chatted to Mary for a while and then made tracks for home. On the way, she kept going through the events in her mind's eye. She'd played it out in her mind before hand and part of her was expecting somewhat of a commotion, certainly more than there was. She actually felt relieved it went so seamlessly. After she'd been to pick the girls up, Mary called her with an update. She explained that all four men, who were in the UK without passports or identification were claiming they were unprepared to speak. Because of this and the police having no idea what country they originated from, Interpol had been engaged. Representatives were due to arrive tomorrow. Mary assured Rebecca she would keep her updated as soon as there was any light.

The next couple of days passed quickly for Rebecca as she focussed her attention on wrapping Christmas presents. Although once more, Rebecca's thoughts had shifted towards the book, again though, she was still not ready. She questioned her emotions several times and as always decided she'd know when the time was right.

It was now 14th December and the girls last day at school before their Christmas break. Over the next few days, Rebecca's attention was on the family, especially as Duncan had taken a few days off. Christmas had been planned for some time now. The closer they got to the big day the more Rebecca was looking forward to what she hoped would be one of the best. Amanda and Ruth were coming with their family, Sam Pochard, her old university teacher and her partner, Judy and of course Roxy, Tommy and his expectant wife, Kaitlin.

This was Tommy and Kaitie's first child and everyone was excited, although when she found out, Rebecca had said, "better late than never, Twit. Let's hope it's a girl." Tommy had responded by fetching a football from his car, and gently tapping it towards Rebecca's legs.

'Moving target, always were, always will be.'

With the big event tomorrow in the main house, Rebecca decided to get the girls to bed early ish. Faith, who'd been out for a long run with Tommy went out with the lights. Gabrielle called her mum back, after Rebecca had tucked her in.

'Mum, will Meredith be there tomorrow?'

'No, Sweetie. What makes you ask?'

'She said she would because she wanted to speak with you about the book.'

Over the last few months, she'd come to expect the unexpected from Gabrielle. This though, caught her completely off-guard. Narrowed eyed and a little taken aback, she asked, 'was this in a dream again, Gabri?'

'Well, it was and it wasn't, Mum. I was in bed, then I was in the big house with Meredith and another woman who I didn't know. She had very long black hair and was very pretty but very sad. She had white skin and bright blue eyes. Then I was back in bed again.'

With her curiosity now heightened, Rebecca asked, 'Can you tell me anymore about the woman?'

'Well, Meredith said the woman needed you to do something I didn't really understand. The woman's name was Minerva. She said she needed you to help her many sisters.'

After Rebecca had said goodnight to Gabri, she went downstairs to chat with Duncan. Gabri's comments had both intrigued her and left her with a lot of questions.

'I am a little confused by Gabri's comments and I need to…' She then paused, realising Duncan didn't know about the book. 'So, when I was getting the Christmas decorations down, I found this old book,' she said and fetched it from the bureau. She placed the book down. 'Right, I am now wondering if Meredith's companion, Minerva was anything to do with this book.'

'Well, I'm used to you being left-field, but I'm not sure how you have conjured up the correlation.'

'Just what I made of Gabri's account, I guess. When she was describing her appearance my thoughts instantly went to this,' she said, pointing at the book. 'It's how it always works for me. I've had this book for a couple of weeks now and although my inquisitive side wanted to dive in, my intuition told me to wait. Oddly though, the time still isn't right. Gabri said something about Meredith speaking with me tomorrow.'

'Christmas Day,' Duncan exclaimed.

'Yep, that's how it works, just when you least expect it, although I often get a kind of signal beforehand. Call it a hunch of sorts, something I feel in my gut.'

'Well, as long as you are back for Christmas dinner,' he said and laughed.

As Rebecca lay in bed that evening, she was actually excited about tomorrow, what with seeing everyone. One thing her parents could do, was lay on an event like this, often with a surprise. *Let's hope the surprise is not me disappearing into the past,* she thought.

Chapter 8 – Christmas Day and…

It was Christmas morning, and with Gabrielle now snuggling up between her and Duncan, bleary eyed Rebecca glanced at the clock. Moments later, Faith came in with coffee for her and Duncan.

'Happy Christmas, Mother, Father, Gabby.'

'Bless you, Faith. Thank you for the coffee, and an early happy Christmas to you all,' she said turning to everyone. She then shook her head, *thinking sixteen going on twenty-five one day and ten the next*. 'Nice and early, six in the morning indeed, not excited, are you?'

'What time is everyone arriving, Muvva?'

'Faith, it's mother, not muvva. And, not until eleven, certainly not at this time.'

'What time is Meredith coming, Mother?' Gabri asked, still snuggling under the covers.

'What's she on about, Meredith?'

Rebecca shook her head. 'You sound like Tommy more every day, Faith, and it's just a little thing between me and Gabri. It's about the paintings in the main house.' She then turned to Gabrielle. 'I'll show you the paintings later and we can chat then.'

Gabrielle just looked at Rebecca, clearly not having a clue what she meant.

With Faith perched on the edge of the bed, they all lay there chatting for a couple of hours. Eventually, around 08:00 am, Rebecca said, 'right you two, in the shower.'

Just as the girls headed off for the shower, Elizabeth phoned.

'Morning, Mother. Happy Christmas. To what do I owe this pleasure, nice and early?'

'Well, Ruth and Amanda just called to say they'd be here early and I thought I'd do one of those Disney style breakfasts. You know, pancakes with all the trimmings. Fancy?'

'Well, the girls are in the shower, then Duncan and myself.' She glanced at the clock. 'Shall we say nine-thirty?'

'Perfect, see you then. Oh, before you go, give Roxy and Sam a call, see what time they'll be here.'

Roxy just text me saying she'll be here in about fifteen minutes. I'll call Sam and then text you.'

'Good job your father put the extra slats in the table last night,' she said and chuckled. 'See you shortly, Sweetie.'

Just as she came off the phone, Sam called to say they were caught up in some road works and wouldn't be there until around eleven. Rebecca let her mother know, before jumping in the shower.

Once everyone was ready, they all strolled up to the house and arrived just as Sam turned up.

'Morning, Rebecca, Duncan, girls. Happy Christmas to you all.' Sam then turned to Rebecca, 'the traffic just vanished, bizarre.'

'If I know my mother, she'll have more than enough breakfast for us all, and some.' She chuckled and greeted Sam and Judy with a kiss.

As they all entered the main house, although chatting, Rebecca kept looking around, half expecting to see some kind of message from Meredith. Once the Christmas celebrations went into full swing, she forced herself to focus her attention on everyone else, and was glad she did. It was the best day ever, what with seeing all these people who were so important to her. To make the day even better, James, her father, had fixed up some elaborate snow machine on the first-floor balcony. Within seconds of him starting it off, everyone was acting like 10-year-olds, throwing snowballs and making a snowman that kept collapsing due to the ludicrously warm weather. A couple of times, Rebecca thought to herself, *global warming if I didn't know any better.* It was around 11pm when both Gabrielle and Faith started yawning.

Rebecca turned to Elizabeth. 'I think these two are ready for bed.'

Gabrielle immediately jumped up. I am fine, can we go play with the snow again?'

'It's a bit late, Sweetie. Maybe tomorrow if that's okay,' she said, glancing at her dad, who smiled and nodded.

Just as Rebecca was helping Gabri with her new boots by the front door, something nudged at her subconscious. Still kneeling down, she glanced up at the painting of Meredith. *Nothing untoward there,* she thought. She finished lacing Gab's boots, stood up, and as she did, Millicent's painting caught her attention. She called out, 'Mum, come and look at this, Duncan, you too.'

As they arrived, she pointed to Millicent. 'Notice anything? Mum, you know these paintings as well as me. Duncan, see anything familiar?'

Elizabeth gripped Rebecca's arm. 'Oh, my goodness, that was never there before.'

Duncan, with his mouth open, glanced at Rebecca and then pointed at the painting. He shook his head. 'Is this how it works? It's the book you showed to me yesterday.' Again, he shook his head.

As Rebecca was about to respond to Duncan, she noticed something in the Meredith painting. 'Mum, grab the magnifier for me.'

With pursed lips and narrowed eyes, Elizabeth nodded, and went to the kitchen. Seconds later, she handed Rebecca the magnifier. 'So, spill the beans.'

Rebecca took the magnifier and peered at the table in Meredith's painting. 'Look mum, the piece of paper on the table. That wasn't even there two-minutes ago.' She then shuddered. Even though this kind of thing had occurred many times in the past, it had never been like this. She peered at the painting, thinking *I could have actually seen this piece of paper appear.*

'You know my eyes, Bex, even with this thing and the lights on. What does it say, if anything?'

'Page one-hundred and thirty-eight. Thirty-eight again,' Rebecca said, knowing this number always meant something was about to occur. Well, it certainly seemed that way, although her gut was telling her there was something more about this number.

'Duncan raised his eyebrows. 'Well, I know what we'll be doing once the girls are in bed.' He then chuckled.

Rebecca tightened her lips. 'Well, I've had the book two weeks, so I am sure it can wait until the morning.' She thought for a second. 'Actually, this book has been knocking around for four-hundred years, so.' Realising she hadn't told her mum, she said, 'By the way, Mother, I found a big old book in the loft of the summerhouse. Remember the old guy in the book shop in town?'

Elizabeth nodded, 'and?'

'Well, I can't be certain, but I'm sure I recall seeing the same book on the shelf behind him the first time we went in the shop.'

'Hmm, one thing I've come to accept over the years is no matter how bizarre it would seem to the rest of the world, with you, everything is par for the course.'

Rebecca smiled. 'I sometimes take it a little for granted, kind of, although I did get spooked the other day when I received a letter from Meredith.'

'You never mentioned that.'

Rebecca then quickly explained how she came by the letter. 'Right, we need to get these girls in bed. Thank you for a wonderful day, Mother. I love you, happy Christmas.' She then turned to her father, 'Dad, thank you for all you did with the snow machine. Happy Christmas, I love you.'

After the girls were in bed, Rebecca and Duncan sat around over cocoa chatting about the book appearing in the painting. Half way through, Rebecca realised she hadn't really talked to Duncan about the paintings, and how things mysteriously appeared over the years.

'You said to your mum about taking this for granted.'

'Yeah, bad choice of words really. I get chills every time something is happening or happens. I think what I should have said is I am prepared and ready, no matter how random events seem. Things do catch me unawares though, like the piece of paper appearing in Meredith's painting. I looked and nothing was there and two minutes later the piece of paper had appeared. Things like that always give me goose-bumps. Generally, though, I get a kind of warning something is about to occur. Gut feeling if you like, so when it does happen, I am as ready as I can be. Also, there are no surprises no matter what happens, because I've learnt anything is possible in this bizarre world I live. The book is a perfect example. How did it end up in the loft, how did Meredith get the letter to a man who lived four-hundred years ago, and then how did I end up there precisely when he was waiting for me? Then you have the book turning up in the paintings and while I was standing there, a note appears in Meredith's painting. To most that would be a bridge too far.'

'Well, handle it you do and very well. What I admire most is the way you never allow it to affect the girls and subsequently raise unanswerable questions.'

Rebecca raised her eyebrows. 'I had years of training, keeping Tommy and his nose at a distance,' she said and laughed.

'So, back to the book, what are your thoughts?'

'It's odd, I should be chomping at the bit to read page one-hundred and thirty-eight. Strangely though, I am still not feeling an inclination. I'm not sure if it's because of Christmas and all. Either way, I'll wait. You know, the thing that has captured my intrigue more is finding out what's happened with those horrid men the police arrested.' She thought for a moment, 'Just saying it aloud has made me realise my subconscious needs a resolution on that before it will allow me to move on.'

The next couple of days went brilliantly for Rebecca, spending time with all her closest friends, who'd stayed over in the main house. It was the morning of the 28th when Mary unexpectedly called with an update. She explained that two of the men were overheard speaking. They'd intentionally put them in a room together for several hours and watched on CCTV. From their few words, they were able to ascertain these men originated from Enchowel.

Having never heard that name before, Rebecca asked, 'Where?'

'Exactly what I asked,' Mary replied. 'Evidently, it's a tiny former Soviet Union country in an area they refer to as the Himalayan Badlands. Anyway, the four men are being extensively investigated and I use that word lightly. We currently see these men as pawns only, which is frustrating. Not to say they won't face a significant custodial sentence. Ultimately, we would like to get at the ring leaders. So, more importantly, I have a name for you in two-thousand and ten, if and when you are back there. I am not sure I understand how this kind of scenario unfolds for you. I suspect from what we've talked about previously, you will only be able to prevent this whole series of events by intervening in two-thousand and ten. Then hopefully, have the main players apprehended. That's if you can find your way to the right place at the right time.'

'Well, here's the thing. In the past, irrespective of the scenario, I always end up in the right place at the right time. Therefore, I have no reason to think it would be any different this time.'

'Well, that's good to know. I must say. I admire your confidence. So, I've been doing a lot of research. I came across a number of occurrences in and around that period. They happened in a number of cities in France, the UK and Germany, among others. What is of great concern is there seems to have been some kind of cover up. I best explain this further. Firstly, the young girls, mostly blond or fair-haired were being trafficked as sex-slaves. Something alarming has come to light and I feel I must share this with you.'

Rebecca could hear Mary take a deep breath.

'Okay, it appears a couple of senior police officers were effectively silenced. It sounds like the script from a ludicrously fictional film. Sadly, I, along with a couple of senior colleagues are taking a retrospective look back, with the cases firmly reopened. At this juncture, it looks very irregular and particularly unsavoury. So, my thinking is it would be advantageous if you had a trustworthy contact in two-thousand and ten. I am going to create a case file. In that file, will be a number of senior people in society, including politicians and business men. All these people were at the heart of these crimes, and indeed were protagonists in the disappearance of at least two senior UK officers, one UK politician and a number of individuals around Europe. So, this leads me to ask if you are able to take items with you when you travel through time.'

Dumfounded by what Mary had just said, Rebecca took a few seconds to gather her thoughts. 'Crumbs, that is a frightening thought. I genuinely didn't believe things like that happened. It sounds like a bizarre conspiracy theory. In answer to your question, if it is right, it will happen. By that, I mean, if I need to take the file with me, the opportunity will present itself.'

'Again, I admire that you are so confident. I guess though, you've been living in this world for most of your life. To us mere mortals, it all seems outrageous. I even feel odd asking you if it is even possible.'

Again, she took a deep breath and Rebecca realised how problematic this must be for Mary, especially bearing in mind her position. 'It must be difficult for you, considering you only ever deal with factual corroborated evidence. My story is hardly that and I guess at best it is circumstantial, hmmm.'

'It is tricky, but only because, as you say, I've had a career path that only ever deals with real-life facts. Sorry, not to say…'

'It's okay, I understand. Even my mother, after all these years, struggles.'

'So, here's the good news. You have already crossed positive paths with one of the senior officers. It was when you met with the prime-minister Mary Scotland. I will give you all his contact details when I bring the file over. That will be at least a couple of weeks to give us time to compile all the evidence. So, don't be climbing the metaphorical spiral stairs just yet,' she said and laughed.

Rebecca spent the next couple of hours chatting to Duncan about her conversation with Mary.

'That is some story. Crumbs, if that was to get to the press, well. Importantly, it sounds like this unscrupulous mob are very dangerous. You need to make sure you take precautions.'

'I thought exactly that. The thing that gets me most is how this is going to change things. You mentioned the space time continuum the other day and it's never been an issue in the past. Now though, well. The kind of senior society players Mary spoke of, if you take them out of the equation twenty years ago, who knows. This could be the one that rocks the boat. Meredith's letter said about changing the future, as we spoke about. I never for one second thought it could be in this way.' She shook her head, considering her own words. 'This could change the world we live in, and I don't know if it will be for the better. For sure, we are best rid of these people, however... Just think for a moment. Say I stop one of the senior people being involved with children. Clearly that person has the ability to cross repugnant lines, where else might their distasteful focus take them?'

'Crumbs, that is a scary responsibility. It was one thing you stopping global warming in the future, knowing no matter, it had to happen. This though.'

'Well, here's the thing, the Witch Book could lead down a road that might impact on the future. I mean, just saying I go back to fifteen whenever and change events.'

'What do you mean, change events?

'Thinking out loud here. Say I stop a witch being burned at the stake and she goes on to, I don't know, invent something, or have a child that... Who knows?' Again, she considered her own words. 'I'm frightened, and I've never been afraid before. I don't mean for my safety; I mean for the consequences of my actions. Say one of those involved is a senior politician in the current government at that time. He gets arrested, the news gets out through the press, which in two-thousand and ten, it will. His party subsequently lose the next general election. Then Scotland gets to have their referendum and leave the UK, then there's the vote on leaving the EU and... The list of possible changes could alter the world.'

'Blinking hell-fire. Sorry, swearing, but...'

'I know, hence why I am more than a tad spooked.'

'Crumbs, the potential scenarios are daunting. How do you deal with this?'

'It's never been like this before. For sure, I've had the odd what-if debate with myself. Nothing like this though. One thing prevails nevertheless.'

'What is that, may I ask?

'I trust Meredith and co to light my way. They always have and I believe always will. My destiny is to keep history on track.'

'What does that even mean?'

'Well, the way I see it, history will take a negative direction given the chance. This is why I believe every generation has someone like me. In essence to stop, as I say, history from going down the wrong road.' Suddenly a penny dropped in Rebecca's thoughts. 'You know, I have just had a realisation. What if one of those witches who was burned in the fifteen-hundreds was of my making. Here's the deal, in that era I would have been seen as a witch. Matilda was, Rebekah was, although neither were burned, but history tentatively suggests they could both see beyond their time. Knowing what I know now, I recognise exactly what that means. Now I have a conundrum, what comes first, the witch or the sex traders? Wow, another idea just jumped into my head.' She shook her head. 'Na, that's daft, too many years in between.'

'You so must explain that.'

'Really, Duncan, just a daft notion.' In the back of her thoughts, she was wondering if saving one of the witches in the fifteen-hundreds could impact on the child abductors even though there was five-hundred years between them. She shook her head. 'Sorry, Duncan. I just had an idea that is so remote it is, as I said, daft.' She then explained her idea.

'I have a very loose understanding of how this all actually works. However, your notion is far from daft. To my mind, if I was watching that scenario as a film, I would expect it to alter the future.'

The two chatted on and off for most of the day and in the end agreed, irrespective of the aftershock, the perpetrators need to be stopped.

As Rebecca lay in bed that evening, her thoughts kept asking the same question. As she lay there, she wasn't so sure her idea she'd dismissed while chatting to Duncan earlier was actually that daft. *What if the witch on page 138 was like her and ultimately, given the chance, could have stopped events in 2010?*

Chapter 9 – Page 138

Rebecca woke up with yesterday's conversation right at the front of her thoughts. With the girls going out for the day with their grandparents, Elizabeth and James, and Duncan heading up to Edinburgh for a meeting, she decided it was time to look at the book.

After clearing up from Breakfast, she bid her farewells to Duncan and the girls. With an odd feeling resonating, she stood staring at the bureau.

Right, she thought, *no time like the present.* She opened the bureau, took the book out and just stared at it, trying to get a grip on her emotions. It was a long time since she'd felt anything like this, and it oddly reminded her of the first time she climbed the spiral staircase. Part of her was hesitant and a little uneasy. Overall, though, just as it was all those years ago, her gut was telling her she was on a path. A path she was destined to follow.

She opened the book on page 138 and started reading. It was difficult at best, being written in Jacobean English. Okay, she thought, put your Shakespeare head on. At university, she'd initially struggled with Shakespeare until her tutor, Sam Pochard had suggested a different way to understand what he was saying. As she read through, she shook her head a few times, unable to believe what had initially read like a foreign language was now legible. As she continued reading, she kept thinking there was nothing there of any significance. Then as she got to the bottom of the page a new section started. It was titled 'The Blacksmiths Daughter.' As she turned the page, she took a sharp intake of breath.

"Rebecca Hewison, hath found guilty of shaping events past wast deem'd a beldams. Th'ref're, on the 7th day of July 1553, the lady shall beest stack'd and burn'd until dead."

Breathing deeply, Rebecca scribbled down on a piece of paper her translation. She read the section over and again.

"Rebecca Hewison, found guilty of shaping events past was deemed a witch. Therefore, on the 7th day of July 1553, she will be stacked and burned."

Not only was it her namesake, the words seemed to suggest this woman could have been a time traveller like her. As spooked as she was, she also felt oddly excited knowing she had a new mission in front of her. When she'd first found the book, her intuition had suspected there may be something of this nature in front of her, but never did she imagine the poor soul would be not only of her making, but also her name sake.

She poured herself a coffee, sat down and read some more from the book. After 20 or so pages, she realised there was nothing more here, for now at least. She then spent the morning pottering about, tidying up as she went. When she realised, all she was doing was moving things around needlessly, she decided to go for a walk.

As she closed the front door, she knew something generally happened when on a walk with the house empty. Today though, she was sure nothing was going to happen. All the usual signals were missing. Although she was aware her intuition might be masked by what she'd read earlier.

As she wandered along the lake edge, she was bizarrely excited by the idea of visiting 15th-century England. With the sun high in a clear blue sky, she tried to focus her attention on enjoying her walk. She headed past the entrance to the wood where the old cottages were and continued along a path never ventured down before. For sure, she'd thought about coming this way in the past, but something invariably got in her way. Today though, there was nothing stopping her. Walking for over 30-minutes, she began to wonder if there was a fence bordering the family's land, or if she would ultimately end up on someone else's property. She shook her head and continued, knowing the nearest property was over a mile away.

She followed the lake path around into a stunning reed fringed bay, and wondered why it had taken her so long to venture this way. As she continued, the path was increasingly buried, to the point where it was almost inaccessible. There was a mass of brittle brown dead reeds and the twisted branches of leaf-less odd-looking willow trees blocking her way. For sure, she'd seen twisted willows before, but none like these. Most seemed to be youthful and certainly no more than 2 or 3 years old. The unusual bit were the twisted branches, which to her mind had an almost cartoon look to them. Every branch was a string of spirals. *Make brilliant Christmas decorations,* she thought.

As she looked forward to see if the path was more accessible, oddly the trees on the other side of the bay were still covered in leaves. It was a sight that jolted her consciousness and to compound these tingling emotions further, the leaves appeared fresh, almost spring like.

Narrowing her eyes, and peering around her, she was at a complete loss. She was certain she hadn't jumped anywhere. In the past, even when her movement through time was unexpected, she always knew something had happened. This was most peculiar, and although her subconscious was a little jumpy, she still felt like she was in her own time. With no visual landmarks, her mood was heightened with curiosity.

She stood there for a few moments. It was as if she was standing amid the corrosion of winter, yet the far side of the bay was full of spring delight. This vision triggered the most bizarre thought. It felt and looked like she was standing in her time, peering across the bay into the future or past. As she regained her composure, she recalled her mood the second time she opened the doorway to the spiral staircase, knowing she was venturing into the past.

'Right, get a grip,' she mumbled and pushed her way forward. She approached a slightly larger willow and as she eased her way around the edge, including getting one of her feet wet, she felt a sudden upward turn in the temperature. The change was certainly enough to make her take her jacket off. This in itself gave her a moment thinking time. Without doubt, she now knew just a few moments ago, she had been peering from her era, into this era. *Whenever or wherever this is*, she thought.

Looking back at where she'd come from, and seeing that too had changed and was also full of spring cheer, a couple of female voices interrupted her thoughts. Cupping her ear, trying to work out where the voices were coming from, she could see a spiral of smoke just behind a couple of tall yew trees. Although this should have alarmed her, what with the stories of witches being burnt, she knew this was perhaps no more than an open fire of sorts. She didn't know why she knew this she just did.

Reckoning the voices may be coming from the area where the smoke was, she continued along the lake edge a little further. She'd taken no more than a few steps when a path to her right, clearly recently trodden, suggested she needed to go that way. Her decision to follow the path was a mixture of intuition and being certain it was heading in the direction she wanted to go.

As she came into a clearing the other side of the yew trees, she could see a wooden cottage of sorts, that had a Canadian log cabin appearance. She shook her head, thinking, *that's reasonable,* knowing a lot of people from this area ventured towards Nova Scotia, Newfoundland and New Brunswick. *Maybe this is where log cabins originated*, she thought, wherever this is. She then took a deep breath, suddenly realising she could actually be in Canada.

Her confused thoughts were interrupted by two women appearing from behind the cabin. One of them immediately started walking towards Rebecca.

In an unusual mixture of early English and modern English the woman said, 'Greetings, Rebecca. I has't did expect thee. Our mutual guardian, M'redith spake of thy arrival h're Pictou.'

That was it, she knew she was indeed in Canada. She'd been doing some homework with Faith very recently and knew Pictou was the original place for the first settlers, mostly from Skye, and the lakes. The thing that was a tad confusing, she was expecting to be in the fifteen-hundreds, but knew it was most likely post seventeen-seventy-three.

'Hello. May I enquire, are we in Canada?'

The woman frowned and tentatively nodded. 'This nation is known as Quebec.' She then squinted. 'M'redith toldeth us thee wouldst knoweth of this colony as Canada. M'redith eke toldeth us thee wouldst needeth to knoweth the year. The year is seventeen-eighty-one and until the British arriveth this nation is still und'r French occupation.'

Rebecca thought for a moment and was sure she knew what this woman had just said. To make sure, she went through it again in her head, in English. *"Meredith told us you would know of this colony as Canada. Meredith also told us you would need to know the year. The year is seventeen-eighty-one and until the British arrive this nation is still under French occupation."*

Rebecca held her hand out to this woman.

The tall, elegant yet clearly adorned by poverty, long black-haired woman responded with a gentle nod while touching Rebecca's hand softly. As she spoke, her translucent blue eyes radiated a tangible appeal. Bizarrely, and as with the original Rebekah all those years ago, it was if she was speaking modern English. 'My name is Belisant. I have a twin sister still at home in Britain who is named Myleesa. We are descendants of Minerva. She was murdered, deemed a witch. Myleesa lives near to your homestead. She knows of a man with the Devil's thoughts. You must find your way to my sister and help her stop this man from taking her existence. He forces her with child, against her wishes. That child's descendants will change life in your time. His life leads to a bigger group of people who abuse children. Your future depends upon your action.'

Suddenly, Rebecca recalled Gabrielle mentioning Minerva in a dream. *Right*, she thought, *notes,* and took a pencil and paper from her pocket. 'Can you tell me again, please Belisant?' she said and smiled.

'Make notes not. Myleesa knows all and with Meredith and Ethernal's help you will find your way to my sister. All I ask, other than your success, is you help my sister find her way to us. A ship, destined for this land, sails from Glasgow six days after you meet with my sister.' Again, the woman touched Rebecca's hand gently. 'Follow your calling and go with strength. Turn now and be home.'

Rebecca nodded, smiled and as she turned, she knew in a second she was back home. She put her winter coat back on, pulled the zip up and considered her frame of mind. She was surprisingly unalarmed. Her only concern was trying to recall everything that Belisant had said. She knew she'd said there was no need for notes, but the way Rebecca felt, her emotions were in a need-to-know process. For sure, there had been many times when she just ended up somewhere without warning. Always though, when she had a mission, which this was, she knew what it was, if not when.

She headed back along the lake side. Just as she turned the corner, she glanced back. Although it shouldn't have been a surprise to her, seeing the trees on the far side of the bay leafless again, still came as a bit of a shock. She shuddered as the impact of what she'd just done and where she'd been hit home. *I'll never get used to this*, she thought. When she'd first seen the smoke, she initially thought it might be something to do with her namesake. Ending up in Canada in what appeared to be a completely different scenario was a little confusing.

Chapter 10 – What Next

As she arrived back at the Summerhouse, the first thing she did was check the time, especially after her last jaunt, which unusually kept her away for hours. *That's odd*, she thought, *it's still early morning*. She squinted, 'hang on a mo,' she mumbled, 'I left at ten-fifteen and it's nine-fifteen. In all her journeys, including her 30 years with Etienne, they only ever took a few moments of her time. There was the odd occasion when she'd been gone a couple of hours, but never had she got back before she had left. Rather unsettled by this, she entered the summerhouse only to find Duncan sitting drinking coffee and the girls sitting out the back. She stood open mouthed, completely dumfounded.

'Umm, Duncan,' she said, unsure what to say. Oddly, he didn't look up. 'Duncan,' she uttered. Again, there was no response. With her spine tingling, her thoughts immediately jumped back to when she was 15-years-old and she'd watched her mother carried to an ambulance after the horrid incident with the boiler. The thing she found a little confusing is that incident was in the future. Clearly this wasn't. She stood there, glancing around looking for something, anything that would give her a clue as to what was going on. Just then, she noticed a pile of greeting cards stacked up on the shelf. They were upside down, so she went over for a closer look. For some bizarre reason, she was unable to pick the cards up, almost as if she wasn't there. Although she should have been alarmed by this, she'd been in this situation with Meredith and her daughter's wedding, when she was there, but unable to interact with anything or anyone.

Crouching a little, she tried to see what was written on the cards. Just then, she got the whiff of that all too familiar smell of almonds. Seconds later she felt someone behind her. Without turning, she knew it was Meredith.

'Hello, my lovely,' came an all too familiar voice. 'the cards celebrate your daughter's seventeenth birthday.'

'What, Faith is seventeen and I've missed it?'

Meredith touched her gently on the arm. 'It was Gabrielle's seventeenth, not Faith's.' She again gently touched Rebecca's arm, almost as if she was aware this sent a shockwave through Rebecca's body.

Rebecca shuddered, going over Meredith's words in her head. She then went to the window and looked at the girls outside. Seeing Gabrielle as a young lady and Faith as a woman sent a spine-chilling tingle through her body. To compound her emotions further, she couldn't believe she hadn't noticed earlier when she spotted the girls out the back. Taking several deep breaths, she turned back to Meredith. A few seconds passed before she was able to speak. 'Why am I here, wherever here is?'

'Look closely at Duncan's face.'

Narrow eyed, Rebecca walked over to the table and peered into Duncan's eyes. Etched was a sadness she hadn't seen since his father passed. She turned to Meredith again with her palms lifted.

'You are with us in the other dimension. The place in your deepest thoughts. The place you've questioned so many times.' Meredith again touched her arm and Rebecca suddenly realised she hadn't felt Meredith's touch for many years. 'You are witnessing a scenario most never see.'

Shaking her head, unsure what Meredith meant, she again lifted her palms.

'You find yourself here after your death in this alternate world. It is a world you were always destined to, but you are here too early. Today is a warning for you to take care. You must understand that you can and will die while on your journeys.' She took hold of Rebecca's hand and squeezed it tightly. 'You will, in time, meet with Myleesa in the summer of seventeen-eighty-one. She has an unsavoury male acquaintance. This man is disturbed by inner thoughts and carries the Devil's factor. He will forcefully impregnate Myleesa with child. That child will go on to have her own children. One of her children will also carry the devil's factor. That factor will lay dormant but carry through the generations. It will show in your time in the year twenty-ten.' She looked directly at Rebecca. 'We spoke of a conundrum and how changing the past would alter the future negatively. All who are in this other dimension have considered all outcomes carefully. We trust your intervention in seventeen-eighty-one to be the only plausible option. Sadly, this journey is littered with danger for you alone. It is, however, the only option that will have a positive outcome. If that outcome is successful, there will be no need for your intervention in two-thousand and ten.'

Although Rebecca was fully aware of her next journey, Meredith's alarmed tone suggested it was fraught with danger and unlike anything she'd experienced before.

'You have a treacherous mission ahead of you like no other. Your only opportunity to stop this man is when he seizes the young girl. He will be armed with a dagger which he carries in his left hand. His right arm is feeble from a previous injury. Be conscious of my words. You will need more than your intuition to stop this man. You will be alone and unless you act with caution, he will murder you. Be aware, he will attempt to gore you in your stomach when you first approach him. Your journey will take you to the door of an alcohol tavern named "The Ship Inn," where he will be standing outside. Trust you will know him and your timing will be precise. You will have a brief moment, so act with stealth and assertiveness. The sky will be in darkness, it will be raining so the ground wet. Although menacing, he is feeble and you are stronger.' Just then the door opened. Gabrielle and Faith walked in. 'Look at the sadness in their eyes. This is not your time. Turn, go with strength, mindfulness, and fortitude. Go back through the entrance door and find yourself home. Remember my words. You have been allowed these brief moments as an insight and a warning. It is a world where you do not belong.'

Rebecca glanced at Duncan and her daughters. She then squeezed Meredith's hand. 'Will I be alone? I ask, because I have always found solace knowing you are always there to catch me.'

'This time, you are alone. Even Minerva's spirit will be powerless to help you. Go now.'

Rebecca gently touched the back of Meredith's hand, turned and stepped through the front door. The instance she did, she knew she was back in her time. She re-entered the summerhouse and seeing it was 12:15 pm, she knew she was back where she was meant to be. Over the next couple of hours, she went through everything that had happened today. She knew she had to keep this to herself and couldn't share this with anyone. Oddly, it now made sense when Meredith had suggested she was alone on this journey.

The afternoon passed silently for Rebecca as she sat going over everything Meredith had told her. Previously, she'd never known what to expect when a trip into the past was on the horizon. This time was different and although she should have been beside herself with trepidation, she oddly felt calm. She considered her mood several times, knowing of the potential danger. Somehow, somewhere in her deepest thoughts, any fears she should have somehow seemed inconsequential considering all the anguish this dynasty had caused to so many women over the years.

Just as she was making her third coffee, her mother rang to say they were staying over at the Alton Towers Hotel with the girls. With Duncan away for a couple of days, she was actually glad of the time to herself. Although she knew it would be unwise to tell Duncan of her upcoming jaunt, she reckoned had he been here, she wouldn't be able to help herself. *No, I need to do this alone*, she thought, recalling Meredith's words.

The following morning, Rebecca was woken early by the sun shining on her face. She'd fallen asleep reading and hadn't drawn the curtains. Bleary eyed, she went over to the window and was somewhat surprised to see a light sprinkling of snow. Although she'd intended on pulling the curtains, it was such a gorgeous scene, she instead sat by the window watching the sun climb in the sky.

She shook her head and thought, *right, coffee.* She headed downstairs and after her coffee and a couple of slices of toast, she decided to take her camera, the one Duncan had bought for Christmas and head outside.

Although the snow covered everything, with the sun high and little wind, it was pleasantly warm creating a rather strange mood. It helped she was wearing a long coat and snow boots she'd bought the last time they visited Canada. In the past, they'd gone to Vancouver. Last year, they'd decided on the east coast Maritime. They'd loved Halifax in Nova Scotia to the point where they thought they may end up emigrating one day, especially as Duncan had so many family members living there. Some of them dating back to the early settlers.

As she was taking her umpteenth photo, something stirred in her thoughts. She pulled away from the camera and shook her head. It was as if she was in the other dimension, even though she knew for sure she wasn't. It was quite an odd emotion she was feeling, almost as if she was there listening to Meredith, Ethernal, Matilda and Rebekah all planning her next journey. Although Meredith had told her she would be alone, she oddly felt she wouldn't be. Looking down at the boots she'd bought in Canada and thinking about her meeting with Belisant, gave her an odd feeling. She then considered her upcoming meeting with Myleesa in the seventeen-hundreds and hopefully paving her passage to Canada. Then there was her and Duncan's decision to visit the exact area Belisant lived just a year before. She shook her head at these bizarre coincidences, all tied together. This was so unlike any of her journeys in the past, including going back to the "Cradle of Civilisation," and all that subsequently followed, including meeting the Queen. In the past, everything that had unfolded invariably seemed down to her actions. Now she was beginning to wonder if she'd ever had any control over any of her jaunts or if, like this one, it was seemingly all planned.

As she wandered along the water's edge, her thoughts were going from one idea to the next. In the past, she'd always believed Meredith was close by to catch her if she fell. Even so, she always felt every choice of direction was down to her. Of late, it was if she was being directed in a play and she didn't much care for that feeling.

'Na, I'm not having that,' she grumbled.

'It was always down to you. We have and always will trust your choices.'

'Meredith,' she said, smiling, thinking I've never seen her twice before. 'Am I with you, or are you with me?'

'You asked yourself that question a moment ago and know you are at home. You know more than any of your predecessors. You are the strongest of our kind. This is why the next mission falls to you. No one has been strong enough thus far. We have waited for you, as we have always said.'

She narrowed her eyes a little. 'Rebekah, surely she was strong enough. She achieved so much.'

'Her fortitude was her beauty and mind alone. It was the same for Matilda. Your strengths are many. You have the beauty and mind; you also are valiant and fearlessly intrepid. Above all, in spite of your slight figure, you are strong physically and mentally. There was one like you, she shared your name. Sadly, she was lost in a time that was not her own. I am here to again advise you at some point in the future you will have an important mission that must remain within your thoughts and you are to share this with no one. Overall, know of the dangers, and do not fall the way your namesake fell. You will understand the importance. Before hand and in the coming days though, you may find yourself in unusual situations. The circumstances of these are for you to learn. You will be alone, although we will all be with you in spirit. I must go now.'

Rebecca stared aimlessly across the calm, almost crystal-like water. With the sun falling like a stone, and along with it the air temperature, she decided to head back to the summerhouse. On the way, she again considered all that Meredith had said. This led her thoughts back to the first day she entered the summerhouse by means of the old key she'd found in the woods. The one she believed had been waiting for her. She shook her head, now wondering if the key had been placed there by someone in the other dimension, knowing she'd find it. The more she considered her own thoughts, her time with Meredith, Matilda, and Rebekah, the more she realised it was perhaps a team effort. *That's it*, she thought, reckoning she called the shots, those in the other dimension cleared the path.

Her thoughts briefly focussed on Meredith's suggestions she would find herself in unusual situations. Although this should have alarmed her, she was strangely excited by the idea. In particular, she wondered what she may learn from these jaunts, if indeed they are that. The only thing she felt certain about was the important mission would involve her saving Myleesa, and helping her reach her sister in Canada. For some reason, although Meredith's warning of danger should have alarmed her, it hadn't. She suspected the entry in the witch diary about her namesake was also a warning. Still, though, she didn't feel like she was in any danger at all. *I know* she thought, *these warnings are just that, warnings.* She nodded her head reckoning without this, she may have gone into this situation without fear and that alone would have put her at risk. *Hmm, that's why Meredith spoke to me twice, to make sure I am careful.*

Chapter 11 – That Door Again

As she approached the summerhouse, something appeared a little odd. As she grew closer, she could see something wasn't right. Just then, she tripped on a fallen fence pole running along the side of the lake. With pursed lips, she shook her head, knowing this fence had been cleared years ago. As she turned back, she could see the old jetty, complete with her dad's boat, the one her and mum had so much fun in. That was 25-years-ago and she thought the jetty, along with the boat were just a memory. As she went to step forward for a closer inspection, her foot was still caught up in a wire that originally run along this old fence. Looking down sent a shiver along her arms, the kind she hadn't experienced since she was in her teens. In place of her Canadian boots were her old white trainers, the ones she'd last worn when she was 15-years-old. 'This is just daft,' she mumbled.

Over the years, she'd gotten used to bizarre sequences, occurrences and events. Even so, wearing a pair of trainers that she had dumped 20 plus years ago was at best daft. The thing was, she just realised she was also wearing her old white jeans. This immediately made her reconsider Meredith's words. 'Perhaps this is what she meant,' she mumbled. She then glanced up and could see the summerhouse was just as it was 25-years ago, although still something a little adrift. This nudged a mental door open, giving her an insight to what might be happening. The question now at the front of her consciousness was not where she was, but why she was here dressed as a 15-year-old. Again, considering Meredith's words, she wondered if she'd missed something all those years ago.

Hmm, she thought, walking over to the water's edge. She'd used the water as a mirror before and each time it was exactly like this, a step into the unknown. She took a deep breath and looked down into the calm water. Although she kind of knew what to expect, it still came as a surprise seeing herself as a young girl once again. The question that kept coming to the front of her thoughts was why.

She shook her head and stepped up onto the decaying veranda. Looking down actually put a smile on her slightly edgy mood. *How did I ever convince my mother this was safe,* she thought as she felt her foot slip on the decaying wood. She looked at the door and although it was as she remembered, there was something a little odd. It was really bizarre, somehow different from what she remembered. It looked older in a strange way. She then put her hand against the side of the door, only for it to crumble away. She stepped back, and again her foot slipped. *This is all very odd,* she thought. She turned to look back up towards the main house. With the grass almost head high, entwined with brambles and shrubs she could barely see the house, although what she could see, appeared derelict.

Okay, she thought, *I'm fifteen and back where it all started.* Clearly though, she could see something wasn't right.

The thing that she was now struggling to get her head around was everything appearing as if they'd never lived there. It looked as if it had all fallen into disrepair, not that it was in great shakes in the first place. This was almost as if she was seeing the house years into the future. It was all very strange and rather confusing. She again considered being clearly where it all started, so how could she be fifteen, yet somewhere so far into the future.

Going over a couple of ideas in her head, she reckoned the best place to start would be up at the main house. The problem was how she'd get there. She'd never minded the odd bramble scratch but her path looked more like a wilderness. Plotting a route, she reckoned sticking close to the edge of the woods might be the best way. At least there, the shade of the huge old conifers would reduce the growth rate of the grass and nettles.

After a bit of back and forth, including re-routing through the woods, she arrived at the old house, nursing several scratches on her arms, muddy white jeans and trainers. She looked up at the old house and spotting ivy clambering down from the edge of her bedroom balcony left her very confused. She knew she was back to being 15 again, and this was her home. *Why does everything appear so old*, she thought. As she stood there looking around, she tried to recall what it was like the first time her mother drove the car here. She shook her head, knowing it was not even close to being this derelict. It was as if they'd never lived here. The confusing thing was her being 15 again but it was if she was looking at the house as if no one had ever lived here. *Well, not since Meredith's time* she thought.

That idea alone sent a myriad of questions cascading through her head. What if I hadn't helped Meredith, what if she'd gone to prison for murdering Millicent. What then happened to George? Did he move away? Did Millicent shoot Meredith instead? She then just as quickly dismissed that idea, only to again think, *what if she did,* reckoning if anyone was capable, Millicent was.

In the end, after considering every possible scenario and some unlikely situations, she reckoned there was no choice but to try and find her way back to Meredith. The one thing that kept occurring to her, was of late, whenever she'd had questions like this, Meredith normally appeared on the scene with answers. The thing that was now a little concerning was Meredith telling her she'd be on her own. She narrowed her eyes, thinking, *did she mean now, or just on the Myleesa mission.*

'Right,' she mumbled, and headed back towards the summerhouse.

After losing her sense of direction in the woods and a few more scratches, she eventually arrived back at the front of the summerhouse. She walked up to the front door, took a deep breath and clenched the handle tightly.

For a second, she felt a rush of emotions, just as if she was doing this for the first time. She then turned the handle, and as the door creaked open, there was that familiar whisper of almond smelling air, kissing the cheeks of her face.

In an odd way, although still spooky, it was also strangely comforting. Stepping inside and seeing the old door at the end of the corridor sent a surge of emotions through her body. The way she physically reacted was really quite strange. Her thoughts were 41-years-old, but her body was physically responding with youthful sensations of discovery.

She shook herself and gingerly made her way down the corridor. The spooky feeling of treading onto the dust laden floor sent a cascade of memories pouring through her thoughts. She paused to glance in both of the rooms but with her mind on the door at the end of the corridor, she was unable to focus. Feeling a little edgy, and unsure what to expect, she pulled at the tiny door handle. Unexpectedly, the door opened easily and through the darkness, she could just make out the spiral staircase. She stood there for a few seconds regaining a little composure. Once more, her thoughts and body were reacting contrarily to each other. Bizarrely, her adult thoughts were focussed on finding an answer but there was an odd naive emotion making her feel hesitant. The only thing she could properly focus on was Meredith telling her she would face unusual situations. This thought made her feel both edgy and intrigued as if once more her youthful innocence was fighting with her grown up consciousness.

Again, she took a deep breath and stepped forward. As she started to climb the stairs into the darkness, her thoughts caught up with her physical reaction to this environment. Not knowing what she'd find on the other side and with the involuntary anxieties of a 15-year-old, she hesitantly pushed at the door on the first landing.

As it did all those years ago, it creaked open. Unable to see her hand in front of her face, cautiously, she stepped into the room. Just as with her first time here, she could see a tiny shaft of light on the far side of the room. Briefly, her 41-year-old thoughts interrupted her youthful emotions, reminding her what happened. Nonetheless, as the door pulled from her grip and slammed shut behind, it still sent a shockwave of emotions through her body. With her eyes clenched tight, she could again see sunlight through her eyelids. *Well, I've been here before, so what's making me so anxious,* she thought, feeling uneasy but determined. Considering this for a few seconds, she knew it was her adult thoughts once again battling with her youthful emotions. *Right, focus.*

She opened her eyes, and was both surprised and unsurprised to see the room exactly as it was the first time, complete with the dandy green dress neatly folded on the bed. If she'd been in any doubt, she knew for sure she was right back where it all started. Considering this for a moment, she realised something was missing. The first time, Meredith had called her name and seconds later appeared at the door. Just as she was going over this in her head, she heard shouting outside. It was Meredith and if her memory served her correctly, it sounded like she was arguing with Millicent.

As a thousand thoughts thrashed around in her head, she hurried to the door on the far side of the room and downstairs into the kitchen. With the argument seemingly more intense, she headed outside. She quickly realised the voices were at the front, so made her way round, concerned what she'd find.

Seeing Millicent pointing a shotgun at Meredith, sent shockwaves through her body. In a flash, she recalled Meredith telling her she could die while on her travels, so reckoned she'd be ill-advised to intervene. As she tried to gather her thoughts, she spotted George hurriedly limping his way towards the ladies. Briefly, George glanced in her direction and it was clear the way he failed to respond she was once more invisible. Considering this, she knew even if she wanted to intervene, she couldn't. She stood and watched as both ladies turned towards George.

Waving his walking stick, George moved towards Millicent with purpose. Millicent turned towards him, and seconds later, George was laying blood covered on the floor. Both Millicent and Meredith, screaming with anguish, rushed towards him.

As she watched the two ladies crouch down, it was clear to Rebecca, George was beyond help. Anguished, she was at a loss what to do next. She felt sure she was a spectator from the other dimension and there was nothing she could do. So, why am I here, she wondered. Something didn't make sense though, because unlike previously, where she'd just appeared in the other dimension, this time she physically climbed the stairs. With Meredith and Millicent arguing once more, something was telling her to head around to the back of the summerhouse. She followed her instincts and as she passed by, she noticed the front door of the summerhouse was open. This sent a flow of emotional memories, and having been in this situation before, she once more followed her gut and entered through the front door.

She wasn't at all sure where she was going and what she was hoping to find. Importantly, she couldn't understand why she wasn't tangled with distress even though she should be. Feeling oddly clear in her head, she made her way towards the door at the end of the corridor. As she did, something caught her attention in the room on the left. It was the room she always considered Meredith's room.

On the far side, she spotted the all too familiar tallboy. In spite of the dinginess, she could see a piece of paper laying on the cabinet. She made her way over and picked up what was a letter. Recognising Meredith's handwriting, she took a deep breath and started reading.

Rebecca.

I am writing this following a dream of you, which told me to inscribe these words. My dream said I would know you in an alternate life but not in my current life. So, although you are a stranger I've yet to meet, I feel life's course will bring us close one day.

If you are reading this letter, you would have witnessed the sad, accidental death of my beloved George.

In spite of my entreaties, Millicent was found guilty of shooting George to death. On the tenth day of October, eighteen-fifty-three, she was criminalised to New Holland.

Reading this left Rebecca confused, knowing only a minute earlier she'd witnessed George being shot, yet this letter was speaking in the past tense as if it had happened weeks or even months ago. Also, she was a little unsure what Meredith had meant about an alternate life. Deciding to look back outside, she could see no sign of Millicent, George or Meredith. Okay, she thought, I have somehow jumped from when it happened to somewhere in the future. That consideration also helped her realise she was seeing a completely alternate existence where her and Meredith's paths had never actually crossed. She shook her head, went back inside and carried on reading.

The sad loss of George. My dear Aunt Rebecca banished to an asylum in the Americas. Millicent's unfair maltreatment. My despair is too deep to stay within these grounds.

It is with heavy heart I bid my farewell to my dearest home, hopeful of finding solace elsewhere.

Go with heart, Rebecca. If my dream is correct, I have no doubt in another life, or dimension, our paths will cross with a smile not tears. For now, though, you have seen one of times many negative possible routes. For everyone of your kind, there is an evil counterpart sending time in a horrid direction.

Be sure, there may be an alternate way. A way for you to correct times negative clock. I know not why I know to write these words. Know I do though. If you look beyond the obvious, you will find a way to correct time and allow it to follow its truthful route.

Meredith.

Now standing out on the veranda, the derelict state of everything, including the main house made sense knowing Meredith had moved away. Rebecca read the letter a couple of times and focussing on Meredith's last words, she knew there had to be another way. It was all very peculiar and unlike any of her previous situations. Here she was with the body of a 15-year-old, the thoughts of a 41-year-old and not having a clue where she was. To compound her emotions, she was aware that she had just jumped backwards and forwards several times, something that had never happened before. She kept asking herself if she was back in her time, in 2007 when she was 15, or at some point in Meredith's time. Because everything was unrecognisable, she was at a complete loss what to think. The one thing she felt she knew for sure was in this world she'd yet to meet Meredith.

She sat down on the veranda, peering across the lake unsure where or what she should do next. The longer she sat there, the more unsettled she felt. She kept speculating what life would be like with no Meredith. This then made her wonder if all of her journeys would evaporate and only be fanciful memories in her deepest thoughts. She shook her head, realising how fine the line was between everything that had happened actually not happening. Part of her wondered if this is what Meredith meant when she suggested there was more to learn and in particular what she'd written about correcting history's negative clock. She reckoned she knew what this meant, however. Somehow though, her gut was saying there was more to come.

Focussing on Meredith's last words again, she thought. *Right, I've got to find a way to fix this.* She remembered an incident in the past where she entered the summerhouse by the kitchen door. This had kept her in Meredith's time, just refocussed her to a time where she could make a positive difference.

With that concept in her mind, she headed around the back. Although she was focussed and her thoughts were positive, she still had feelings of uncertainty. As she approached the kitchen door, she was a little surprised to see it closed. In the past, her gut had always led her towards an open door. Considering this for a moment, and trying to focus her thoughts to her real age, she realised she was perhaps better off thinking naively. This way, she'd be able to follow her intuition openly, instead of blinding her gut with unimaginative adult thoughts. *That blinking common sense again.* She pushed her shoulders back, and opened the door.

Stepping through the narrow entrance, she wasn't sure what to expect. Even so, she was now feeling confident. *Well,* she thought, *nothing ventured.* There wasn't anything jumping out at her in the old kitchen, so she headed upstairs. Briefly, she paused by the green dress on the bed. She then went through the door where she'd originally came in, down the spiral stairs and outside onto the veranda.

Within a breath, she knew she was in 1853, except this was the 1853 she knew. Just then, she heard Meredith calling her from the back of the house. The odd thing was, it was the same tone Meredith had used the first time they met all those years ago. She headed around unsure what she'd find, although she realised, she'd seamlessly jumped from the negative past to the past she knew.

'Aha, there you are dear girl. I've been looking for you.' She then paused for a moment. Looking down and shaking her head ever so slightly, she looked up and smiled. 'I have the strangest of thoughts in my head.' Again, she paused.

Recognising Meredith's expression, Rebecca reckoned she knew exactly what was happening. As in the past, Meredith's conscious thoughts were catching up with her subconscious dream memories. 'Although you see me as your daughter, you are aware I am not. Part of your thoughts see me from another life, and these thoughts are tucked deep in the recesses of your brain nudging your consciousness. We have met many times and you know this, but are unaware why you know this. It will all become clear. Although I am from a world many years from now, we share a similar path through life. Let us walk and allow yourself a moment to gather your thoughts.'

Meredith smiled, although still appeared a little uneasy. Almost involuntarily, she took Rebecca's hand. 'Let us indeed walk. My thoughts are cloudy, although the sky is clearing.'

Silently the two walked towards the main house. Although Rebecca was unsure if this felt right, it was almost as if Meredith was leading her. As they approached the main house, Rebecca spotted Millicent. This caused the strangest sensations because it was exactly the same scenario as the first time that she'd met Millicent. Just as she was contemplating going through the same dispute with Millicent, Meredith stopped dead in her tracks.

'We have been through this situation before. I do not know why I know this; however, I do.' Appearing a tad perplexed, she again paused. 'I have a message for you that appeared in my thoughts. It is from someone I am yet to meet. Although, I know this person. This is most unusual.' She nodded, seemingly much more comfortable with her inner thoughts. 'In another time, we will meet with Millicent and that meeting will unfold the way it is meant to. Today's meeting allows you to see how history could have played out if it had not been for your intervention in my life. Our time together is for that reason alone. To help you see your own destiny. Therefore, it is time for you to return to your world. I will walk back with you.'

As they headed back, Rebecca considered Meredith's words. Thinking about how anxious she was when she saw Millicent shoot George, and again thinking about what Meredith had just said, she felt closer to truly understanding her life's destiny. Occasionally in the past, she'd considered the path she was on, never really sure why. Now though, she knew her life was always destined to keep history on track. She also realised all the events of the morning, seeing the main house in total disrepair, George being shot and her yet to resolve the situation between Meredith and Millicent was just showing her how the world would spiral down a negative path without her kind.

As they approached the front of the summerhouse, Meredith let go of Rebecca's hand. Instantly, Rebecca knew Meredith was gone and she was once more back to her own reality. She stood there for a moment considering all that had just happened, and especially jumping back and forth between alternate times. Although this should have confused her, focussing on what might be, she was able to concentrate on the one overriding message that her life was a continuing journey and her destiny was to keep history on its true path.

She entered the summerhouse, made herself a coffee and sat down to consider all that had happened on this day. Ever since effectively saving humankind from self-destruction, she'd understood the implication of her journeys. Never though, had she truly fathomed the significance of her kind. Over the years, she'd been aware there were others of her making and circumstances had suggested there was one of her kind in every generation and she now truly got why. The nagging thought at the back of her head was why her generation had two, her and Gabrielle. That was if Gabri was of her making. Considering this, and thinking about her own mother's tentative jaunt into Rebecca's world as a child, she reconsidered Gabrielle's involvement. The more she thought about this and recalling Meredith suggesting they'd waited generations for one as strong as her, she assumed perhaps there were many of her making in every generation. She nodded, realising conceivably there was only ever one at a time who was strong enough, not that she liked the word strong. Maybe some step forward and some push their ability to one side, cast it off as a dream, or worse still, as was the case with her mother, have it frightened out of them.

Looking up at the calendar, she realised Elizabeth and James would be home with the girls tomorrow. After all that had happened, she was looking forward to seeing Faith and Gabrielle, and especially as Duncan was home early later tomorrow. In an odd way, she was in no mood to talk about her last couple of journeys, which was just as good because Meredith had suggested she shouldn't tell anyone.

Chapter 12 – Focussed

The next few days passed quietly, well as quietly as could be expected with two girls full of tales about their adventures at Alton Towers. This actually helped Rebecca refocus her attention on Duncan and the girls. A couple of times, while chatting to her mum and dad, her father had asked poignant questions. He'd done this in a way suggesting he knew something had happened, as he'd so often in the past whenever she'd been anywhere. Even though she was momentarily tempted to tell all, Meredith's words and her intuition knew she should keep quiet, for now at least.

As the days turned into weeks, in what felt like the blink of an eye the first signs of spring were showing. The daffodils she'd planted last November had bloomed and were now closing their eyes for another year. With Duncan once more in Scotland and the girls having gone back to Alton Towers with Nan and Grandad, Rebecca took her coffee outside and sat on a rocking chair her father had bought for Christmas. At the time, she'd thought it was a little grandma-ish for her, but it had become her favourite place to watch the world. As she sat there doodling some pixies and fairies for a wallpaper she wanted to make for Gab's room, her phone rang.

She glanced at her phone screen, a little surprised to see the call was from Mary Simmonds. 'Hello, Mary. How are you?'

'I am fine, thank you. I have some news for you, which is all very odd. Two days ago, the four men apprehended were being taken to Stansted Airport for transportation to Interpol Central, Lyon, France.'

Rebecca could hear Mary breathing heavily. 'Are you okay, Mary?'

'Yes, I am fine, thank you. Look, I think this may be better if I came to see you personally.'

'I'm free all day,' Rebecca said, her curiosity at bursting point.

'Okay, shall we say in around thirty minutes?'

'Excellent, you've left me wondering. I'll have the coffee on.'

'Sorry. I am wondering too. Apologies, that statement doesn't help does it?'

'No worries, see you soon.'

Rebecca had just made some fresh coffee when she heard a car pull up outside. By the time she was at the front door, Mary was standing just about to ring the doorbell. The look on her face told Rebecca this was important. 'Hello, Mary. Come into the kitchen and I'll pour us a coffee.'

The way Mary sat down with a puzzled look on her face intrigued Rebecca. Although she was keenly interested in what Mary might have to say, she knew to wait until she was ready to speak.

Mary sipped her coffee, glanced up at Rebecca and offered up a rather uncharacteristic smile. 'So, I have some very odd news for you and I am hoping you may be able to share some of your wisdom. The four men were being transported in a secure vehicle heading to Stansted Airport. Now, I say secure for a reason. When the vehicle arrived at the airport, well, it never arrived. The vehicle including the four men had vanished.' She shook her head. 'I am at a complete loss. I saw the four men as they were placed in the vehicle and the doors locked. The two drivers were senior officers. This is where it gets odd. When I started to investigate, all records of these men had vanished. In fact, there was nothing. When I spoke to the two officers about their journey to the airport, they looked at me with a blank expression.' She raised her eyebrows. 'That was awkward, I had to make up an excuse. Anyway, I even checked my phone records relating to this incident. Gone, as if it never happened.' She then lifted the palm of her hand, clearly perplexed.

Rebecca narrowed her eyes as a bizarre idea came to her. 'So, have you spoken to anyone else about this?'

'No. I don't see how I could. There are no records of this ever happening, anywhere. As I said, including my phone. In fact, I had to look up your number as it was no longer in my phone, even though…' She shook her head. 'I hope you can make sense of this and by the look on your face, I suspect you might have some ideas.'

Just as Rebecca was about to speak, Mary held up her hand. 'Sorry, this part is very important. So, I checked the records of previous abductions and everything is as it was. It is just this incident that has, for want of a better word, disappeared.'

'Okay, I can't go into details, however.' She then thought for a moment. 'So, early in January, I experienced a couple of jaunts into the past. These were all designed to show me how things might look had I not intervened with history. I use this term lightly, but stay with me. After these episodes, for the first time I truly understood my mission in life. That mission was, is, all about keeping history on track. I have been advised history is perpetually bound for a negative direction.' She paused and seeing Mary was with her, she continued. 'So, I am now wondering if this is something to do with that. Perhaps someone else intervened in the past. By someone, I mean one of my kind. Subsequently, the group that controls these men never came into existence.' She shook her head, unsure about her own words.

'That doesn't add up though, because…'

Nodding profusely, Rebecca said, 'Yep, just thought that. Hmm, so perhaps someone just intervened with these four men, or even stopped them heading to the station.' She shook her head. 'The thing is, someone could have travelled not just from the past, but also from the future. If say one of my kind got wind of what these men did, they could have jumped back and stopped them snatching the girl from Liverpool Station. I use that purely as an example.'

Nodding, Mary said, 'well, here's the thing. Thinking about this, I wondered about the girl they were trying to apprehend. So, I phoned the mother.' She shook her head ever so slightly. 'She never went to the station because their car had two flat tyres. By the time that was sorted, they decided to take their trip on another day.'

Nodding Rebecca said, 'that'll be it then. Someone else from another time has intervened. The question is from the future or past.' She thought for a moment. 'Must be from the future because Meredith knows all about this event and she would have stopped anyone from the past interfering. Hang on, that doesn't make sense because she would have stopped them even if they were from the future. Well, someone would have stopped them, I would think, although I am kind of guessing.'

Appearing rather captivated, Mary asked, 'Does it or can it work like that?'

'The one thing I've learnt over the years, nothing is out of bounds. Just when I think I've seen it all, there's a new twist. A prime example is all that happened in January, wherein I got a glimpse of a negative world, showing how it would be if I hadn't intervened.'

'That must keep you on your toes.'

She nodded, 'I am used to being surprised, so I kind of expect it, which results in me not being caught off guard. In essence, not being surprised even though I should be. I get chills for sure and sometimes it takes me a moment to gather my thoughts. Overall, though, I am always able to kind of work out what is going on and where it is leading me.'

The two sat and chatted for a while about some of Rebecca's early jaunts into the past. After some lunch, Mary headed off.

'Thank you, Rebecca.'

'I will let you know as soon as I can find anything out.'

After Mary had left, Rebecca sat around wondering what could have happened with the four men. Every time she thought she'd come up with a solution, just as quick her common sense dismissed it. At a complete loss what to think, her phone ringing brought her down with a bump.

'Hello, Mother. How are you, dad, and the girls?'

'Hello, Sweetie. We are having fun, thank you. Do you know a girl named Katherine?'

Rebecca thought for a few seconds wondering why her mum would ask this. 'Err, no I don't, why do you ask?'

'Well, the day before yesterday, Gabrielle said she'd been playing with a girl called Katherine. It was all a little odd, but she said the same again today. The thing is, she hasn't been out of our sight. Well, no more than a few seconds. Anyways, Gabrielle said Katherine had let down the tyres on a car.'

Instantly, Rebecca's brain went into overdrive. 'Mum, did she say she'd been actually playing with her, or was it in a dream?'

'No, Bex, she said she'd been with her. When I asked her the other day, she said it had been when your father and I were getting some coffee. Gab was with Faith, no more than ten yards away. When we got back, Faith had her head in her phone and Gabri was sitting on the bench with her legs up. Here's the thing, her knees were muddy, as if she'd been kneeling down.'

'Okay, Mum, don't worry. I know what it is and I'll tell you when you get back.'

'Rebecca, you can't leave me hanging like that.'

'Sorry, Mother. So, you recall when I was young and I told you I'd been with Meredith and you said I'd only been gone for a minute. This, I suspect, is the same. I spoke with Mary, the senior police officer dealing with those men from that incident. So, here's the thing, the men disappeared along with all records of them ever being detained. Anyways, when Mary spoke with the woman, she knew nothing of the situation, saying she never got to the station because someone had let down the tyres on her car.'

'Flip, that's spooky. So, you think Gabrielle let down their tyres. Is she capable?'

'I've known for some time she's been speaking with Meredith. The thing is, it was only ever in a dream. This would be the first time she'd been anywhere, certainly that I know of. Well, it stacks up. Look, I'll see you tomorrow and we can chat to Gab about it all. Have a lovely time, and thank you for calling. You've answered an unanswerable question. I love you, Mother, give the girls and dad a kiss.'

After Rebecca came off the phone, and with her thoughts going from one thing to the other, she decided to go and watch the sun set over the lake. It had been a delightful spring day and without a cloud in the sky, she set her camera up on the veranda.

As the setting sun magically changed the sky with threads and curls of orange, yellow and red, she started clicking on her camera. After a couple of dozen shots, she moved the camera to capture the sun setting behind the island. She took a test photo and checked the image. Nearly choking, she looked back and forth between the island and the image on her camera. In the camera was a small boat surrounded by mist, and it was right next to the island. The thing was, there was no boat and definitely no mist. She took several more shots, but the first was the only one with the boat.

Although confused by the image, she wasn't as shocked as she should be, having seen this boat twice before. In the past, the appearance of the boat had preceded an incident of sorts. Indeed, the first time was soon followed by her first meeting with Meredith. The more she considered this, she wondered if this was a sign that Gabrielle was about to meet Meredith for real, as opposed to in a dream. Rebecca actually found this notion a little uncomfortable. Although she was fine knowing Gab was of her making and the idea of her stepping into her shoes was exciting. The issue she had was Gab being only 10-years-old. She mumbled, 'I was fifteen and barely old enough to deal with all that happened.'

'Deal with it you did though,' came a whisper. 'Fear not, the door will not open for your girl until she is ready.'

Rebecca was used to Meredith creeping up behind her and whispering, but whoever this was, it wasn't Meredith. She turned around and no one was there, and she could sense whoever it was had now gone. She stood there for a few seconds, unsure what to think. She glanced back at the image on the camera. As much as it should have been a shock seeing the image minus the boat, it didn't really surprise Rebecca. With the sun now set and the temperature dropping, she put away the camera. As she picked up the tri-pod to head inside, a piece of paper dropped to the floor. She picked up the paper and turning it over, could see some childlike writing.

My name is Katherine.

I will look after Gabrielle.

We stopped the bad men.

My aunt wanted us to stop them in case you did not.

You know my aunt, Belisant.

Goodbye

Rebecca stood peering at the letter, unsure what she felt. On one hand, she knew for sure, Gabrielle had effectively stopped the mother and daughter going to the station. Subsequently, she'd put a stop to the men seizing the daughter. Importantly, she'd done so without any issues. She shook her head, confused how Katherine's aunt could be Belisant. Belisant lived in Canada in the seventeen-hundreds, so how could Gabrielle be with this woman's niece. She then shook her head realising Katherine's timeline wouldn't stop her being with Gabri. *After all*, she thought, *I was with Rebekah 4-thousand years ago.* She grinned at herself for even speculating about such things.

After a lazy pizza, she decided on an early night.

The following day, the girls arrived home. Rebecca had a brief chat with her mother, choosing not to mention the boat. She did however, show her the letter from Katherine.

'Well, you were right then about Gabrielle. Seems she is of your making.'

'Yeah, Mum. Initially, I was worried about Gab, what with her being ten and all. Then I heard a whisper.' She shivered. 'I should be used to this kind of thing, but this caught me off-guard. In the past, whispers have only ever been occasionally Ethernal, but mostly Meredith. I didn't recognise this female voice and it spooked me a little. Importantly though, this woman said the door wouldn't open for Gabri until she was ready.'

'Makes me think about my brief interlude in the past.'

'It did me too, Mum. I have kind of come to a conclusion. Something Meredith said to me about me being strong enough to deal with everything made me think. In the past, my understanding was there was only ever one of my kind in each generation. Now, the only reasonable explanation is there is only ever one who actually does anything.' Seeing her mum appearing a little confused, she said, 'like with you, Mum. Your father frightened it out of you. Maybe there are several of our kind and only one steps forward. Although, that doesn't quite add up, because it would appear, we have me and Gabri both affecting the past. I really don't know what to think.' Then a penny of sorts dropped. 'So, maybe Gab isn't actually doing anything in the past, she is only there witnessing events, the same as what happened with you. You were there, but never changed anything. You saying Katherine let the tyres down would confirm Gab was seeing and not actually doing anything.'

'That makes sense and actually helps me feel a little better.'

'Me too, Mother.'

They continued to chat for a while, believing Gabrielle would only follow in Rebecca's footsteps if it was right.

Later that day, Rebecca mentioned Katherine to Gabri.

'She's my new friend, Mum. She is naughty and wears funny clothes.'

'Naughty, in what way?'

'She said we had to let the tyres down on the car, and said her mother had told her to do it.' She then chuckled. 'She is funny. She speaks with unusual words. I don't always know what she means, but I get her.'

Narrowing her eyes, Rebecca asked, 'does she say things that sound like, holla, mine own nameth is kath'rine?' The way Gabrielle grinned and nodded Rebecca realised Katherine could well be Belisant's niece.

'She talks like that all the time. Her aunt does too.' Gabrielle turned her bottom lip up a little. 'I won't see them for a long time though, Mum.'

'Why do you say that, Gabri?'

'Katherine's aunt said I had lots of things to do before I could see them again. She said I must listen to you and do all I am told.'

Although Rebecca continued to chat to Gabrielle it moved onto Alton. For sure, she wanted to know more about Gab's time with Katherine, but recognised she'd found out all she needed to. She was also aware Gab had said all she wanted to for now. Realising Gab was more intent on talking about Alton kind of endorsed her being just ten-years-old. It also made Rebecca realise Gab was taking her trips into the past as the norm, which caused mixed emotions, but also settled her nerves a little.

Later in the afternoon, Duncan arrived home, and suggested going out for supper. It was just what Rebecca needed as the last thing she felt like doing was cooking.

Chapter 13 – Where next?

The next few weeks passed quietly for Rebecca mostly taken up with helping Faith prepare for her exams. This had proved a little difficult at one point. After a county football match, Faith had been approached by the Manchester City Ladies team. Although they'd agreed with the club that Faith would concentrate on her exams, it had nonetheless distracted Faith a little. Fortunately, Tommy had spoken with Faith and told her she had to focus on getting her grades. This helped greatly. The club had also spoken to Faith about the same thing, stressing it was important she got good results, suggesting it was their policy.

In the blink of an eye, the girls were finished school for the summer. As a present to Faith for getting excellent exam results, Elizabeth and James had suggested to Rebecca, they would like to take the girls to Disney in Florida. Although initially, Duncan and Rebecca had considered going along also, sadly the timing wasn't right for Duncan who had a very important business merger to oversee. Several times, he'd said he could get someone else to cover, but Rebecca knew this was his baby.

After dropping mum, dad and the girls off at the airport Rebecca returned home. Duncan had flown out to New York for his business meeting and this meant she would be on her own for a few days. After so much going on at home, she was actually rather looking forward to some down time.

As it was such a beautiful day, on a whim, Rebecca decided to take the boat over to the old Bear-Lodge. After a few attempts, the outboard eventually started. This brought a smile to her face, reflecting on her time with her mum in this boat. On the way across the flat calm lake, she thought about the first time she and her mother found the old lodge. Recalling it as if it were yesterday, she remembered speaking to her mum about bears around here, and saying, "there's none that we know about." The look on her mother's face when they eventually found the lodge, only to discover it was called the bear-lodge made them both laugh out loud. She didn't really know why the old lodge had captured her imagination after so many years, but capture her thoughts it had and as always, she'd gone with her intuition. For some time, she'd had her impending meeting with Myleesa at the front of her thoughts. Often, since she'd learnt of Gabrielle's time jaunts, she'd become increasingly concerned that Gab might get involved with Myleesa. Her biggest concern was Meredith suggesting that actual meeting would be fraught with potential dangers. She'd never minded a bit of danger herself, but her meeting with this man had spooked her, so the idea of Gabrielle getting involved just wasn't an option.

There were times in the past when she was able to generate something happening. Especially after Meredith had told her she just needed to focus and it would happen. Coming over to the lodge, she felt she was actually forcing the issue, albeit she was also following her gut. For some reason, she was feeling a tad hesitant, and reckoned it might be because she hadn't forced the issue for a number of years. Over the last few months, Rebecca had to some degree unwittingly avoided situations that may end up with her jumping. She was sure it was after the incident with Millicent and George, which had left a horrible taste in her mouth. With the girls and Duncan away, she'd decided to follow her intuition and make something happen. Today's trip was exactly that, a calculated intuitive trip into the unknown.

With only remnants of the old jetty left, she had no choice but to beach the boat as best she could. Fortunately, there was a long ish rope in the boat, which was just long enough to reach a slender branch. She wasn't at all sure it would hold the boat if the wind got up, but as there was no sign of wind, she headed off into the woods none too concerned. Trying to recollect her foot steps from 25-years ago, she knew her path would at best be laboured. Bizarrely, the path was actually quite clear in places and she wondered if perhaps it had been trodden down by a dear, 'or a bear,' she chuckled. Laughing at herself, she soon arrived at the front of the old lodge. When they'd first found it all those years ago, it was derelict at best. Oddly, it didn't look any worse, if anything, the door she remembered hanging off its hinges appeared to be up-right.

Narrowing her eyes, she moved for a closer look. As she did, she heard something or someone thumping around inside. Even by her standards, this spooked her. Frozen to the spot, she wasn't sure what to do or think. She was sure it wouldn't be a bear, even so, the sound coming from inside suggested something more significant than a squirrel or bird of sorts.

Seconds later, the door creaked open and a weather-worn face, masked by long wispy grey hair and a bedraggled beard appeared at the door. In a flash, she knew she recognised this face, but couldn't focus enough to know where from.

'Rebecca,' came an educated, distinct Liverpool voice. 'You appear confused. You know me, although I see from your expression from where you know not.' He then chuckled. 'The old book shop in town.'

With her mouth open and her palms lifted, Rebecca didn't know what to say. For her, this elderly gentleman had seemingly vanished many years before, perhaps into time. Here he was though, back and apparently no older. This confused her emotions, leaving her speechless.

'Words elude you.' He smiled. 'Come inside, I have tea ready. I knew I would see you today, now you are once more open to intuition. The intuition that has always opened your door to this world.'

Rebecca followed the man inside, still unsure what to think or say. Her indecisiveness was compounded entering what was essentially a derelict building only to find it rather homely. The man offered her a seat. Sitting opposite him, she asked, 'so, how long have you been here? Last time I saw you was in the old book shop and, well...' She narrowed her eyes. 'Have you been here since?'

He placed a cup of tea in front of her, smiled and nodded. 'I have indeed, awaiting your return. I have been happy here with my old books. You may recall me suggesting there was more for you.'

She nodded. 'I do although I thought that meant more time jaunts.'

'And so, it did. There is however, more reading for you.'

Although still a little befuddled, his words focussed her thoughts. Narrow eyed, she went to speak but hesitated seeing him hold his hand up.

'I suspect your thoughts will be confused with many questions. I have a book and an entry in said book that you should read first.' He then went to a dust-laden book shelf and lifted down a huge book. Placing it on the table, he put both hands on the book. 'The entry in this book will refocus your attention. Before your meeting with Myleesa, there are other issues you must consider foremost. Please,' he said, opening the book, 'read these pages first.' He then turned the book towards Rebecca.

She sat staring at the chapter title, The Witch Register Consequence. Immediately, she suspected this would relate to Minerva and her two descendants. As she started reading, she was a little surprised to see although they were mentioned, the chapter was centred around a 12th-century woman named Evanora. Although this woman was deemed a sorceress, she was never vilified as a witch. The more she read, the less she understood where this was going. After stumbling through several pages of Jacobean English, she glanced up at the old man.

The way he pointed at the book and told her to read on intrigued her. Narrow eyed and with heightened curiosity, she continued reading. After a couple more pages and wondering if she'd missed something, she again glanced up. Once more, he nodded and pointed to the book. She turned the page and continued reading. The chapter then took a different turn, stating Evanora was a niece to King Stephen. This instantly rang alarm bells with Rebecca. After her time with Queen Matilda, she'd done some research on that period. King Stephen's accession to Henry 1st had resulted in a bitter civil war with Empress Matilda as she was then known. A war that cost the lives of many innocent villagers in the area between the Scottish borders and Lakeland, the area where she now lived.

Rebecca sat back and considered her time with Matilda, and having effectively saved her life, believed her time with this gracious woman was over. Clearly something had occurred following her time with Matilda. With a need to know more, she read on. After a few more pages, she looked up at the elderly man. 'So, this Evanora, horrible name I might add, anyways, she was a thorn in King Stephens side. If I've read it correctly, she instigated his pursuit of Matilda.'

He smiled and nodded. 'Your interpretation is correct. In this world, for every one of your kind, there is an evil counterpart. Evanora was exactly that. Often with her kind, especially in the dark-ages they are deemed a bad witch and murdered. Because she was of Royal ancestry, the only person who was prepared to challenge her was your lady, Matilda. After you effectively saved her life, her pursuit of Evanora continued fruitlessly. This resulted in a bitter civil war. Further to this, Evanora's son became an advisory to King Stephen's accession Henry 2nd. His throne led to the Constitutions of Clarendon. A set of laws which resulted in the wrongful trials of members of the Church of England.' He then paused. 'I can see from your eyes you are speculating if you can affect the outcome. As with this incident and others of its kind, your intervention would be of no consequence. Wars and such like are and always will be part of humankinds learning. As unsatisfying as that is for your kind, it is the path of life.'

'So, why am I reading this? What part can, or should I play?'

'For all time, there have been your kind, maintaining a natural inoffensive path for history. Alongside your kind have been the likes of Evanora. Their journey is to disrupt history's peaceful path.' He appeared to think deeply. 'I understand your conundrum. You feel, as with your predecessors, a desire to stop evil acts such as war. All you can do is alter the path of individuals whose destiny is evil bound. To this point, Evanora's descendants maintained a position within the Royal family. This led to the birth in the eighteen-hundreds of a callous, evil individual. You will know of this individual as "Jack-the-Ripper." This is where your kind can alter history's negative path. Alas, to approach this evil man would be fraught with too much danger. Therefore, there may be another way, through a door that may take you back to Perth Priory.'

Dumbfounded, but nonetheless intrigued by this man's words, Rebecca was unsure where this would lead and how she could alter history in Matilda's era. In the back of her thoughts, she knew she still had an impending issue to resolve in Myleesa's time. Now though, at the front of her consciousness was a notion the door to Perth would mean meeting once more with her beloved Matilda. She looked at this man unsure what to say.

As if he'd read her thoughts, he said, 'agonise not. I know of Myleesa. As always, Ethernal and Meredith will open the doors for you when the time is right. As with all your journeys, trust your intuition, after all, it brought you to me today. For now, our time together is over. Know the darkest paths always have light.' He then stood up and opened the door. 'Before you go, I must give you this letter. You should keep it about your person at all times. One day, you will indeed find yourself back with Empress Matilda. This letter will then serve you well.' He then frowned. 'Avoid temptation and do not open the letter until that time.'

Rebecca took the letter and placed it in her coat pocket. As she did, she knew she would struggle with curiosity, the cat and all that. 'You said for now, does that mean we will meet again?'

'History will determine that, Rebecca.'

As she made her way back to the boat, she kept going over everything in her head. Trying to focus and recall all she'd read and everything he'd said, she had a realisation. She shook her head, knowing she didn't need to remember everything, it was cast in history. Her job was to alter that history for the good of all. As she arrived back on the beach, she was somewhat pleased to see the boat still tethered. On the way back across the lake, she wondered how history would respond if she was to rid it of Jack-the Ripper. In a flash, she thought about Gabrielle letting down the tyres and the subsequent result. She pursed her lips and muttered, 'he'll just disappear from history.' This then led her to wonder about the women he murdered and if they could or would somehow change the future.

Mooring the boat and making her way back to the summerhouse, she reckoned, as with everything else she'd been through, there will always be a cause and consequence, it was just if the resulting change would be nondescript, positive or negative. Unusually apprehensive, she sat drinking her coffee, and considered her actions over the years. Realising her every involvement had seemingly had a positive outcome, helped her find a comfortable thought process. After all, she reckoned, Meredith was always there and importantly, she said those in the other dimension had considered all outcomes. Just then the letter from the old man came into her thoughts. Finding it still in her pocket, she breathed a sigh of relief. Thinking about all the elderly man had said, she decided to put the envelope in a sealed water-proof bag. She then placed it in her new outdoor jacket, the one she'd worn of late whenever she went for a walk, and zipped the pocket closed.

She went to bed that night, and although still considering her meeting with the book-shop man, she felt settled.

After a good night's sleep, she woke early, again with the sun shining through the window. After a shower and a couple of coffees she decided to go for a walk. Just as she was heading out the front door, something nudged at her inner thoughts. She went back inside, put her phone, camera and bag on the table. Of late, every time she'd been out, she'd always had one of these items with her. Remembering back to when she was young, she'd never jumped anywhere if she'd had anything of this type with her, even down to a plastic bag. *Unless it was meant to be*, she thought, remembering the medicine she'd taken to Matilda. She then patted the letter in her pocket and thought, *it will be if it is meant.*

She stood on the veranda not knowing which way to go. *Right*, she thought, *back to the Spry wood*, realising the last time she ventured into the woods with purpose was years back with her mother and that was to show her the fallen oak. She then went inside to fetch her sketch pad and pencil. She wasn't sure why she'd decided to take these, other than going with her gut, something she hadn't done as often as she did when she was younger. Also, part of her was trying to find a way back to the innocence that drove her decisions as a 15-year-old. This notion had occurred to her when the elderly man had said she should trust her intuition.

Arriving in the clearing by the fallen oak brought an evocative surge of emotions to the front of her thoughts. Even though it was 15-years since she'd last been here, it appeared exactly the same. Narrow eyed, she looked at the young willows, reckoning they should be fully grown trees by now. She tightened her lips and again narrowed her eyes as an unexpected thought occurred to her. Every time she was here, it looked exactly the same and that included the willows. The first time she was here 26-years ago, these trees were 3-years-old at most. They were the same when she was here with her mother, 15-years ago, and still haven't aged all these years later. As she leaned back against the old oak, she got a whiff of that all too familiar almond smell. *How have I missed that, it always smells like this*, she thought, again shaking her head in disbelief. For sure, in the early days, she'd smelt almonds, mostly around the summerhouse. Smelling it today jolted her memories, realising it always smelt that way in this wood, she'd just never noticed it before.

This sudden awareness changed her mood completely. With her consciousness scrambled, she wasn't at all sure what was going on. Then something bizarre occurred to her, suspecting this place could perhaps be some kind of half-way house between her world and that other dimension. She sat there considering her thoughts, reckoning that made complete sense. Searching through her memories, she realised most times she had spoken with Meredith's spirit, it had been hereabouts. She recalled standing in this exact spot the first time she saw Meredith, but couldn't cuddle her.

As she considered her emotions, something was telling her to head down to the stream. She shrugged her shoulders and followed her instinct. Arriving by the stream sent a reminder up her spine. For the first time, she realised it looked exactly the same as the stream that ran behind Perth Priory in the woods. It was a place her and Matilda had escaped to so they could chat freely. As she was considering this, she faintly heard a woman's voice singing. Although the voice was some distance away, she knew instantly it was Matilda.

Heading off in the direction of the voice, she came across an opening. On the far side, she could see Matilda. She made her way towards her, calling. Seconds later, she heard several men's voices shouting, and before she had time to think, five kilt clad men had surrounded her. One of them, a huge brute of a man, pushed her to the ground, shouting in a broad Scottish accent.

She screamed for Matilda several times but there was no response. As one of the men dragged her to her feet, she again called, but Matilda didn't turn, clearly unable to hear her, which was odd because she wasn't that far away. Distraught with both fear and frustration, she continued to call as the men dragged her towards the Priory. Her pleas to the men clearly fell on deaf ears. They pushed her through a small door at the back of the Priory, then forced her down a narrow damp corridor. The horrid clanking sound as they opened the door to a damp, horrid smelling cell sent fear spiralling through her thoughts. With no words, they pushed her inside the cell and locked the door. Before leaving, one of the men pointed at her aggressively and ran his hand across his throat.

Chapter 14 - Locked

Fraught with fear and trying not to cry, Rebecca stood at the back of the cell. The floor was covered with sodden, horrid smelling straw. She'd never been this frightened in her life and shaking with hopelessness and anguish, she tried to focus her thoughts. She kept wondering why Matilda hadn't heard her calls. Then the most bizarre memory occurred to her. On her previous meeting with this woman, whenever she'd spoken to her, she'd always turned sideways. 'Was she deaf in one ear,' she mumbled.

In an unsteady, odd accent that somehow reminded her of Liverpool, she heard a man speaking close by.

'They heard your Sassenach accent. They assumed you were of English King. There is no escape, and no redemption.'

Looking around, Rebecca couldn't work out where the voice was coming from. 'Where are you?'

'I am in the cell next to you. I came to this area four years since, my aim, to help Matilda. As with you, they heard my English accent. The law in these parts is an ancient Scottish law, Yr Hen Ogledd. As such, we have no voice. If you are believed guilty, you are guilty.'

Fearful and anxious, she was struggling to focus her thoughts. Almost unwittingly, she moved to the front of the cell and without thinking, held her hand out through the bars. 'My name is Rebecca.'

With a hand, red with sores, he touched Rebecca's hand. 'I am James. They will bring you dirty food and filthy water once a day. They will not respond to your appeals.'

'Surely there must be some way. I know Matilda and she is a good person.'

'I too know she is a good person. I came here to warn her of the evil intent of King Stephen and his malevolent niece, Evanora. Sadly, my message was never relayed to Empress Matilda.'

Suddenly wide eyed and alert, Rebecca took a deep breath. 'I am here also to warn of Evanora.' *Right*, she thought, taking the letter from her pocket. Hesitantly, she looked at the letter, recalling the book man had insisted she shouldn't open this until she'd met with Matilda. For a few seconds, she considered her options. 'I have a letter for Matilda but I am only to open it when I see her.' She shook her head, unsure why she'd just told this man the letter was only to be opened in Matilda's presence.

James asked, 'did you see Matilda today, if so?'

'I did,' she said, realising she'd seen her and that was enough. She leant back against the wall and peeled the envelope open. Inside were two sealed letters. One headed "open now" and the other, "open when with Matilda." Still tormented with fear, she took a deep breath, opened the letter headed open now and stared at the heading. It had the Royal Crest of Matilda at the top. Scanning through the words, she realised this may be redemption for her and possibly James. 'I am going to read the letter to you.'

"I, Empress Matilda, write this for those in possession of this dispatch.

Under any consideration, the person carrying this memorandum should be respected as my ally and advocate.

I am to be contacted immediately upon receipt of this communication.

Queen and Empress Matilda."

'That will be your salvation. How did you come upon this letter; may I enquire?'

'That, James is a long story and one I will explain when I have sorted out this mess. Once I see Matilda, I will make sure she frees you also. She trusts me with her life, so…'

Almost on call, a grumpy looking man, one that reminded Rebecca of a character from the Braveheart film came to the front of the cell. He sneered at Rebecca and placed some rancid looking bread under the bars.

Holding the letter up, and in her best Scottish accent, the one she'd practiced on Duncan, she said, 'Look, I have this from Matilda.' She then watched as this man peered at the letter, his long moustache twitching. By his reaction, she suspected this man couldn't read. Clearly though, from his response, he seemed to recognise Matilda's crest. He huffed, kicked the bar and returned to where he'd come from.

She leant back against the wall and sighed. 'I think he couldn't read. He seemed to recognise Matilda's crest; I hope. He has gone now.

'He may return,' James said with an air of positivity in his weakened voice. 'I can only hope. The thread of my life is shortening with every sunrise.'

Now focussed, Rebecca banged on the bars continually. After several minutes, and just as she believed it was to no avail, a smart looking, clan dressed individual appeared in front of the cell. In an odd and calming way, his appearance reminded Rebecca of Duncan.

Holding his hand out, he demanded, 'Communiqué.'

Hesitantly, Rebecca held the letter up to the bar. She kept a tight grip, knowing this was perhaps her and James's only escape.

He glanced at the heading, seemed to read the letter. His austere appearance changed and with a somewhat magnanimous expression, he held his hand out for the letter. 'I will take this to Matilda. It seems you are a friend and ally.'

The last thing Rebecca wanted to do was hand this letter over, but realised she had no choice. She looked the man in the eyes, then apprehensively handed him the letter through the bars.

The way he nodded with the slightest glimmer of a smile, made her feel a little better. He took the letter, nodded and turned away.

He seemed to be gone for hours and as darkness fell, weary, Rebecca wondered if she could stand up for any longer. With no intention of sitting on the sodden floor, she propped herself up at the back of the cell. Just as she was getting to the point where she actually couldn't stand any longer, the man returned. He opened the cell door causing a horrid rusty clanking sound. Then, with an odd smile of sorts, he indicated for Rebecca to follow him.

'James in the next cell,' she exclaimed. Sadly, this fell on deaf ears. She pulled at his arm, and pointing back, she said, 'James is my ally, and is here to help Matilda.'

His somewhat calm expression changed and frowning, he pulled his arm away. 'It is Empress Matilda. You will speak with her presently, and should address her correctly. You can speak of your ally then if the Empress deems it so.' He then put his finger to his lip.

He led her around a number of dingy corridors. Eventually, they came into a well-lit, clean area more befitting of an Empress. Again, he turned to Rebecca, held his finger to his lip and opened a huge gothic like arched door. He indicated for Rebecca to stay still and entered the room, closing the door behind him.

She put her ear to the door, and then realised she was being watched by several regally dressed people. She pulled away from the door, and drew comfort from recognising the tartan worn by all. It was the same tartan Duncan wore. This helped settle her nerves further. Moments later, the door opened and the man beckoned her inside. Then with a nod to Matilda, he left and closed the door, leaving the two of them alone.

Getting to her feet and with open arms, Matilda hurried towards Rebecca. Although, as with the first time they met, she was speaking in a twist of Scottish and Germanic, Rebecca understood her clearly. 'My dear, Rebecca. I have awaited your return. I know not why I know this. I have certitude you carry a message from the Book-Keeper.' She then hugged Rebecca.

With both her hands gripping Matilda's shoulders, Rebecca smiled. 'I have thought of you often.'

'You too have been in my thoughts. You saved my life, although King Stephen is still in pursuit. Therefore, I am almost a prisoner here. Fear not, I find solace in my writings. I have also known of your visit for some while and have smiled often.'

'Before I go any further, there is a man in the cell next to mine. His name is James and he is an advocate for you. Like me, he was jailed because of his English accent.'

Matilda nodded. She then went to the door and beckoned a man towards her. After a few words, she closed the door and turned back to Rebecca. He will be looked after and I will speak with him presently. So, you are older, what hand has life given you?'

Rebecca smiled. 'Thank you, James is a good man. So, my life since we last met. For you, I believe it is one year. For me, it has been…' she thought for a moment, '… twenty-five years. I am married to a Duncan Fergusson.'

Narrow eyed, Matilda held her hand up. 'I too know of a Duncan Fergusson. You met with him on our journey back to safety. He is my close friend and confidante.' She then held up her palm in a questioning manner.

Grinning, Rebecca said, 'my Duncan is a direct descendant. Bizarrely, he has an identical appearance. Seems we both have good taste when it comes to our men.'

Nodding, Matilda squeezed Rebecca's hand. 'Seems we do. Are there offspring?'

'I have two girls, Faith who is sixteen and Gabrielle who is ten.' She then briefly explained about Gab's ability.

The two then chatted about their lives since their last time together. Rebecca told her how she had read her writings and said she should draw comfort, knowing her words will become revered and respected more so in eight centuries.

'Well, at this time, they are just a few thoughts scribbled although...' She then thought for a second. 'I have been urged by my close friend Mary to write seriously.' She then nodded. 'This I will do.'

'Right, I have a letter for you from the Book Keeper.' She then handed Matilda the other letter.

She took the letter and then handed it back to Rebecca. 'will you read this for me. It is written in your tongue. I can understand your words but am unable to read them.'

Never for one second had she considered this and caught a little off guard, she took the letter and started reading.

'Empress Matilda.

Luis, the Laird of Dunbar has reason to travel to York on September 26th 1124.

Whilst there, he will meet with an adversary of King Stephen.

In attendance will be Princess Evanora.

In the evening at fifteen minutes past nine, Evanora will walk in the grounds of York Minster. York Minster is yet to be built in your time. There is however, a sixth-century church standing in its place and is known as York Church.

Your ally, Luis should know she is to be smuggled away and interned within Perth Priory. He need not be present though when she is taken. Evanora is a danger to you. Importantly, her descendants, if she is not stopped, will carry evil in their blood. Therefore, she should be held at Perth in solitude until she is after child birth.

If your approach is with stealth, after inspection, King Stephen will have confidence Evanora was taken by vagabonds. Be mindful, if he suspects anything, his trail may lead him to Perth.

Your servant, The Book Keeper'

Appearing somewhat taken aback, but still clear minded, Matilda seemed to think for a moment. 'Okay, I must send word to Luis. It is September fourteenth now. In your time, it takes a breath to communicate. In our time, we are horse and weather dependant.' She then again went to the door and spoke with a man, this time at length. She then came back and sat opposite Rebecca. Holding both of Rebecca's hands, she said, 'Word will reach Luis.' With a smile, she continued, 'so, tell me more about your two daughters.'

'Well, Faith is sixteen-years-old,' she said, and suddenly realised she'd be 17 in a week. 'She will be seventeen soon, when she returns from America.' The way Matilda looked at her, she realised what she'd just said made no sense to this woman. 'Err, America is a country a long way from here. In your time, it is yet to be discovered. It is west from here, some three-thousand miles.'

Matilda grinned. 'I heard about this place from Meredith.' Again, she smiled. 'she often visits me from that place she lives.'

A little surprised, but not shocked, she asked, 'Do you mean the place Meredith calls the other dimension? Oh, and we named Faith, Faith Matilda.'

She moved forward and squeezed Rebecca's hand. 'Thank you. Yes, she does refer to her place as the other dimension, although I've never really understood this notion.'

'Me neither, but I believe it is a place where our kind go, once we have departed this life. By our kind, I mean those of us who have this ability to speak with others from a different era. There are some of our making who have evil intent. For every good soul, there is a bad soul. Our destiny in life is to stop history from taking a negative path. Princess Evanora is exactly that, an evil soul. Importantly, one of her descendants will cruelly and viciously murder a number of innocent women. This is why she needs to be apprehended and held beyond her child bearing years. Evanora is one of many who must be stopped. Without our intervention, time will take a negative path. An ultimate path of damnation.' She breathed out heavily.

'You seem troubled telling this tale.'

'I have another mission I must complete and it is fraught with danger. Speaking to you has brought home how much danger I could be in. It was compounded when I was locked up here and had it not been for your letter, I could have perished there without you ever knowing.' She then nodded. 'Your laws should give captives a voice. I was imprisoned only because of my English accent. This was the case with James. He ventured here to warn you. He is an advocate, one that has been jailed for four years.' Again, she shook her head. 'It is not for me to tell you how Scottish law should be. Although, perhaps me being here, in your time, serves two purposes.'

'I will change this. You are correct in all you say. I now have a greater understanding of my life, why you were sent to save me, and our kinds purpose. The likes of Rebekah, Ethernal, and Meredith move between worlds maintaining a balanced and fair equilibrium. It is our job to act upon their directives.' She then seemed to think deeply for a moment. 'When Meredith told me of the America's, I considered sending a fleet to discover this land. I was told this should wait for humankind to be ready for this journey. My intervention would upset the very equilibrium we are here to protect.'

Matilda's words hit home to Rebecca, compounding her understanding of how this all works. Seeing Matilda was appearing a little perplexed and understanding it was a lot to take on board, she decided to change the mood. 'So, with my husband, Duncan, being a direct descendant of your confidante, I wanted to name my first born after you. My other daughter, who is ten-years-old, is named Gabrielle Meredith.'

Again, squeezing Rebecca's hand, she smiled.

Biting her bottom lip, Rebecca narrowed her eyes a little. 'I am curious why I am still here. It is lovely that we can talk freely. Normally though, I have a mission and once that is complete, seamlessly I return to my time.' She thought for a moment. 'No matter when, where or with whom, it is job done and home. Sounds a little emotionless, and frankly, I've never considered this before. There was one time when I spent many years in an era sixty years before my own. I was married and gave birth to two boys. At the time, I thought I was there for ever. The thing is, as soon as one of my sons discovered a cure for a horrid virus, I was back home. No goodbyes, nothing, just one moment I was there and the next... Now the strange thing is, I felt no sadness. It was as if it never happened.'

'That must have caused your emotions to tangle.'

'It did. My father helped me find solace. You see, I was upset, but only because I felt no detachment. He suggested, although I seemingly lived every moment, I wasn't actually there.' Seeing Matilda appearing a little confused, she said, 'I best explain. I have been on many journeys through time. Some I feel I am there and some I feel as if I am watching from afar. There have been times when nobody could see or hear me. It is all very confusing. That said, it is the only explanation. In essence, there are times when I am invisible, seemingly only there to observe. Then there are times, as my father suggested, when I am there, but actually only seeing that world through another's eyes, as was the case when I had the two boys. Alternatively, there are times like now, when I am me and undoubtedly here with you, no question or ambiguity. So, I was fifty years old when I was with two sons. The second I came back, I was twenty-one once more, the age when I left.'

'I believe I follow. I now find my inner thoughts considering what may lay in front of us two. As you suggest, you are still here, so there must be more.' She then appeared to think for a moment. 'I wonder if the man in the cell next to you has a part to play. Forgive me, his name eludes my thoughts.'

Nodding, Rebecca said, 'His name is James. You may be right.'

'I will vorladung him.'

'Sorry, you will what?'

She smiled. 'I will have him brought to us. It actually means to summon someone.' She turned her head slightly to one side. 'To summon someone is somewhat demanding. I will ask if he would like to join us.'

'I knew what the word meant, it just seemed odd hearing it in Germanic.' Rebecca shook her head. 'May I ask you a question?'

'Of course, ask whatever has your curiosity.'

'When we were first here, which was a year ago for you, our one-to-one meetings were all behind a smoke screen. What has changed?'

'After you left, I knew many things had to change. I had become detached from my people. Alongside this, my people, I thought, expected me to be detached.' She shook her head. 'A year since, me speaking to a commoner would never do. Not that you are a commoner, but I felt at that time you would be seen that way. So, I changed things. Now, I speak with anyone. I am still finding my way, but I want to be the peoples Empress, Queen and ally. I have a long journey and it is one you have helped me start. For that, I thank you.'

'That is interesting. After I returned to my own time, I thought a lot about you and our meeting. It bothered me that you, who are in charge, actually wasn't even in charge of your own destiny. In my time, we had a princess whose husband was air to the throne. Her name was Lady Diana. She was a princess to the people and was loved the world over. She cast off starchy tradition and affectively broke the rules. Sadly, this was not appreciated by those in power and her life was short, her demise surrounded by conspiracy theories. The point is though, even many years after her untimely death, she is still loved.'

'I need to follow this path and as head of state in Scotland, unopposed, I will embrace my people. My only menace is from England and King Stephen.'

'Just chatting like this has conjured an idea. I wonder if James actually could bring something to our table. I think rather than chatting and becoming side tracked we need to speak to him now.'

Nodding profoundly, she said, 'I agree. I will ask him to join us.' She then again spoke with someone at the door.

Chapter 15 – Unlocked

A few minutes later, there was a knock at the door.

'Enter,' Matilda called out.

As the door opened, Rebecca took a sharp intake of breath. The man, presumably James, who'd just entered the room looked like a dishevelled twin of her father. Although now clean and with suitable clothing, his sunken eyes told a horrid story. As he drew closer, and knelt before Matilda, the sores on his skin appeared painfully infected.

Matilda offered him a seat. 'I am sorry you have had to suffer such indignity. I plan to change the way our legal system works. In future, those of your kind will be given a voice. Importantly, not judged by their accent.'

He offered a weary nod. 'Ma'am, I am here now and all is behind us. I carry a message for you.' He then looked down briefly. 'I was visited by a sorcerous in a dream. For me to carry this message to you may be perceived by many as foolhardy.' Again, he hesitated.

Without thinking, Rebecca took a small pack from her inside pocket. 'James, I was the girl in the cell next to you.'

He offered a fatigued smile. 'I understand your engagement resulted in my release. I thank you. I knew you were unlike others. An ambiance surrounds you, one that is similar to the sorcerous who visited me. I could even feel your strength through the cell wall.' He nodded, somehow appearing a little more comfortable.

Although Rebecca was desperate to quiz this man on the sorcerous, she felt a need to help with his sores first. She glanced at Matilda, who seemingly read her thoughts, and nodded. 'I have something that will help your sores.' She then opened a sachet of antiseptic wipes and some penicillin tablets. Again, she glanced at Matilda.

'I suspect this is the medicine you used to aid my recovery.'

Rebecca nodded. 'Ever since our meeting, I always carry with me a small medical kit. Although, mostly I am unable to move items from my epoch to another, it seems this is acceptable.' She then started to bathe the sores on James's arms and hands. As she did, she could almost feel him thinking. 'I suspect you have a question, James?'

He nodded. 'Again, you are like the sorcerous, able to read my thoughts. How can this be. In addition, you spoke of another epoch.' Again, he appeared to go deep inside his thoughts. 'The sorcerous, Rebekah, visited me in a dream, although I was not asleep. She too spoke of another epoch, a world many years from mine.'

Wide eyed, Rebecca glanced at Matilda. She then thought carefully about the words she could, or should use to allow James an insight to their world. 'Both Empress Matilda and I know of your sorcerous. We are all of the same making, breed, type. We are messengers through time. Our destiny is to keep the lives of all settled and straight.'

James nodded. 'I should not comprehend this, I do, although I know not why.'

'Perhaps, in some way, you are of our making. The only difference, you are a messenger who only moves in your own time,' Matilda said, glancing at Rebecca.

Rebecca looked at Matilda and nodded. 'I was thinking exactly that.'

He tore the lining of his dishevelled hessian coat and produced a folded scroll of sorts from the lining. 'A messenger, I am. I carry warnings from Rebekah. She was passed these notices by, excuse me if I say his name incorrectly, Ethernal.'

'Ethernal is correct,' Matilda said, with Rebecca nodding.

It was one thing being here in the eleven-hundreds with Matilda, someone she'd last seen 25 years previously. To compound her senses, James's words were unexpected and heightened her intrigue. Animated, she wondered where his message might lead her. With her emotions at bursting point, she had to curb her eagerness to know more, aware of her surroundings and so forced herself to hold back a little.

'James, again, I apologise for your imprisonment. Please tell me of the message you carry.' Matilda then glanced at Rebecca and she could see this woman was equally intrigued.

James carefully unfolded the scroll, which appeared sodden. 'I hid this message when I was apprehended. I am unable to read the uncommon words therein.'

For some reason, she suspected it may be in English, although she didn't know why she would think this. She glanced at Matilda who responded in a way that suggested she had a similar notion. As she picked up the parchment, she was instantly aware it wasn't just wet, it was saturated. She looked at James, realising how horrid his existence would have been without her intervention. 'Before we go any further, can we get James some new clothing? If this message is anything to go by, his cloths must be soaking wet.'

Matilda nodded, went to the door and again spoke with someone. 'I am sorry, James. New attire will be here imminently.'

He lowered his head, 'thank you, Ma'am.'

'Thank you, Matilda' Rebecca said. She carefully laid the message on the table in front of her and started reading.

Empress Matilda.

A descendent of Princess Evanora will aim to stop a treaty that will be known as the Magna Carta. The descendant's name is irrelevant. The princess is destined with three malevolent children, born with wicked blood. These births must be stopped.

The Magna Carta, also known as the Great Charter of Freedoms, will be agreed and implemented by King John of England at Runnymede, near Windsor, on 15 June 1215. The charter is to make peace between the unpopular king and a group of rebels. It will promise the protection of church rights, protection for the barons from illegal imprisonment, access to swift justice for all, and limitations on outdated payments to the Crown. Initially, all sides fail to agree and many years of conflict will follow. Although this charter will face conflict, it will set the provenance for a fair legal system in years to come.

One of the outcomes, many years on, in 1381 will be a Peasants' Revolt. It is destined to be a major uprising across large parts of England. Social and economic issues following the Black Death pandemic in the 1340s will be a catalyst. In addition, high taxes resulting from the conflict with France during the Hundred Years' War, and instability within the local leadership of London will play a part. The final trigger for the revolt will be the intervention of a royal official, John Bampton, in Essex on 30 May 1381. His attempts to collect unpaid poll taxes in Brentwood will end in a violent confrontation. It will rapidly spread across the south-east of the country. Many will rise up in protest, burning court records and opening the local prisons. The rebels will seek a reduction in taxation, an end to the system of unfree labour known as serfdom, and the removal of the King's senior officials and law courts.

Neither the war, the uprising nor the pandemic can be halted. History is ordained with many negative events. These events are part of humankind's learning. Through many tragic events, mankind will step forward. Ultimately, charters such as the Magna Carta will create a fair and just legal system throughout.

Therefore, the Magna Carta must not be interfered with in any way. Matilda and Rebecca, you are ordained with apprehending Evanora and preventing her pregnancies. She is a negative counterpart of your kind. She does not belong in history. Her make appeared out of sequence at childbirth, where she should have been stopped. Her evilness did not manifest until she entered her twentieth year. Our kind is not to kill these negative travellers, just to stop their progression. Allowed childbirth, history will spiral uncontrollably and become littered with many negative events.

A warning: When Evanora is apprehended, furtiveness must be the highest priority. If stealth is *not used, her capture will lead King Stephen to Perth Priory.*

Rebecca turned to Matilda. 'This is obviously why I am still here. We need to make sure Evanora is captured and that we do it away from any prying eyes.' Just then a thought occurred to her. 'How far is Dunbar?' She then had a change of thought. 'Actually, how far is York? I know roughly how long it would take to get there in my time, but…'

Narrow eyed, Matilda said, 'Four to five days. Why, may I enquire?'

'I am unknown to anyone in your time. I could apprehend Evanora. If I was seen or detained, there would be no repercussions back to you or Perth Priory.'

'I cannot allow you to risk yourself in this way.'

'I do not think we have a choice. I could travel with a couple of your men who could aid the return of Evanora to this Priory. I have something in my medical kit that with one breath, will render Evanora unconscious.' She shook her head in disbelief. Some days earlier, she had the mind to pack a safe alternative to chloroform. At the time, she didn't have a clue why. Again, she shook her head, coming to terms with how this all works. 'When it is right, it all falls into place. Me being here with you, at the same time as James. Also, with enough time to travel to York. To compound this all, only three days ago, I packed this medicine that will aid Evanora's safe capture. When I packed it, again, I was following my intuition. It strikes me, this is how my journeys work. So, no debate, I am going to York. It is meant to be that way.'

Glancing around the room and clearly considering Rebecca's idea, she turned back to her. 'You have twelve days before Evanora arrives in York. I will again send word to Luis to explain the change of plan.' She smiled towards James. 'Thank you, James. I will see that you are fed and treated for your injuries.' She then showed him to the door.

'So, it is just us two,' Rebecca said. She then noticed the parchment. The words had vanished, not faded, but completely disappeared. She shook her head and pointed at the paper. 'This is so weird. I do however, take it as a message.'

Appearing quizzical, Matilda asked, 'How so?'

'It has just occurred to me, no sooner we had agreed that it was right for me to travel to York, the words seemingly vanished. I do not know why I think this suggests our plan is right, but I do. I suspect, if it was not right, the words would still be here. If I am here until Evanora is captured, hopefully all will be well and I'll return home. Alternatively, if we miss this opportunity, I may be here for many years. Importantly, if we do miss this opportunity, she may give birth. That in itself would bring me back to this day and we would need to start over. That pattern will continue until we stop Evanora. To my mind, that is how it is all planned out by the likes of Rebekah and Ethernal. It has taken me many years to understand, or even accept this, however… The good, like us, must stop the evil time twisters, for want of a better term. So, we must be successful in our pursuit of Evanora and get it right the first time.'

Nodding, Matilda said, 'I concur. I have learnt, mostly through you, we are part of a bigger plan.'

Over the next couple of days, the two made ready for Rebecca to travel. With Rebecca's appropriate clothing sorted, three men selected and several small details considered, the two decided to go for a walk in the grounds. This time, with Rebecca dressed fittingly, there was only the occasional glance in their direction. This highlighted to Rebecca just how much had changed since the last time she was here.

'A lot has altered since my last visit. You seem comfortable openly being with me. Importantly, no one is staring. Although, I do suspect this may be because I am dressed in clothing more fitting for your domain.'

'I believe, many of the issues were exasperated by my detached behaviour. My people never saw me among their kind. I only ever appeared holding court with the highest dignitaries. I changed that after you left. I quickly became aware the people were happy to see me speaking with my maid and others in a similar position on level terms. Once aware, I ventured amongst my people, and held court with all.'

'I am pleased you see the importance of engaging your people. History is littered with royals who have detached themselves from their people.' She then thought for a moment about what she wanted to say. 'You are Queen, Empress of whom, your people, so be their Queen.'

The way Matilda reacted left Rebecca unsure if she'd said the wrong thing. Matilda then nodded and smiled. 'Your words, Rebecca, are well considered and perfectly observe my position. They were difficult to hear because they are true.'

As they headed through the woods and towards the stream, Rebecca felt a chill, followed by that familiar smell of almonds. Instantly, she knew that could only mean one thing. She stopped dead in her tracks and looked around. Touching Matilda on the arm, she said, 'Meredith is here, although I believe she is in her spirit form.'

'I am indeed,' came a voice from behind them.

Recognising the voice of her beloved Meredith, Rebecca turned, pulling Matilda round with her. 'Sorry, I am so excited, I pulled your arm a little hard.'

'Worry not. Meredith, to what do we owe the pleasure of your company?' Matilda asked.

'I would love to embrace you both. I am though, here from the other dimension. I carry an important message for Rebecca from Ethernal. Rebecca, your powers to move through time are at their strongest when you are near water. In time, you will learn how to use this power to move freely between era's and indeed, dimensions. Alternatively, your evil counterparts, such as Evanora are at their weakest when close to water. Evanora has already learnt to move between her evil dimension and this world. If you try to apprehend her away from the water's edge, she will jump into a dimension where she will be untouchable. She is, however, unable to move from one year to another. So, your only chance to apprehend her will be when she sits by the lake at the back of York Minster. It is important that you comprehend, the cathedral you know of Rebecca is yet to be built. The grounds are sacred and a sixth-century church stand in this year. On the north side of the lake is a circular flint open folly structure. Directly in front of this structure is a flint and mortar seat next to the lake. This is an innocuous and safe distance away from interfering eyes. This will be your only chance. Behind the folly is dense woodland. The path through this wood leads unobstructed to the River Ouse. From there, you can head north in safety. Lastly, be mindful, there may be problems near the border with Dumfries. Rebecca, trust your instincts as always. You will be alone on this journey. The safe passage of history is dependent on your success. You are strong enough and in you we trust.'

Before Rebecca had time to react, Meredith was gone once more. She turned to Matilda. 'In the early years, I always thought the door to my journeys was via an old spiral staircase. Never did I consider the lake near my home as a doorway. Thinking about it now, it all makes sense. It was by the lake where I found you. The first place I saw Meredith, also where I found the key that started my journey, all by the lake. Although, according to Meredith, it is water.' Even my door to you this time, was this stream,' she said, pointing. She then realised half of what she'd just said to Matilda wouldn't make any sense. Over the next couple of hours, she explained all about her journeys, including seeing Meredith as an apparition on the lake and finding the key that started her journey.

The days passed quickly and waking on the morning of the 18th September, Rebecca felt confidant she was doing the right thing, travelling to York. She'd had one or two restless nights, mostly because of her intrigue and anticipating how it might pan out. Each time, she reckoned what will be will be. After breakfast with Matilda, and with the horses ready, Rebecca bid her farewells to Matilda.

'Be safe, my dear friend. I await your return, confidently. In you, I trust.'

Chapter 16 – The Journey

As Rebecca reached the edge of the priory's ground, she slowed her horse and took a look back. Seeing Matilda, surrounded by people, waving passionately caused an odd feeling in her stomach. As she and the three horsemen headed into the woods, she considered her reaction to Matilda. *Her world has changed,* she thought, *and I've played a positive role in that.* It was around eight in the evening when one of the men suggested an upcoming manor near to a wooded area would serve as a harbour.

'Ma'am. The folk in this house know of our arrival and will offer us safe shelter. They are the McCreery Family, supporters of Empress Matilda. They detest the English.'

'Thank you. Firstly, may I ask your name, and indeed the others. Importantly, please call me Rebecca. We are on this journey as equals.'

He nodded and smiled. 'I have been advised of your sincerity and free speech. You have changed the lives of all within the Estate of Perth and surrounding area. My name is Peter. This,' he said pointing, 'is Mark and Jonathon. We will shield your life with ours if need be.'

'Your words are good reward for my endeavours. I too will protect your life with mine.'

He nodded, brandishing a radiant smile. 'All that was said of you by our Empress was the truth. Your spirit is that of a clansman, and for that I thank you.'

Seconds later, they were greeted by a goliath of a man. Sporting a purple and green tartan, he was followed by two pipers. This created a strange feeling inside Rebecca and oddly reminded her of the time she visited Queen Elizabeth at Buckingham Palace when pipers were in the grounds. The sound of pipes had been something she'd loved ever since.

That evening, the McCreery family served an incredible meal, including haggis, something she'd loved from the first time Duncan cooked it for her. After an interesting chat, what with the different dialect and language variances, which caused much laughter, she headed off to bed. The thing that pleased her most was even though Peter had suggested this family detested the English, they'd welcomed her openly.

She was awake early and was miles away considering the day ahead, when a young girl, perhaps in her mid-teens, entered the room. As she made her way towards Rebecca, she was unable to take her eyes away from this girl. Her flowing locks of sunset red hair and soft pale complexion exaggerated her natural beauty. Her high cheek bones and bright jade eyes enhanced her appearance further. She placed a hot drink beside Rebecca's bed, and then nodded a little uncomfortably.

Reading this, Rebecca sat up, pulled the edge of her bedding back and indicated for the girl to sit next to her. 'I am Rebecca. Thank you for the drink. May I ask your name?'

Hesitantly, the girl perched right on the edge of the bed. My name, Ma'am, is Mary.'

Rebecca, pointed at the bed, moving over a little. 'Please, Mary, sit comfortably and do call me Rebecca.'

The two chatted for a few minutes, then out of the blue, Mary said, 'I see your life, I see your doors, I have seen beyond my world. I am frightened by these events. I hope you can show me an alternative mood.'

Startled, Rebecca sat for a few seconds with her mouth open. She knew instantly there was something different about this girl, if nothing else, she was able to understand every word Rebecca had said. For all that, she never saw this coming. 'I too was frightened the first time I stepped through the doorway to this world. I was fifteen-years-old and can recall my emotions as if it were yesterday.' She then thought for a moment.

'I too am fifteen.'

'Mary, your spirit is strong, you must cast off your fear and embrace what you have been graced with. This life and all life previously and in years to come depend on our kind. We keep an equilibrium of peace.' The two then chatted for a few minutes more. As much as Rebecca wanted to stay talking with Mary, she knew it was time to make tracks.

As she mounted her horse, Mary dashed over. '

'I have seen your safe return. I will see you in ten nights. In two days, change your horse before he becomes lame.'

'Thank you, Mary,' she said and reached down offering her hand. 'Continue to accept your destiny. It is an amazingly beautiful journey, sometimes full of laughter, and occasionally tears.'

Hesitantly, Mary too offered her hand.

Rebecca squeezed her hand. 'I will see you presently.'

'Be safe.'

Over the next couple of days, things passed off peacefully. As Mary had suggested, just as they entered Dumfries, Rebecca could tell her horse wasn't moving freely. As they drew close to the final stop at the McCray family home before entering England, her horse now seemed fine. Nonetheless, she spoke to Peter and arranged for her horse to be changed, explaining he was limping a little. No sooner she'd dismounted, her horse appeared noticeably lame. This not only saved her from continuing with this horse, it confirmed Mary was of her making.

The following morning, they entered Northumberland. The stallion like horse Rebecca had been given was a feisty character. Although initially, his temperament was strong, Rebecca talked to him and showing a strong arm, she let him know who was in charge. It had helped, she'd ridden a similar horse sometime back while on holiday in the Highlands.

Their journey through Northumberland and into Yorkshire was surprisingly peaceful, excepting the occasional glance from the odd farmer. It clearly helped they'd changed out of their Scottish clothing and to most onlookers perhaps appeared as passing Englishmen.

On the evening of the 25th, they took refuge in a dense wooded area 15 miles north of York. Because it was a mild evening, Peter suggested they camped without fire, thereby avoiding a smoke trail. The following morning, after Rebecca had established the nearby river was the Ouse, she told Peter of Meredith's message and directed him towards a pathway along the river. Although Meredith had only suggested using this path as an escape route, she reckoned as it was right by them, it made sense to use it both ways.

Everyone agreed it was a good plan and so they followed the somewhat remote route. After a few twists and turns along the meandering river, guiding the horses around the odd fallen tree, they eventually arrived directly behind the folly Meredith had told Rebecca about.

Peter dismounted his horse and offered his hand to help Rebecca down. 'Your ally knows this land well.'

Rebecca smiled. 'I am going to take a close look at the folly. I suggest you men wait here.' She then made her way down to the lake edge. Arriving by the water caused a strange sensation. If she didn't know any better, the way she felt was as if she was about to jump somewhere. Thinking about her feelings, she realised it was her being by the water that was creating this mood. She turned to investigate the folly. It's curved shape, open front, which faced the water, and undercover seating, reminded her of the Victorian covered seating she'd seen in Scarborough along the sea front. Deciding to take a closer look at the 4-foot-thick walls, she was a little surprised to see a small door, inside the folly, almost out of sight, just to the left of the structure.

With her mind now in overdrive, she tried the door handle as an idea occurred to her. To her delight, the door opened easily, and importantly, quietly. Inside, although slightly dusty, she reckoned she could hide beside the four oars that stood in the corner.

She returned to Peter and explained her plan to hide and apprehend Evanora as soon as she entered the folly.

Peter shook his head. 'Ma'am, sorry, Rebecca, how do you know Evanora will enter the structure?

She thought for a moment. 'We have a confidante who is close to King Stephen and Evanora.' The way he narrowed his eyes, she wasn't sure he'd bought her story. Nonetheless, he nodded. 'So, I suggest you men wait here in the woods. I will hide in the building. When you see her walking towards the building, wait until she enters, then make your way to the back of the building.'

'With respect, Rebecca, you are of slight build. The heart of a lion. However, we understand Evanora is powerfully tall.'

Smiling, Rebecca nodded. 'Worry not, I have a plan that is infallible.' It wasn't infallible, but she felt confident if she timed her approach right, her idea would work seamlessly.

With the men hiding in the woods, Rebecca hid inside the folly, leaving the door ajar. Although she was certain of what she had to do, her heart was beating through her chest. She took several deep breaths and eventually calmed herself, only for her heart rate to jump again as soon as she saw a woman heading towards her. Instantly, this woman reminded her of Morticia of the Adams Family TV show, which actually made her smile. Not only did this woman look like her, she was dressed outrageously similar, to the point where she wondered if the creator of the Adams Family hadn't somehow seen Evanora.

Feeling a tad more relaxed, she watched as this woman appeared to glide across the grass, her long black dress whispering around her legs as if it were made of some supernatural material. She then stopped at the front of the folly, her eyes dancing from one side to the other, almost as if she sensed something.

Rebecca held her breath and put her hand against her chest in a vain attempt to slow her heart rate. She stood there, watching this woman, unsure if she should move now or wait.

Then Evanora turned her back to face the water.

With as much stealth as her heart would allow, Rebecca opened the door and moved towards Evanora, with the knockout cloth in her hand. As she approached her, lifted her hand, this woman whispered, 'water, my weakness.' Rebecca placed the cloth over Evanora's mouth and within a breath, she'd slumped to the ground. Seconds later, the three horsemen bundled her into the woods as Rebecca kept a watchful eye. Hurriedly, they galloped the horses along the path they'd came in by. Arriving back at the entrance to the woods as the sun was coming up, they all agreed on a change of tact. Instead of travelling by day, they decided, until they reached Scotland, they'd travel under the cover of darkness.

Just as they were setting up camp, Evanora regained consciousness. Fearful she would scream Rebecca took her cloth from her pocket.

Evanora held her hand up. 'I will not shout. You, my alternate image, are an adequate adversary. I have always been aware this day would arrive and accept my destiny.' She then nodded to Rebecca. 'My mortal kind have one purpose, to damagingly disrupt man's path. You and those of your making have an alternate destiny and that is to maintain man's safe journey. You have won this battle. There will be many others. I will not fight and accept my journeys end. She then put something in her mouth and seconds later slumped to the ground.

Shocked, Rebecca wasn't sure what to do or think. She narrowed her eyes and going on a gut feeling, tentatively leant forward to check Evanora's pulse. She was dead, although for some reason, Rebecca was suspicious. Something in the back of her thoughts reckoned her evil counterpart wouldn't go that easy.

'Peter, tie her hands.'

'She is dead, Rebecca.'

She shook her head. 'Something is telling me she is disguising her death. Trust me on this and tie her hands.'

Hesitantly, Peter tied Evanora's hands.

'I can sense your uncertainty, Peter. Something in my gut is telling me this is not over yet. I have come across this type of woman before. You must understand she is a sorcerous, witch or wizard, and as with others of her making, capable of a disguised appearance.' She then thought for a moment. 'At any point, she could change her surroundings. We must keep her tied at all times.' Then a thought occurred to her. 'I need you to keep the large water vessel we brought with us close to her body.' Seeing him and the other men appearing perplexed, she said, 'water is her weakness. If we fail to watch her closely, and she is allowed to use her powers, she will be gone.'

Frowning with obvious curiosity, Peter asked, 'How do you know all of this?'

'I have met her type before. They are at their most dangerous when away from water, and at their weakest near water. I am not sure the water vessel will work, but it is something we must try.'

Over the next two days and nights, there were no signs of life from Evanora and Rebecca was beginning to question her judgement. Towards the end of the second night, there was a horrid hiss from Evanora as she regained consciousness. Although Rebecca found this sound quite objectionable, she reckoned this woman was only reacting like this because of the water, which was seemingly rendering her powerless.

Peter shook his head. 'It would seem you were right about this creature.'

It was only my intuition, I did not actually know for sure, just…'

'Well, your intuition served you well.'

Once they were across the border and in Scotland, they made good pace, especially as they were now travelling during daylight. Arriving back at the McCreery estate brought a smile to Rebecca's face, looking forward to seeing Mary once more.

Greeting Mr. McCreery, Rebecca explained the situation with Evanora.

He then took Rebecca to one of the out buildings that contained a huge water butt. 'Will this work?'

'This will be a perfect place to hold this woman.' She then noticed a large cage affair in the corner of the barn. Although she knew this cage would be an ideal place to hold Evanora and certainly big enough, she still felt a little uncomfortable with the idea. Pointing, she asked, 'that cage, can it be moved closer to this water container?'

Mr. McCreery raised his eyebrows, took a few steps and dragged it surprisingly easy towards the water. 'Will this work for you?'

Tight lipped, she nodded. 'I am a little uncomfortable locking her in this cage, however, Evanora is a dangerous woman.'

Standing at least a foot taller than Rebecca, he nodded. 'Mary, my daughter, explained what we should expect with this woman. A callous sorcerous, I believe.' He then shook his head, his long grey beard swaying. 'Mary is keen to talk with you. I believe you two have a similar hidden forte.' He grinned and said, 'even for a Sassenach, it is pleasing to have you around.'

Rebecca thanked him and turned to Peter who had joined them. 'To be safe, we perhaps need to cage Evanora.' Even though Peter agreed, and she knew it was the right option, she still felt uncomfortable.

Moments later Peter, with one of the other men returned with Evanora. She took one look at the cage, glanced at the water butt and hissed horribly at the two men and Mr. McCreary.

She then turned to Rebecca. 'For now, you have control. One error and I will elude your grip.' She nodded, her eyes showing her obvious frustration and belligerence. She then entered the cage. 'One slip and I will haunt you.'

Peter placed a cloth on the floor for her to sit on, and tied her hands to the bar of the cage. He then locked the cage.

With a horridly evil look on her face, she glared at all and again hissed. She then turned her back.

Mr. McCreary beckoned her and Peter to the door. We need to guard this creature throughout the night. I, along with your men can take shifts.

An idea occurred to Rebecca. 'I have my medicine cloth and if Evanora struggles, this will render her unconscious.' She then thought for a moment. 'Maybe it would be best if I stayed here throughout the night.'

Both Peter and Mr. McCreery shook their head. 'Under no circumstances can I allow that.'

'I agree,' Peter said. 'I will take the first assembly. Rebecca, go and enjoy supper.'

She reluctantly agreed although her intuition was telling her otherwise. 'I am not at all sure,' she said, glancing at the two men. 'Right, I will be back shortly. Watch her closely.'

Peter nodded. 'I have seen what this woman is capable of and will watch her every move.'

On the way back to the main house, she turned to Mr. McCreery. 'May I ask your first name?'

He nodded. 'My name is Robert.'

Very appropriate, she thought. 'Robert, will Mary be joining us?'

'I would be unable to stop her. She has wandered around without intent since your departure, awaiting your return.'

Rebecca smiled, and nodded a little. 'I know those emotions well, aimlessly awaiting someone's return. I may commandeer your daughter's attention.'

He nodded, 'and she yours.' He opened the huge arched oak doors leading into the house. Then, he led Rebecca into the dining room.

Seeing Mary sent an unexpected surge of emotions through Rebecca's consciousness. It was as if she'd known this girl her whole life. She made her way around the back of the table.

Mary, with the biggest smile, stood and cuddled Rebecca.

For Rebecca, it felt as if she was meeting up with a life-long friend. Standing back a little and holding both of Mary's hands, she said. 'You were right about my horse, my lovely. Was this how you envisaged my return?'

'It was exactly.' She then seemed to recoil into her inner thoughts briefly. 'Evanora's characteristics and deportment are what I anticipated. Strangely though, I never saw her in my vision, so know not why I have these thoughts.'

Intrigued by this comment, she asked, 'so what did you see exactly, and how did it appear to you?'

'Well, I am still unsure if I was in a dream.' Again, she appeared to think deeply. 'I was here, exactly like this, although I was aware it was a vision of the future. It was strange. I was here sitting next to you and we were having this conversation. Even suggesting Evanora's appearance was as I expected, even though I am yet to see her.' She shook her head. 'It is the most unusual emotion.'

'I understand your feelings. I have lived in this world for many years and still am shocked by my own emotions, and reactions. I have had incidents when I have known a person's appearance even though I cannot see them. It is as if they are a shadow, one I recognise. It is difficult to embrace this weird world as normal. For us though, it is the life we live. Like me, you must find a way to accept it as normal. Never be surprised by how often you are surprised. May I ask, have you had any other incidents since we were last together?'

'Three nights since, I had the strangest emotion, but no vision. I felt you cradling death. Not yours, but another's demise. Now this is where it was most peculiar. The death you cradled was not as it appeared. It is difficult to explain. It was as if you were tending to someone who appeared dead. For some reason, I knew they were not. Does that make any sense at all?'

Rebecca took a sharp intake of breath. 'Three night since, Evanora swallowed a pill of sorts, which appeared to kill her. Somewhere in my deepest thoughts, I knew she wasn't dead, even though she was breathless and without heartbeat. It was indeed, the strangest of feelings. Two days after, she breathed again. It would seem, you saw this event.'

The two continued to chat between courses. Once they'd finished their meal, they felt it would be good to engage with the others.

She turned to the maid who was clearing dinner away. 'I have had Salmon before, but never like this. Please tell the person who cooked our supper it was the best I have ever had.' In the back of her thoughts, she was thinking, now that's fresh Salmon, unlike the local supermarket *plastic* fish.

Rebecca spent a brief time speaking with Robert about Mary and her dreams. As best she could, she suggested, although Mary's accounts may occasionally sound outlandish, he should embrace her thoughts and visions with open arms. Without going into too much detail, aware witches and such like were recognised in this era, she explained that some sorceresses were evil. As a counter balance, there were those like her and Mary who were virtuous alternatives, keeping a fair balance. He'd responded, suggesting they refer to them hereabouts as either a White Witch or Black Witch. Before she headed to bed, she decided to check on Evanora. To her relief, Evanora was sleeping.

Michael, who was taking his turn, said, 'No chance of me falling asleep with that horrid cawing sound she makes.' He then raised his eyebrows. 'A wife of mine who slept this way would be my wife no longer.' He then chuckled in a childlike way that didn't suit his powerful character and demeanour.

'Has she stirred at all?'

Shaking his head, he said, 'nothing, other than this dreadful sound that comes from her often.'

She bid goodnight and reluctantly headed off to bed. She then lay there tossing and turning for around thirty minutes. Finally, wide awake, she got dressed and headed downstairs and outside to the barn. When she got there, Robert was on his stint.

'I expected you. Your valiant, intrepid persona is strong. Sit, lets speak, over this maddening sound this creature makes, if at all possible.'

The two continued to talk about Mary and what may lay ahead for her. Surprisingly, Robert appeared to take all Rebecca said in his stride. Peter then entered to take over.

'It is okay, Peter, Rebecca and I will see out the remainder of the night.'

No sooner Peter had left, Rebecca could feel eyes burning at her back. She turned sharply, only to see Evanora sitting up staring at her. Instinctively, Rebecca got to her feet, walked over and sat right in front of the cage, staring back at this woman. 'You can hold your thoughts. They carry no fear for me. You face many years imprisoned so your evil intent is kept silent.' Just then, she noticed the water butt. She turned to Robert, 'the water is leaking out.'

He hurried over, and after a few seconds, he pointed to a hole right by Evanora's tied hand. Somehow, she'd made a hole.

'She is waiting for the water to drain away so she can jump. I will explain what I mean by that in a moment. Can we fix this hole?'

He then hurried outside and seconds later, returned with a burning torch, and some material that looked like a kind of rubber. 'This is sheep intestine, and I can use this to seal the leak.' He opened the cage and tied her hands in a different position so she couldn't again reach the water butt. He then set about resealing the leak. All the time, Evanora was hissing and glaring at Robert.

Rebecca stayed with Robert for the remainder of the night. The following morning, after Rebecca had spoken to Mary and bid her farewells, they set off. During the remainder of the journey to Perth, there were no further issues with Evanora. All the time though, Rebecca suspected this woman had more to offer, knowing she wouldn't go that easily. At the entrance to the Priory, they were met by Matilda and two huge tartan clad men. Rebecca followed as they marched Evanora to a dingy, damp cell. In an odd way, Rebecca didn't much like the idea of this woman being caged here for the next 30-odd-years. In spite of her evil intentions, she felt no one deserved this kind of torturous existence, especially as Rebecca had suffered in this way, albeit only for a short time.

'Matilda, I am not at all comfortable with this cell. As evil as this woman is, no individual deserves this. I realise in your time, this kind of treatment is normal, however…'

Narrow eyed, Matilda glanced around clearly considering Rebecca's words. 'We have some outbuildings adjacent to the main building and I can arrange for one of those to be made secure. I appreciate your compassion, although…'

'I am not sure I could go back to my time knowing Evanora was being kept in these conditions. In my time, even the most horrid of individuals are allowed a level of dignity.'

'I accept your opinion and, as with many issues in my time, we need to change.'

As Rebecca explained about Evanora's weakness when near water, she could feel her staring at her through the cell bars. She turned, glanced in her direction and offered half a smile. She wasn't at all sure why she did this, it was just an instinctive reaction.

'You are a strong adversary. Your compassion weakens me. We may cross paths again.'

Rebecca nodded and although she felt sure their paths would not cross, the comment left her a tad uncomfortable. She then glanced at Matilda, indicating she wanted to head back up to the main building. On the way, Matilda suggested showing Rebecca where she planned to hold Evanora. She then led Rebecca to a thick-walled wooden outbuilding with narrow windows and a heavy cage door.

'This is perfect,' Rebecca said looking around. 'With it being directly next to this brook is ideal.' As they headed back to the main building, Rebecca started wondering why she was still here. Contented with Evanora's holding cell, knowing she would be at least moderately comfortable and importantly there was no chance of her escaping, she wasn't sure what to think. After some food, her and Matilda talked about the differences between the way criminal minded individuals were treated in Rebecca's time.

Narrow eyed, Matilda said, 'so, even if an individual murders someone, they are not put to death. Surely though, as the religious scripts suggest, it is an eye for an eye.'

Rebecca shook her head slightly. 'The issue with that is too many people have been found guilty, put to death, only to discover they were innocent and wrongly accused.' She then thought for a moment. 'If it is wrong for someone to kill another, how can it then be right to kill that person. That is double standards. James, by example, was imprisoned because he spoke with an unfamiliar accent.'

'To my mind, the issue with James was a catalyst for further change. I had already measured my position as Queen since we last met. I have made many changes towards my people. By example, we were taking unfair taxes from hard working farmers and this has now been stopped. Being so detached from reality, I was not aware of such injustices.'

'In my world, we are still bridging the gap between the masses and minority groups and only just understanding how unfairly some people are treated. Often for their diverse opinions on religion, government, mostly though because they appear dissimilar.'

Matilda appeared to be considering Rebecca's comment. 'We have similar issues in my time. By example, the warring clans, who all hold a dissimilar view on a number of matters, fight endlessly. To this point, I have invited two of the local clans to meet with me and my council. I would appreciate your input.'

Maybe this is why I'm still here, Rebecca thought. 'I would like that very much. When are they due? She asked, wondering how much longer she could be here.

'This very afternoon. The most influential clans here abouts are the MacDonald family, who have a moto, "Forget Not."

Also, the Sinclair family and their moto, "Commit Thy Work of God." So, it should be stimulating.'

Nodding slightly, considering Matilda's words, she said, 'stimulating it will be. What time are you expecting them to arrive?'

'Well, one of the clans go by the position of the sun and don't use time as we do. I sent word for both clans to be here when the sun is behind the Priory Spire. Without me going into detail, they both comprehend this.'

The two continued to talk about the void between those who govern and the people. They also discussed how individuals discriminate against others, often because of the things they were taught by their forefathers. After some lunch, there was a knock on the door.

'Enter,' Matilda called out.

'Ma'am, the MacDonald and Sinclair family are in the court awaiting your attendance.

Waving the man away a little dismissively, she said, 'I will attend.' She then turned to Rebecca.

A little uncomfortable with the way Matilda responded, she asked, 'can I say something?'

Nodding, and smiling, Matilda said, 'I am intrigued.'

'It is not for me to say, however.' She then thought for a moment. 'So, we have spoken about the void between you and your people.' She could see Matilda nodding and suspected she knew what Rebecca was going to say. 'The way you addressed that man just a moment ago was rather indifferent and dismissive. My father once said to me consider the way you speak to people. Put yourself in their shoes and hear your own words. If you would react negatively, then so will they. I believe the most important thing you can do is to address them by name.'

Matilda appeared to be thinking deeply. She looked up, her eyes flitting around the room. She then nodded. 'Your father has a valid perspective. I will make a conscious effort to address my custom. Shall we head downstairs, my dear friend?'

'May I ask why you invited these men other than to show them your thoughtful approach to governing?' She then thought for a moment about something that had been niggling at the back of her thoughts ever since she'd returned from York. 'So, in time, the English will invade Scotland. In the process, they will slaughter many. I am not proud of this, being English, but their approach will be callous and lead to many years of horrid conflict. As you have two of the most powerful clans here today, it would be good if you could get them to work together.'

'We already abhor the English, as you know only too well. Scotland was first invaded by Æthelstan in nine-hundred and thirty-four. That resulted in the death of many around the borders. Subsequently leading to Scotland's abhorrence of the English.'

Chapter 17 – The Clans

Rebecca followed Matilda downstairs. In the courtyard was a huge wooden table seating around 20 people. Her eyes immediately focussed on the dozen warrior like men sitting opposite each other. In the middle of each group was an elderly looking individual. Both these austere looking men, with their long grey hair and beards reminded Rebecca of a television programme about fighting clans she'd seen some time back.

'The men in pale blue and green tartan are the Sinclair family, and those in dark blue and red are the MacDonald family. They command authorities for miles around Perth and beyond. If I can gain their trust and soften their approach towards these lands and the folk here abouts, we could take harmonious steps forward.'

Matilda sat at the head of the table. Then, as if she'd taken Rebecca's suggestion on board, she addressed every individual by name, introducing Rebecca as a virtuous advocate. 'I have asked you here for a reason. We continue to face conflict with the English, especially around the Dumfries border lands. I have it on good authority the English will invade again and head north. We must act as one in defence of our lands and heritage.'

A lot of slightly ominous eye contact between the two clans followed. Then one of the Sinclair family spoke. 'Good authority. Who?'

Matilda glanced towards Rebecca. 'It is Rebecca, she is an English ally. She has abilities, considered beyond most.'

All the men instantly glared at Rebecca. 'This waif of a creature?' the MacDonald leader said, pointing at Rebecca.

His words and attitude were like a red rag to a bull. Rebecca jumped to her feet and although she could feel Matilda pulling at her sleeve she bellowed, 'Waif? I will give you waif. My name is Rebecca. Your attitude is weak, your manner feeble. I am here to help you all,' she snarled, glaring at the leader of the McDonald clan. 'As with Scottish people, there are good and bad. It is no different in England.' She shook her head and banged her hand on the table. 'Carry on the way you are, fighting with each other. It will be easy for the English to take your land and slay your heritage.' She then got up and walked around the table. She didn't know why she did this, but the reaction of these powerful men astonished her. As she passed each, they barely managed to make eye contact. 'Right, let's get some things sorted,' she said, placing her hand gently on the shoulder of one of the MacDonald family members. 'My name is Rebecca Fergusson. Yes, a Scottish name, my husband's name. I want to know all of your names.'

One of the clansmen stood up and turned aggressively towards Rebecca. Although inside, her heart was pounding, she knew this was no time to show weakness. She moved towards him. He stood a foot taller, and this reminded her of her childish battles with Tommy. Although that was 25-years ago, it settled her nerves completely. Without flinching, she made eye contact in spite of his arm waving. Appearing frustrated, he put his hand on his sword. As he did, the Sinclair leader, stood and pulled him away, mumbling something in Gaelic.

'Empress Matilda knows our names. No need for introductions,' one of the other MacDonald men snarled.

Rebecca stood directly next to this individual. 'That is fine then. None of the other people here matter. If one of the Sinclair members said this you would react negatively. Everyone here is here for a reason, so all deserve the same respect. How will you collectively battle against the Sassenachs if you are still fighting with each other.' She shook her head, leaned forward, placing both hands on the table. She then made eye contact with every individual. 'Consider your thoughts and words, introduce yourself.'

There were a few grumbles and after a couple of moments, the leader of the Sinclair family stood up.

He looked around the table, then nodded towards Matilda and Rebecca. 'My name is Haimish Sinclair.' He then turned towards Rebecca. 'I hear your words clearly within my thoughts.' He then glanced at the other clansmen. 'A waif you are not. Your spirit is strong, your opinion considered.' He then nodded. 'If you were a Scottish daughter, I would be proud.'

Rebecca shook her head. 'You see, that is the problem. You judge me by my birth place, rather than who I am.' She again put both hands on the table. 'Do you judge a horse by its colour? Or do you select said horse for its speed and strength? It is that simple. If you afford a horse that much consideration, why not your fellow man?' She could see by most reactions her words had made some inroads. There were nonetheless still one or two who appeared disapproving. 'Look across the table at your fellow counterpart. Consider your view of this person. Then put yourself in their position. You would draw swords. How can that be when you both want the same thing, to keep this land for you and your Scottish family. How will you do that if you continue to squabble with each other over what, something your father told you? This is time to step into today with solidarity, work as one, and keep the Sassenachs at bay.'

This time, the leader of the MacDonald Family stood up. 'This fearless woman is stronger of mind than us all together. Her words have changed me. It is a new day. Together we must step forward. My name is Malcom MacDonald.'

Over the next few minutes every individual introduced themselves, although one or two were clearly still uncomfortable.

Malcolm turned to Rebecca. 'Your words and character are stronger than the sword. Were you taught this or were you born this way?'

Malcolm's comment caught Rebecca a little off guard. She thought for a moment. 'The first time I faced an unexpected, challenging scenario, was when I was fifteen-years-old. I was aware there were probable pitfalls ahead of me. I also knew this potentially difficult situation laid before me for a reason. Without fear, I stepped forward and followed my intuition. Ultimately, my instinct didn't let me down and subsequently, I have always followed my gut. Now, all these years later, that same instinct led me here.' She thought for a moment before turning to Matilda. 'You have two simple choices in life. If you walk away from a demanding predicament once, then you may end up walking away forever. Or, alternatively you choose to step forward. There will be misjudgements and mistakes along the way, but these should be a catalyst for learning. Throughout our life, we store reasoned actions, behaviours and events deep within our memories. When faced with difficult situations, those memories nudge at our subconscious thoughts, either telling us to walk away or step forward. I suggest to you, we most often ignore that quite voice of reason.'

Matilda put her hands together. 'Some of you will know this, and some will not. Rebecca saved my life. I had been wounded by King Stephen's guard. This woman brought me from the lakes of England to this priory a year since. She acted selflessly and without fear for her own welfare. Therefore, I trust her. She has shown me an alternative way to lead these lands. To be your Empress, I must know you all and understand your life. My obligation is to work with you all to advance our journey. I did not know the name of those nearest to me, and this intrepid, free-thinking woman helped me see. We are in this together and together we must act to save our legacy. It is a legacy that is best served together.'

Rebecca could suddenly smell burning. Seconds later one of Matilda's guards hurried into the court.

'There is a fire in the outer building,' he shouted, pointing.

Rebecca followed the others through the court and towards the building holding Evanora. Although there were many people dousing the building with water, she could see the fire was out of control. With her emotions going in so many directions, she was unable to think clearly. She stood helplessly and watched as the building burned ferociously. She turned to Matilda. 'Is Evanora still inside?' she asked, feeling horridly emotional. Although she knew this woman was evil, she'd struggled with this whole scenario. The way Matilda nodded, she could see from the look on her face, she too was struggling with this outcome. Then a thought occurred to her and keeping a good distance from the bellowing heat, she headed around the back to see if Evanora had perhaps escaped. Shielding her face with both hands, she arrived by the stream to get a better look at the back of the building. The strangest sensation came over her and she was suddenly aware there was no heat. She pulled her hands away from her eyes and instantly knew she was back by the stream in her own woods. Emotionally exhausted, she sat on the damp moss by the stream, her head in her hands, wondering if Evanora had died in the fire. After a lot of back-and-forth deliberation, she shook herself and stood up. As she made her way back towards the summerhouse, she was struggling with her emotions. One minute, she was standing with Matilda, fretting over the sorrowful demise of Evanora. Now, she was back home, those emotions evaporated. As she made her way through the woods, she thought about her time with Etienne and their two children. One minute she was the fifty-year-old wife and mother of two young men, the next she was back to being twenty again with no emotional detachment. The more she thought about how she felt now, the more she realised her father's view on her journeys were right. Although it felt as if she lived every minute of every journey, she was only ever seeing that world through the eyes of another.

Arriving back at the summerhouse, she opened the door and headed to her bureau. Before any of this had happened, she had printed off an internet article that referenced Jack the Ripper.

Her intention was to show Mary if she'd been successful in changing history. She stood looking at three blank pieces of paper. She then spent a few minutes searching every drawer trying to find the papers she'd printed off even though she knew where she'd put the article and the paper was now blank.

She then opened up her laptop and searched Jack the Ripper. After several minutes, and finding nothing, she sat back, reckoning Evanora must have died in the fire. After a coffee, she decided to look up Scottish history, hoping to establish if she'd made any inroads with the clans. She didn't really know what she was looking for, so narrowed her search down to Matilda's era.

Although there was nothing specific, she did establish aside from the tenth century invasion Matilda had spoken of, the first time the English successfully invaded Scotland was two-hundred and fifty years after Matilda's rein. This got her to thinking about Meredith suggesting war will remain in history and is part of mankind's learning. She sat there for a few moments wishing she'd known more about Scottish history. In the end, she felt she'd done her best to stop the inter-clan fighting and maybe that was why it took the English so long before they actually made any headway.

After some lunch, she again searched the internet for anything relating to Matilda. Reading through a myriad of articles, she was unable to find much at all, leaving her feeling a little frustrated. On a hunch, she decided to search Edith of Scotland, remembering one of Matilda's maids addressing her as Edith on more than one occasion. She'd meant to ask Matilda about this, but... After another thirty odd minutes, she discovered Matilda's first name was actually Edith. In the early history, Matilda was often referred to as Matilda although as the years passed, she was seemingly known as Matilda Edith and then just Edith. Establishing she'd lived into her seventies and stayed within Perth Priory, she felt extremely pleased with herself. Although she couldn't remember exactly, she'd looked up Matilda's history after she first met with this woman.

Although she didn't have the details in front of her, she knew for certain that Matilda had died at the tender age of thirty-eight and was buried at Westminster Abbey. Now there was nothing on the internet that related to this incident. After an unsuccessful search for anything to do with Evanora, she decided on an early night even though it was only 8pm.

    As she headed upstairs, it occurred to her, she'd been with Matilda for 20 days. Although mostly her jumps only ever lasted a few seconds in her own time, irrespective of how long she'd been gone, of late, there were one or two where this wasn't the case. Staring at her watch and realising it was the same day as she'd left, she nodded, quietly relieved. In spite of all that had happened, she was in need of some company and importantly, someone she could discuss her journey with. With Duncan, her parents and children away for another two weeks, she decided to give Mary a call, who said she'd love to come over for a chat. They agreed on 11am the following day.

Chapter 18 – Just a chat

Lying in bed, she kept thinking about how things had changed, what with Jack the Ripper seemingly disappearing from history. She'd planned on speaking with Mary about this, but knew that was going to prove difficult. She shook her head, got up and spent another half-hour looking for the paperwork she'd printed off, unsuccessfully. She'd planned to show this to Mary as a kind of evidence how things changed when she intervened in the past. She knew she didn't have to prove anything, but had felt this would show exactly how it all works.

Now back in bed, she kept jumping between telling Mary about Jack the Ripper or just keeping the conversation about her time with Matilda. When she woke the following morning, the first thing that came into her thoughts was this gang of child snatchers and if there was any more news. After a shower where she spent most of her time thinking about Matilda, she headed downstairs to prepare some lunch for her and Mary.

Right on cue, as always, Mary arrived at 11am. 'Morning, Mary. Come in, boy have I got a lot to tell you.' She then showed Mary through to the kitchen. 'Coffee?'

'Love one thank you.'

'So, how are you?'

'Things have been oddly quiet. So, with some time on my hands, I've been doing a lot of research on that horrid group. That can wait though. By the sound of it, you have a lot to tell me, I'm intrigued, tell me more.'

Rebecca put the coffees down and sat opposite Mary. 'Oh, we can come onto my story later. I need to hear someone speaking in my language.' She could see Mary's intrigue jump up a level. 'Sorry, that was a little unfair,' she said and smiled.

Mary raised her eyebrows and shook her head slightly. 'It's okay, I am used to you throwing me a curve ball. So, it would seem this gang have gone to ground. I looked right back to when they first started, and it would seem there is uncorrelated evidence of their activities as far back as the nineteen-seventies. With that in mind, I've set up a task force to look at every incident since nineteen-seventy and further back if needed. At this point, we are unable to point a finger at any nationality or main group. Indeed, the key players seem to come from all over the world. There is however, one key aspect that joins them all together. It is always blond girls over ten and under twelve-years-old who are taken.'

'That must be so interesting when you unearth something like that. I am not sure interesting is the right word, but you know what I mean. Correlating all this must be a huge task. I recall seeing something on TV that over one-hundred thousand children go missing every year in the UK alone. The figure that hit home was one child reported missing every thirty seconds. I found that all very disturbing.'

'Well, a lot of those children are thankfully found, or come back home on their own. That said, the figures are alarming. To that point, we have two-hundred people now working on this here in Liverpool alone. Similar teams are being set up across every city in the UK. We also have all the major players in Europe, in addition to Canada, the US, Australia, well, every world body has signed up to a G-Eight type group. It is going to take some time to correlate everyone, however…' She looked down for a second. 'Quite frankly, I cannot believe it has taken us until now to create an international task force. For sure, we've worked together in the past, but never on this scale.'

'All this kind of makes my mission pale into insignificance, aiming my time arrow at one group. By the sound of it, there are groups like this all over the world'

'Far from it. This particular group, it would seem so far, is responsible for the disappearance of over ninety percent of all blond girls between the ages we mentioned. Now, here is a worrying trend that I've uncovered in the last few days. It is early days, but my team are uncovering evidence that there are similarities with red-heads. It is not for me to say, however...' She again seemed to think for a moment. 'Okay, so, there is some historical evidence of fair-haired girls being trafficked to certain destinations.' She shook her head. 'And this goes back many years.'

Taken aback by Mary's comments about red-heads hit home how important it was for her to find a way to stop this group. 'So, who set this task force in motion?' She'd known for some time how important helping Myleesa was, but this just compounded her responsibility.

Grinning, Mary said, 'it was me. The day I first met you, I started digging. Well, the hole has become an abyss. So, tell me your story. Enough of my intrigue knocking the blinking door down.'

Rebecca thoughts were focussing on how her actions in the twelfth-century had immaculately extinguished Jack the Ripper from history. Although this had worked, she was also aware that this group was part of a much bigger operation and she wondered if taking one man out of the equation would have any effect. Then suddenly Belisant's words surrounded her consciousness. *"His life leads to a bigger group of people who abuse children."* At the time, she had comprehended what she'd said, but she wasn't aware just how significant it was. Considering this, she wasn't sure where to start. 'Stop me if I jump about a bit,' she said and laughed with a tad of irony.

'You've never lost me before, although...' She sipped her coffee, and chuckled. 'You are not obliged to say anything, although I must caution you that anything you say may be used in evidence.'

The two then laughed out loud. 'Well, Ma'am, sipping from an empty cup won't work on me.' She then picked up the two cups and made some more coffee. While she was waiting for the coffee beans to grind down, she asked, 'have you ever heard of someone named Jack the Ripper?'

Mary narrowed her eyes. 'Now that is so weird. A couple of weeks ago I was digging up some old paperwork while down in London at the Black Museum. It is in Scotland Yard and effectively is an historical collection of horrid events. Anyways, I took some photos of stuff relating to the murders of young women on the streets of London during the eighteen-eighties. Now, here's the weird bit, yesterday, I was talking to a senior officer about this very case. He had never heard of Jack the Ripper, which I thought was very odd, especially as it struck me his name was synonymous with the murders of young ladies of the night. So, I took out my phone to show him the photos I'd taken and, well, I nearly swore. Actually, I did swear. Now, get this, I'd watched a film on TV about Jack and when I searched for it, there was nothing anywhere, even on the Internet.'

Although Rebecca knew exactly why Mary had sworn, she still wanted to hear it. 'What made you swear, although I suspect I may have a similar tale.'

'Well, the photos had vanished. When I say vanished, I mean there was no record of them having ever been taken. Because of my job, every photo I take has a log number. Now I took around thirty photos. The thing is, not only had the photos disappeared, there was no gap in the number sequence.' She shook her head. 'I know with certainty I took those photos.'

Rebecca held her hand up. 'She got up and placed three blank sheets of paper in front of Mary. 'I printed out three articles on Jack the Ripper. You're looking at them.' She then explained about her time with Matilda and the demise of Evanora.

'So, no sooner you'd affectively stopped Evanora from having children, Jack the Ripper disappeared…' she seemed to think for a moment. '… seven-hundred and fifty years later?'

'In a nut shell, yep. You see, the thing is, Evanora had an evil gene that would pass through the generations and manifest itself all those years later. It is difficult to get one's head around it, but in essence for every good individual of my making, and there have been many, there is an evil counterpart. Although much of my time in the past was changing events, of late, my direction has changed.' She could see Mary appeared a little perplexed. 'Okay, so throughout history there have been many of my kind. You may recall me telling you about the first documented Rebekah four-thousand years ago. The cradle of civilisation and all. So, for every one of my kind, there's always been an evil counterpart. Their job is to disrupt history and send it down a negative pathway. My job, along with others of my making, is to keep history on track.'

With pursed lips, Mary asked, 'could you stop things like war?'

'Well, I thought that. So, wars are part of humankind's journey. They are there, as frustrating as it is for me, so man will learn from their mistakes and hopefully, eventually, finally, move on.'

'Considering all you've achieved in your wonderful life, especially saving the planet from its self-destructive road, not being able to stop wars must be frustrating.'

'Well, initially it was. I've since come to terms, accepting some things are there for a reason.'

Over lunch, they chatted more about Rebecca's journey, and what may lay ahead for her.

'In the past, I never knew what was in front of me, it just occurred and I dealt with it as it happened. Lately, I have been given an insight as to what will happen. By example, I have that issue with Myleesa in seventeen-eighty-one, the one we talked about last time we met. Never in the past have I known what is in front of me.' She then thought for a moment as something occurred to her. 'I knew about Evanora because it was potentially dangerous for me. It is the same with Myleesa.'

'Dangerous, in what way?'

Rebecca then explained about her time with Meredith and how she'd warned her about this dangerous man.

'Does that frighten you?'

'Yes and no. It is all rather odd the way I feel. I am fully aware of the dangers. However, every time in the past, I pushed my shoulders back and got on with it.' She looked down for a moment. 'It is what it is. It is part of my destiny. The thing is, I've always felt Meredith would be there to catch me if I fell. On this one though, she told me I was on my own.' Again, she thought for a moment. 'I have to do this, irrespective of the dangers.'

'That is very brave. Just a thought, couldn't you take something like a taser with you?'

She frowned. Although this made sense, it went against her ethos. 'It is not something I've considered. Hmm, I am against taking modern things into the past, although there have been one or two unavoidable scenarios where I've had no choice.' With tightened lips, she narrowed her eyes. 'This might work actually. There is no need for anyone to see it and importantly, there will be no evidence left behind. It is not like I have to stop this man forever. I just need to stop him raping Myleesa and subsequently stop her falling pregnant.'

'Exactly. If things become dangerous, you could stop him in his tracks. I have one in my car. Sounds a little odd, but because of my position in the force, it is a must have. I'll get it for you before I go. On that subject.' she said, glancing at her watch, 'I must be heading off, dear girl.'

After insisting on helping Rebecca tidy up, Mary fetched the taser from her car. She then spent a few minutes showing Rebecca how to use it correctly. 'So, keep it on charge, but take it with you every time you go out on one of your walks to, well, who knows where you'll end up. I'll speak with you soon, especially if we come up with any information about that group.'

After Mary had left, Rebecca placed the Taser on their baker's shelf by the front door, and then attached a bright pink post-note to it. "DO NOT FORGET THIS."

She then returned to her computer and continued reading up on Matilda. She shook her head, remembering an old Scottish history book Duncan had come across in an antique shop. She went upstairs and oddly it was right at the front of their book cabinet. It was as if someone had placed it there intentionally. Picking it up, she thought, *this is a bit weird.* She was certain it wasn't there last night, knowing she would have seen it, what with it being out of place.

She opened it up and scanned through the faded index. Although she was unable to find Matilda's name in the index, she did come across the MacDonald family 1100s. She opened it up on page 338, and thought, what is going on with this blinking number 38 again. She started reading and soon established throughout the 12th-centruy, they'd battled endlessly with the Sinclair family. After reading a little more, she reckoned she needed to cross reference this book with the internet. Over an hour passed and she was unable to find anything that related to this century long battle. In the end, she hoped Matilda bringing these clans together had changed history for the better. *Well, we dowsed Jack the Ripper from history, so why not,* she thought.

She then typed in the year she first met Matilda, 1123. Staring at the computer, she couldn't believe what came up at the top of the search. She had to scan down before actually coming across the year 1123. Returning to the top, she opened the article up and started reading.

Guardian Angel Number 1123 inspires you to step forward toward a life-changing event. It reassures you to get things in order so that history will run smoothly and as planned in your life.

Unable to believe what she'd just read, she opened up other similar articles. Most were just a variant on words. She then noticed an article she'd missed. It was headed Old Testament's meaning for 1123. The first section simply said it means strong. She then typed in biblical 1123. Buried in one article she came across a section that sent a chill through her body. It attributed the number 1123 to Rebekah. She always felt there was an unfathomable link between her, Matilda and Rebekah. So why is Meredith missing from this link, she wondered. She continued to search a little more, but now becoming bleary eyed, she decided she needed some fresh air.

Chapter 19 – Daughter from Another Life

Deciding to go for a walk to the left of the summerhouse, a direction she'd bizarrely never been before. She'd always meant to go this way but the path along the lake edge had constantly been under water and any alternative route appeared completely overgrown. With the lake level down a couple of foot, standing at the front of the summerhouse, she could see a possible route. She started making her way along the path, then stopped dead in her tracks and went back to fetch the taser. She still wasn't sure she felt right taking this with her, but Mary's comments, and knowing she might be in danger, had left her with little choice. Raising her eyebrows, she headed down the path. After a few minutes, she came close to the old willow where she'd first seen the mystical boat on the lake 25-years earlier. Arriving by the side of the tree triggered the strangest feeling.

She stood there for a few moments considering her emotions. Unable to understand her feelings, she reckoned her mood was just because she was standing by this tree. In the past, whenever she'd felt similar, something normally happened. She checked her pocket for the taser and then tried to find a way around the tree. It didn't help that behind it was head high brambles and nettles. To the front, the tree branches hung twenty or so foot over the water's edge. She considered turning back, but as quick dismissed that idea having waited so long to walk this path. In the end, taking her shoes and socks off, she decided her only option was wading under the twisting branches of this huge willow.

As she made her way through the ankle-deep water, and with her emotions further heightened, she wondered what may lay ahead of her. Arriving at the other side of the tree, she could see the path continued around a huge bay that was out of eyeshot from the front of the summerhouse. Making her way around the lake edge, she kept stopping, trying to regain a levelheadedness. This area was generating the most peculiar mood. It certainly wasn't spooky in any way. It was just weird. As she headed a little further, she came across an old bench, which just added to this odd mood she was feeling. Easily pulling away some new-shoot bramble and inspecting the bench, she was surprised by its exceptional condition. *This is odd*, she thought, reckoning it must have been here for many years. Walking around the front, she stopped dead in her tracks. Pulling away the bramble had revealed a slightly grubby brass plaque. Searching her pocket and not having a hanky or tissue, she decided to use one of her socks to clean the plaque. She read the message, which left her unable to move or think clearly. She read it again.

For Rebecca, my daughter in another life.

She breathed out through pursed lips not sure what to make of this. Then in the corner, she could see what looked like a number. Again, rubbing with her sock, she revealed the year 1853. This was the year she first met Meredith and knowing this sent a shiver of curious emotions through her body. Considering all that had happened today, she couldn't but wonder if there was more. In the past, without fail, occurrences like this always led somewhere.

Still contemplating the plaque, she looked around to see if she'd missed anything else. With the path overgrown and no way forward, she sat on the bench wondering if this was actually leading anywhere. As soon as she sat down, the most peculiar chill run down her spine. She was sure there must be something else. Contemplating what she believed was some kind of message, she started thinking about the first time she met with Meredith. It oddly felt as if it were yesterday and she could remember almost every detail. When she got to the part when the two of them met Millicent, something occurred to her. When Millicent had shown aggression towards her, Meredith had defended her as if she was her daughter. At the time, she'd believed Meredith was just seeing her as a daughter and this was why she'd been so defensive. Thinking about it now, maybe there was another reason.

Over the years, through every turn, Meredith had always been there when she needed her most. Because of this, Rebecca had always considered Meredith as her guardian angel. Continuing to go over her times with Meredith wasn't giving her any answers. She kept jumping between different notions. On one hand, she was certain Meredith had only seen her as a daughter that first time, and that was only because Rebecca had appeared to Meredith as her daughter. Since though, what with Meredith knowing Rebecca was from the future, their relationship had been more an alliance. She turned again and looked at the plaque. *What does this mean*, she thought?

In the end, she decided it was a beautiful message indicating Meredith's love and no more. She had another look around, and guessing there was no more here for her, reluctantly headed back. She took a couple of steps, turned to look once more at the bench and then glanced further along the lake edge. For sure, she could wade her way through the head-high nettles, but there was nothing pulling her in that direction. She considered her thoughts briefly and reckoned her gut would tell her if she needed to go any further. She did wonder if seeing this bench and the message was sending her emotions in the wrong direction and perhaps somehow shielding her intuition. 'Na,' she muttered, 'I'd know.'

Just to make sure, she tried something that had worked in the past and called out to Meredith. There was nothing, no answer, no mood change, no smell of almonds, nothing. Now content there wasn't any more here for her, she headed back to the summerhouse. She went inside, made herself a coffee and sat on her rocking chair on the veranda. With the warmth of the sun kissing her face, she put her cup down and closed her eyes thinking about the message.

Shivering, she woke up abruptly wondering where she was. It was pitch black and seemingly late in the evening. It must have been around 2pm when she'd nodded off. Doubtful she'd slept this long she went inside to check the time. 'Where's the blinking clock,' she muttered? Shaking her head, she was starting to feel quite odd. Looking around, everything was just so, apart from the clock. She then started to pull out the cabinet to see if the clock had fallen down the back. Before she'd moved it an inch, she noticed there was no sign of the clock ever being there. Because it was a big old Victorian clock, Duncan had fixed it in place with a wooden batten, which was also missing. It was one thing the clock disappearing, but this just wasn't adding up. Still curious what the time was, she headed upstairs to check her phone. After a few minutes searching unsuccessfully, she turned to her laptop. 'Now this is getting weird,' she mumbled. She knew for sure her laptop was on her dresser because she'd left it open before she went out and had come back to close it down.

There were times in the early days when she'd felt a little spooked by certain situations, but it was only ever because something unexpected had happened, like a door pulling from her grip. The way she was feeling right now was something altogether different. Feeling this spooked was making it difficult to think straight. She went downstairs and searched for her phone or laptop even though she knew they had been upstairs when she went out.

Right, she thought and went outside to look at the position of the stars to gage the time, something Duncan had taught her. Seeing heavy cloud cover, she knew that wasn't going to work. Over the years, she'd experienced many different scenarios, but nothing like this. She knew she was in her own time, well at least it felt that way, *so what is going on*, she thought. Famished, and trying to give herself time to focus, she went inside to make a sandwich. Everything was just where it should be, so she knew she hadn't changed times. Or have I, she wondered? Scratching her forehead, she looked around at a complete loss what to think.

Desperate to find out what was going on, she decided to head up to the main house. *Too many clocks to disappear*, she thought. As she headed up, and not having a clue what to expect, she focussed her attention on establishing the time. With her parents away with the girls and Duncan in the US, she was surprised to see light coming from inside the house. She put her key in the door, and was shocked to find it unlocked. Narrow eyed, she pushed the door open and could hear the voice of her mother coming from the kitchen. Before she had time to think, she then heard her own voice. With her spine burning and her thoughts blinded with curiosity, she opened the door to the kitchen.

Seeing her mother, father and herself sat around the table sent a shockwave through her body. Realising she was once more invisible and perhaps seeing events from the other dimension, her thoughts jumped back to the time she saw her mother's accident. She then noticed some odd-looking cards on the far side of the kitchen. Before she had time to go and investigate, her mother started talking.

'Rebecca, we will get through this together. You must focus all your attention on the girls.'

She then listened to herself speaking, her voice trembling with grief, but oddly certain. 'I know, Mother,' she said, appearing strangely detached. 'I am besieged with concern, seeing my girl's world without their father.'

Dumbfounded but weirdly calm, she made her way over to the cards on the sideboard, wondering why she wasn't overwhelmed with anguish. Importantly, she couldn't understand why her mirror image also appeared to be taking it almost in her stride. Unable to touch the cards, she peered inside the first one. She could see it was a sympathy card for the death of Duncan. She leant this way and that, trying to peer inside the remaining cards, hopeful of finding a clue to what had happened to Duncan. The cards only expressed sympathy. Desperate to find out what happened, she stood by the table listening. Then, remembering the old clock in the hallway and knowing it showed the date, she stood by the door, still listening, while trying to peer at the clock. It was the 17th July and she knew that was three days after Duncan was due back from America. She then suddenly realised she needed to know what year it was. Heading back over to the cards, she could see what looked like a couple of discarded envelopes in the bin. *They'll have the Date*, she thought. As with the cards, she was unable to touch the envelopes, so bending down to get a better look, she was able to establish it was the same year.

She stood there listening for an hour when suddenly Rebecca's tone changed.

'I told him I could feel the front wheel wobbling.'

That was all she needed to hear. Just before Duncan had left for America, she'd used his car to pick the girls up from school. That evening, they'd had an unusually heated debate about the car. Duncan was adamant it was okay, what with it being only 3 months old. A couple of days later, when he left for America, Duncan had taken the car and parked it at Liverpool airport.

With her emotions tangled, although oddly calm, she headed back to the summerhouse knowing she had a good chance of preventing what had happened. Although she hadn't felt any sensation, opening the front door, she knew between the main house and here, she'd jumped back into her own time. The first thing she did was look for her phone. After unsuccessfully turning the house upside down, frustrated, she slumped down at the kitchen table. Glancing up and seeing the clock had reappeared made her feel rather odd. Seeing it was 11pm, she reckoned she couldn't do much now. Then she realised it would be around 6 in the evening in New York. 'Right, I need to phone him,' she mumbled.

Again, she turned the house upside down, still unable to find her phone. Frustratingly, what with Duncan having a brand-new phone, with a new number, the only way she had of contacting him was with her phone. *Why didn't I ask him where he was staying*, she thought, *stupid or what?* Then an idea occurred to her and she headed up to the bedroom to find the box the phone had come in. Halfway upstairs, she could visualise herself putting that box out with the rubbish. Using the house phone, she called up Duncan's service provider, and although she explained how important it was, they would not give out Duncan's number. She slammed the phone down, but in the back of her thoughts, she knew Duncan was always very strict with his number and had actually threatened a previous provider with legal action because they'd given his number out.

Over the next couple of days, she tried everything she could think of, including phoning her father. She hadn't gone into details other than she'd lost her phone, but could tell from his tone, he knew something was going on. They hadn't heard from Duncan for a couple of days, when he'd phoned to speak to the girls. Frustratingly for Rebecca, his number had shown up as withheld, as it always does. James went on to say Duncan would evidently be busy in meetings and may not be able to phone often. In the end, she told her father how her phone had mysteriously vanished, and although she said it was important Duncan called her, she still didn't go into details. Before coming off the phone, she said, 'tell him to call on the house phone when he calls back.'

'He said he'd tried the house phone but it failed to connect.'

'Right, thanks, Dad, I'll check the phone. Bye, love to everyone.'

After finishing the call, she spent a few minutes going through the call register on the house phone. Bizarrely, other than her call a moment ago, there was a 5-day gap in the incoming and outgoing calls. She quickly called her father back and asked if he had tried to call the house phone.

'I did a few times but as with Duncan, it wouldn't connect. I thought the problem was my end, especially as I had trouble getting through on your mobile. When I discovered Duncan couldn't get through either, I sent you an email, but oddly that bounced back. I was actually relieved when you called just now. So, young lady, tell me what is going on.'

'Dad, I am not really sure I understand what is going on and why I can't contact Duncan.' Although she didn't want to alarm her father, she knew she had no choice, so told him about the scenario she'd experienced. 'Maybe there is a reason I can't contact him, but I can't possibly imagine why.'

'That must have been horrid witnessing that and not being able to do anything there and then. Importantly though, I can't possibly imagine why the powers that be would stop you contacting him. I must say, your phone, laptop, and even the clock vanishing has all pointed you in a specific direction. Not that I know what direction that is, although I am confident you will find answers, you always do.'

'I will, Dad. I have a few days yet.'

She came off the phone and with her father's words resonating in her thoughts, she focussed her attention. Oddly, something deep in her thoughts was telling her to be patient, as annoying as that was.

The next two days followed a similarly frustrating pattern. Duncan, who hadn't phoned her father, was now due home in two days. Considering everything over the last couple of days, a conspiracy theory was starting to form in her head. She now found herself wondering why she'd been handed all this information and then subsequently unable to contact Duncan. It just didn't make sense. As she was thinking, she noticed a set of car keys on the kitchen sideboard.

Getting up, she could see they were Duncan's spare set. 'Now that is plain daft, I washed this side down this morning.' She sat back down twiddling the keys. She didn't have a clue which car park he'd used, or if he used the drop off service where they park the car somewhere else. Over the next couple of hours, she called every drop off car service and none of them had a record of Duncan. Knowing there was a short stay, 5-day maximum, plus two huge long stay car parks, she reckoned she had to go and search both the long-stays for his car.

Seeing it was just after midday, she jumped in the car and headed off to the airport. On the way, she considered phoning Mary to see if she had any ideas, but without her phone that was a non-starter. Arriving at the first car park and looking across a sea of cars, she knew this was going to be almost impossible. Nonetheless, she started trudging up the first aisle of cars. After around 500-yards and halfway along the first isle, she glanced to her left. It looked like there were hundreds of aisles and she knew this was going to be impossible on her own. Then she remembered she had written Mary's number on a scrap of paper. She headed back to the car, grabbed the paper, then went to the car park kiosk.

'Hello, is there a public phone nearby.'

'Sorry, Madam, it's been vandalised.' He then narrowed his eyes a little. 'Madam, I hope you don't mind me saying, but I recall reading about you in the paper some years back,' the elderly man said. 'You can use my phone, but it is stuck on loud speaker.'

'Oh, that is so very kind of you. I wouldn't normally, but this is so important.' She then smiled, 'you may well recall seeing me in the paper.'

'Thank you,' he said and handed her the phone. 'And, thank you for giving my grandchildren a future.'

Rebecca called Mary and explained the predicament she was in. Mary, offering to help, said she'd be there within the hour.

After she came off the phone, the elderly man turned his computer screen around. 'I overheard your conversation. If you know the approximate time and day your husband parked his car, I can find where he parked it on our CCTV records. I didn't mean to listen in, and was going to go outside, but as soon as you said about your husband's car, I knew I could help.

I could use number plate recognition but that won't tell us where he parked.'

Thinking for a few seconds, Rebecca said, 'it was the fifteenth and he left home around eleven am. It takes around an hour.'

By the time he'd come across the footage, Mary walked in.

'Hi, Rebecca.' She introduced herself to the man and then lent over Rebecca's shoulder peering at the screen. 'I thought of this on the way.'

After around 20-minutes, they found Duncan's car right at the back of the car park.

'On foot, that would have taken me days to find that,' Rebecca said and laughed. She then went outside with Mary and briefly outlined her story.

'Crumbs, that is so scary, but at least you can prevent it ever happening. Right, I will arrange for the car to be taken back to the showroom, checked today and brought back before Duncan returns home. I reckon as soon as they know who I am, they will do what I ask of them. In the meantime, fancy a coffee?' After phoning the car company, the two headed off to the airport lounge. On the way, she said, 'the car company have a depo just around the corner, which is handy.'

Sipping her coffee, Mary shook her head. 'After all you've been through with this, I am surprised you managed to focus. Knowing your husband could die, you must have been distraught with panic. I am very impressed how you've managed to focus.'

'Thank you,' Rebecca said, although in the back of her thoughts, she found herself again wondering why she wasn't besieged with grief.

Half way through their second coffee, Mary's phone rang. After she came off the phone, she looked at Rebecca. 'That was the main mechanic and he said two of the wheel nuts had broken. He said the car is very dangerous in this condition and they were shocked the wheel hadn't caused a crash already. He also said, because the company have taken complete ownership for the fault, they will bring a new car and park it in the same place. They will then arrange for someone to wait for Duncan. He then asked me what time Duncan's flight was due. I told him I'd call him back.'

'Without my phone, or Duncan's flight number, all I know is he is due back on the twenty-ninth.'

'Not a problem,' she said taking out her laptop. I will check all flights from all New York airports. After scribbling down a few notes, she looked up at Rebecca. 'There are eight flights due. Annoyingly, the first one lands at six in the morning and then they are spread out through the day. It is going to be a long wait for the car people.' She then called the car company back and explained the situation. After finishing the call, she said, 'the guy I spoke to sounded a little miffed. When I again explained who I was and that they could have been responsible for the death of Duncan, his tone changed, as you would expect.'

'I must say, Mary, I listened to you on the phone, and well, I thought if I had been him, I wouldn't have debated it with you,' she said and chuckled. Before they headed off, they went back to the car park kiosk and explained the situation.

'I must say, Rebecca, we make a great team. Do you want to come and work for me? We could solve a lot of crimes with your intrepid, fearlessness and insight to the past and future.'

'Well, we are working together, although, like you, I don't see it as work. On that subject, any news on the child abduction group?'

Squinting, she nodded. 'Still oddly very quiet. I must say, I found myself wondering if this group had anything to do with... Evanora, was it?'

Tight lipped, Rebecca considered this notion for a moment. 'Now, there's a thought. I might have to do some checking. I guess it is possible, although, going on past events, I suspect I would know by now if the Myleesa situation had changed.'

'Myleesa?'

Realising she hadn't mentioned Myleesa in any detail, she explained the whole scenario.

'Oh right, I see, I didn't recall you mentioning her name before and thought it might be another job, if that's the right word. Now you have told me the story, I do recall you saying something in passing. Anyways, make sure you keep your taser with you.'

There it was again, that word, anyways. 'Mary, may I ask you, you use the word anyways, as do I and my mother.' She'd heard her use this word before and having only known a couple of people use it, thought it was time she asked. 'Importantly, Meredith used that word also. Now I don't know if I got the word from Meredith and my mother copied me, or the other way around. Hearing you use it made me wonder.'

She could see Mary thinking. 'Umm.'

Surprised by Mary's response, she held her palms up.

'I think I may have picked the word up from you.' She paused briefly, again clearly thinking. 'I suspect you're not going to accept that, are you?' she said and narrowed her eyes a little.

With her thoughts jumping around a little, Rebecca wasn't quite sure what to say. 'So, I get the notion you want to say something but are hesitating for some reason. Anyone listening in would say it's just a coincidence that you both use the same word.' She then pursed her lips a little. 'We both know that is not the case, so out with it, tell me what you have to say.'

'Long story. I met a psychic in America some time back. Well, that is a label they put on people who can see beyond the obvious. So, I was over there investigating a number of similar crimes that had occurred both in the US and here. The NYPD often use psychics, clairvoyants or whatever you prefer to call them, to help solve crimes, unofficially. Anyways,' she then chuckled, 'I met with this woman who claimed she could see into the past. At the time, and I am eternally sorry for this, I dismissed the notion as nonsense. That said, I got on very well with this woman. She had a lovely tone, style, and manner. She used anyways and it stuck. When I met you, I tried to contact that woman to say I was sorry I hadn't believed her story. Not that I ever let on I didn't buy in.'

'Okay, so did she help you solve the crime?'

'Well, here's the stupid bit on my part. Once I was back in the UK, the NYPD had acted on her suggestions and apprehended the criminal. Sadly, annoyingly, at the time, I still dismissed the notion that they'd solved the crime because of her suggestions. Retrospectively, I was far too fastidiously blinkered and well… Then I met you. I must say, when I met you and heard you use this word, I wondered how long it would be before you asked me why I use it also.'

Scratching her head, Rebecca wasn't sure what to think. 'Maybe it is like a secret handshake word, like a gang,' she said and laughed. The two continued to chat a while longer.

'Right, must dash. And, if you plan on going anywhere, take the taser.'

Chapter 20 – Two Days

Rebecca pulled up in front of the summerhouse feeling relieved. As she made herself some supper, her thoughts were jumping between what Mary had said about the Psychics and the plaque on the back of the bench. Then from the corner of her eye, she could see her phone on top of the microwave. She shook her head, unable to believe what she was looking at. She'd briefly thought the day before her phone going missing was part of a bigger plan. Because she'd never experienced anything this material before, she'd kind of dismissed the notion that Meredith or Ethernal had hidden her phone. Now she knew for sure and in an odd way, found it rather comforting. She went and picked the phone up and could see an endless list of missed calls from Duncan. Checking the time, she could see it was ten in the morning in New York, so called him. Initially, there was no answer. Then as she put the phone down, he rang back.

'What happened to your phone, Sweetheart? I was so worried until I spoke with your father and he told me you were okay.'

Rebecca went through the story about his car, and mentioned about her phone going missing and then mysteriously turning up just a moment ago. Duncan, as always, accepted her tale without question. The two chatted for over thirty minutes and agreed to meet at the airport at 4pm. After taking the flight number, she called Mary with the details so she could pass them onto the car company.

As she sat there, finishing off her now cold pizza, which actually tasted better, she felt relieved Duncan had accepted her story without question, not that he ever debated any of her tales. This series of questionable incidents though was a whole new level and she could recall feeling exactly this way when she first got her father to believe her story about the boiler.

After finishing her pizza, she decided to sit down and watch TV. Scrolling through the channels, she couldn't find much. Starting again at the top and just about to read a book instead, she spotted a film called About Time. Reading up on the storyline, she decided to give it a go. Because it had already started, she used the green button to watch it from the start. That in itself made her smile, thinking it was like having a TV time machine. Several times during the film, she found herself shaking her head at the similarities between her and the father, and in particular the way he handled this family gene.

After it was finished, she sat there staring at the blank screen thinking about all she'd been through and how differently people had responded over the years. This again brought her back to the time when she convinced her father she could travel through time and how he'd changed since. Bizarrely, she still had the drills with the hole cut in the pocket. Even though they were tattered and now far too small, she could never bring herself to throw them away.

As it was such a warm evening and not in the least bit tired, she took her glass of wine outside and sat on her rocking chair. Looking at the stars, she started thinking about all that had happened over the last couple of days. One or two things had stayed rumbling around in the back of her thoughts. When she'd viewed, seemingly from the other dimension, her mum, dad and herself talking about Duncan, it had bothered her a little that she wasn't tearful. For sure, she'd felt a huge amount of anxiety, but at no point did she feel tearful. She'd questioned this at the time and often since. Mostly, she reasoned her emotions were driven because she was sure she could resolve this. Niggling though, something was telling her this odd detachment was because of some other reason she wasn't aware of. These conflicting thoughts made her again consider her time with Etienne and how unemotional she was then, in spite of leaving a husband and two children behind.

For sure, her father's suggestion she had witnessed the entire event through another's eyes had helped her re-evaluate her feelings. The thing that was bothering her most was she'd felt similarly detached when she learnt about Duncan's demise. Yeah, for sure she'd witnessed the whole event from afar, even so, she should have felt more than she did. With Etienne, she had only ever seemingly witnessed that world through another's eyes, so wasn't actually involved. The love for Etienne and the two boys was another's love, not hers. Duncan was her husband and she wasn't seeing this from someone else's perspective. It was her world. So why do I feel so detached, she kept wondering? In the end, she forced herself to believe she felt this way because she was able to fix everything. Still, though...

Considering these supressed emotions, the plaque on the bench came to mind. *My daughter in another life*, she thought, *what does that even mean?* At the time, her initial reaction believed it was just simply a message from Meredith because she had seen her as a daughter the first time they met. Now though, she was questioning if there was more to this. She wondered if Meredith had seen her as a confidante, and used daughter as a term of endearment. All this considered though, there was still something suggesting there may be more hidden in this message? This made her think about the word anyways. She always believed she'd picked it up from her mother. She was now wondering if her mother had gotten it from her. *If so, did I get it from Meredith*, she thought, *and if I did, when?* Everything considered seemed to be pointing in a very specific direction. The problem with this, Rebecca's thoughts didn't have a map and she just couldn't come up with a rational answer for her disconnected emotions. There was a tiny spark right at the back of her thoughts that tied a knot between Meredith and her. At this juncture though, she wasn't prepared to consider this notion even though it made sense.

Feeling rather perplexed, she again considered the word anyways and decided she'd copied it from Meredith and no more. After finishing off her wine, she headed up to bed and tried to think about something else. The next thing she knew it was 11 the following morning and once again, her brain was full of confused thoughts and emotions. After some toast and orange juice, she decided to do some research on the internet.

She opened her laptop up and typed in witches, not really sure what she was hoping to find. After scrolling through a myriad of fanciful images and stories that were at best, guesses, she decided she needed a different approach. Thinking about the book she'd seen in the old bear lodge, she typed in witch-register. This again produced endless speculative notions and ideas. Unsure if she'd forgotten the date Minerva was around, or hadn't ever known, she typed in witch-register 1700s England. After again scrolling through endless drivel, she found an article in Wikipedia that appeared to relate to facts rather than speculation. Reading, she was horrified to discover that a Witchcraft act was introduced in 1563. This act presented a legal death penalty for any sorcery used to cause someone's death. She then read it was reformed, *a very inappropriate word,* she thought, to include anyone having made a pact with the devil. She went on to discover the last noted witch-trial was for a mother and daughter named Mary and Elizabeth Hicks in 1716. There was however nothing referring to Evanora or Minerva. Unexpectedly, she came across an article that told of an incident in Liverpool by the docks. It went on to say that a vagabond girl named Myleesa murdered a distant member of the royal family, had been convicted and put to death. This rang alarm bells in her head. She knew that when the door eventually opens to Myleesa, she must not only save this girl. It was now also imperative she helped her reach Glasgow docks and subsequently take the ship to Canada and join up with her sister. With her intrigue heightened, she started reading more on the Internet.

After a few minutes, she stumbled across an article labelled "Polygamia Triumphatrix," which suggested in the 6th century one "holy father," insisted "women cannot, and should not, be called 'human beings." Adding to the suggestion that 99% of witch trials involved women, she felt incensed. Thinking about this, she remembered one of her school teachers referring to the early 1900s as the female dark-ages. Considering how Rebekah, some 4000 years ago had been revered, she wondered where and when things changed. She then recalled Duncan's father saying, when they were talking about woman in history, that largely men are weak and subsequently fearful of strong women. For sure, there were exceptions such as Joan of Arc, Elizabeth 1st, and Zenobia, an Empress in Syria, some 2000 years after Rebekah. Largely though, you could count them on one hand. Most recently there was Margaret Thatcher, who although highly respected and revered, was still seen as a threat by many leading, older-generation, political men.

Miffed, and unable to concentrate any longer, she closed down her laptop and decided to go for a walk. She stood in the hallway looking at the taser wondering if taking it with her would effectively stop her resolving the issue with Myleesa. With Duncan due home the following afternoon, she knew she couldn't take any chances. She reckoned if it stopped her going anywhere, so be it, but also, if she did jump, and knowing of the potential dangers, she also had to give herself some protection. Nodding, she popped the taser in her pocket and headed off for a walk in the woods. In the back of her thoughts, although eager to resolve the Myleesa issue, she knew, as always, time was and would always be on her side. *Doesn't actually matter if I help Myleesa today, tomorrow or next week*, she thought.

She'd been walking for a couple of minutes when she heard voices coming from the direction of the main house. *Bit odd,* she thought, and headed in that direction, knowing it was actually more than a bit odd. The closer she got, the louder the voices. She then heard a horse whinny. With her curiosity now taking over, she hurried through the woods. Arriving near the main house, she could see a number of people at the front of the house standing near a six-horse carriage. With her focus on the people and carriage, she suddenly noticed the house was half the size it was in her time. Looking at the structure, and going on what she knew about her home, she reckoned she'd possibly jumped to the late-1700s. This in itself stirred her focus, knowing this was Myleesa's period. In the past, whenever she'd jumped anywhere, it had always been to the right place at the right time. So, if I am here to help Myleesa, why am I here and not in Liverpool, she wondered.

Keeping a good distance from the people, she tried to work out what was going on. Once more, she considered her mission with Myleesa. The thing was, that was in Liverpool by a dockside pub called The Ship. Tight lipped and a tad confused, she mumbled, 'how am I going to get to Liverpool.'

'You need to take the carriage to Liverpool, Rebecca,' came a voice she hadn't heard for a long time. Knowing it was Ethernal, she didn't turn.

Looking down at her clothes, she wondered how she would get on the carriage without causing a reaction.

'Worry not, you cannot be seen. Hurry.'

She could sense he had gone, so hurried towards the carriage. As she drew closer, one woman turned and looked directly in her direction, which caught her off-guard. The woman then seemingly looked straight through her. Standing by the carriage, she watched as people climbed aboard, clearly unaware of her presence. With no seats, she looked around for somewhere she could hitch a ride. She then noticed a platform at the back. Reckoning that was her only option, she pulled herself up, gripping a metal rail near the top. Within a couple of minutes, the carriage pulled away, nearly jolting her off. Getting a better footing, she held on tightly wondering how long this journey would take.

As the carriage rambled through miles of huge conifers, she started wondering how she would get back. Remembering Meredith telling her she was on her own on this one, she started feeling a little concerned. After going over a number of scenarios in her head, she reckoned she was just stressing. Thinking about her time with Matilda, she decided to do what she always did, and take it as it comes. After around 4 hours they reached the outskirts of Liverpool.

Mesmerised by all the old wooden buildings, her consciousness was broken by one of the carriage drivers bellowing, "Next, The Ship Inn."

Well, that couldn't have worked out any better, she thought. As the carriage jolted to a halt, she jumped off and looked around. It was just getting dark and so she made her way over towards the Inn. Aware she was still invisible and was perhaps going to witness events from that other dimension, she wasn't sure how she could change anything.

She'd been standing there for around an hour when it started to rain heavily. Watching people hurry for cover, and now standing outside alone, she reckoned this downpour might actually help. Taking shelter under a small wooden canopy, she wondered how long she would be hanging around. No sooner she'd thought this, she heard a girl's voice screaming from the back of the Ship Inn.

Hurrying around the back, she could see a black-caped rogue of a male pushing a young pretty, but raggedy looking blond girl against a tumble-down wooden fence.

Unsure how she could stop this man, she moved closer. As she did, the blond girl turned and looking directly at Rebecca, cried, 'Help me, Miss.'

Taken aback, not only could this girl see her, she was able to speak to her also. Aware the man was oblivious to her presence she took the taser from her pocket, and tried to place it in the girl's hand. As she did, the man pushed the girl again and took a knife from his pocket. Unable to hand it to the girl, she held the taser up. With the girl looking, she pointed it at the man and pressed the button in an attempt to show the girl how it worked.

Unbelievably, the taser had worked and she watched as the man dropped to the ground. With her mouth open, she looked at the girl.

Shaking her head, the girl touched Rebecca on the hand. 'Thank you, Miss. How did you do that?'

She was aware to most, including this man, she was invisible. This girl being able to see her, and also speak to her confused her a little. She'd been in this other dimension before, but had always been invisible to everyone. This scenario was not only unexpected, but somewhat baffling. The fact that her taser worked added to her confusion. She forced a smile through her muddled thoughts. Seeing the girl staring at her, she smiled. 'My name is Rebecca. Are you Myleesa?'

Appearing a little surprised, this beautifully sharp featured, but grubby girl shook her head. 'My name is Myleesa, how could you know, Miss?'

'I know your sister, Belisant. You must come with me.' She then lent down to the man who still appeared unconscious. As heavy as he was, she tried to turn him over. As she did, she noticed a pool of blood and could see he had fallen on his own knife. Thinking about the cloaked message she'd found on the internet she knew she had to get this girl away from here. She checked the man's pulse and he was dead. 'You must come with me. Hurry.' She then led the girl down towards the water's edge. She didn't have a clue where she was going, but as always, was trusting her gut.

Arriving by the dockside, and seeing a number of small sail boats moored up, an idea occurred to her. A couple of years back, she'd learnt how to sail a small boat, with the idea of using one on the lake by their house. Hearing a commotion of voices behind her coming from the direction of the Ship Inn, she reckoned there was no time to think. She turned to Myleesa, put her finger to her lips and indicated towards one of the small sail boats.

The two of them clambered down a wooden ladder at the side of the dock and into the boat. With as much stealth as she could muster, Rebecca untied the boat and eased it away from its moorings. As quietly as she could, she used the oars to head away from the dock. As the Ship Inn disappeared into the darkness, Rebecca pulled the main sail up.

'Are we safe, Miss?'

'Please call me Rebecca. Yes, we are safe. I am going to help you get back to your sister.'

'She lives many miles from here, are we going to sail?'

Grinning, Rebecca thought, not across the Atlantic. 'No, we are going to Glasgow. There is a ship destined for your sister's country.'

With a gentle breeze, and a clear night, Rebecca tried to use the stars to guide her way. She reckoned Glasgow was around 150-miles by boat. She didn't have a clue how long it would take them though. Before she'd left to go for a walk, for some obscure reason, she packed a couple of sandwiches and two bottles of water in to her back pack. At the time, she hadn't a clue why she was doing this.

As so often in the past, she'd just gone with a hunch and was now glad she had. Even so, knowing the ship destined for Canada was leaving in 6-days, she didn't think they had anywhere enough food to last that long, but at least she had something.

With a good wind, they were soon leaving the Mersey Estuary and heading out into the Irish sea. The wind was a little stronger and in a good direction. Sitting chatting to Myleesa, she suddenly recalled a conversation she'd had with the instructor who'd taught her how to sail. He was going on a charity sail and was aiming at 1500 nautical miles in 10 days. Importantly, it was in a craft a similar size to this one. Doing some maths in her head, she reckoned on reflection they could be nearing Glasgow in around 2 to 3 days. That would give them enough time to locate the ship that was bound for Canada. The problem was getting a ticket for this girl.

'Miss, what did you do that stopped that man so easily? It was as if you used the light I see in the sky on stormy nights. It looked like it was coming from your hand.'

Caught off-guard, Rebecca wasn't at all sure how she was going to explain this away.

Almost as if the girl could see Rebecca was unsure what to say, she said, 'my grandmother told me you would help me and my sister.' She then went quiet.

Focussing under a full moon, Rebecca touched the girl's hand. 'I spoke with your sister and know of your grandmother.'

'My Nanna is dead now. They thought she was a witch because she warned people of things that had not happened. I was a little girl when they took my Minerva away. She said you would come from tomorrow and help me. Are you from tomorrow?'

Caught emotionally unprepared, she again touched Myleesa's hand. 'I am here to help you. Your Nanna was right, I am from tomorrow.' She then showed her the taser. 'This is also from tomorrow and it helped me stop that man. It does use the flash you see in the sky on a stormy night. You should sleep now; we have a long journey.'

'How will I get a passage on the ship?'

Rebecca wasn't ready for that question even though she'd thought about this predicament. It certainly wasn't something she'd considered long enough to come up with an answer. Thinking about it now, the only thing she had of value was her gold wedding ring. She twiddled the ring on her finger and decided she had no choice. She then took the ring off and put it on Myleesa's finger. 'This is very valuable and you should be able to trade this for your passage.' She then thought for a moment about what she'd just done and again found herself wondering why she didn't feel any emotional loss, even though she knew she probably should. In the end, she told herself it was because she could replace the ring. Still though, there was that nagging feeling again at the back of her thoughts.

With a steady wind and the sun rising, the sea started to become a little rough. Now hugging the coast line, Rebecca was starting to struggle keeping the boat on an even keel. With the boat pitching around and Myleesa looking rather scared, Rebecca steered very close to the beach. Late in the afternoon and after nearly capsizing, Rebecca followed the coast line into a bay and down a meandering river unsure what she was hoping to find. Once again though, she was following her intuition. As darkness fell, and the tide dropping, she felt she had no alternative other than to moor the boat in a small fishing harbour. Clambering out of the boat, they were greeted by an elderly, rather grumpy looking man. Looking at his appearance nearly made Rebecca chuckle as she thought, *now that is what a sea-dog looks like.*

'She is too rough for ya little boat. Where ya heading?' he said with an odd accent which seemed to be neither English nor Scottish. 'You, a waif of a lass should not be out alone in this sea.'

Realising he was only speaking to Myleesa and reckoning she was invisible to this man, she said to Myleesa, 'ask him where we are.'

'Sir, where are we?'

He narrowed his eyes a little. 'You is in Carlisle. Where is ya heading, Miss?'

'We are going to Glasgow.'

He shook his head. 'Too far for you alone. This sea is here for many days.' He then appeared to think for a moment. 'You said we. Did ya mean you and your little boat?'

Myleesa glanced at Rebecca. 'I did mean me and my boat, Sir.'

With his words resonating, Rebecca reckoned they needed to find another route to Glasgow. 'Ask him if we can buy a horse around here.'

'Sir, can I buy a horse around here.'

Again, he narrowed his eyes. 'Are you running from someone?'

Myleesa nodded. 'A man tried to hurt me. I pushed him away and he fell on his knife.'

Instantly, his appearance and voice softened. 'I lost my niece to a man of this manner. Follow me, I have an old nag in my yard. She can work no longer, but she is a good lady and will help you get to Glasgow.'

She glanced at Rebecca, then turned to the man. 'Thank you, Sir.'

'I just have two questions for you, Miss. Why Glasgow and why do you keep looking to one side as if there is someone with you?'

'There is a ship going to my sister in Newfoundland. It is in a few days. I must get back to my sister.' She then paused, clearly thinking. 'I am still frightened and look to one side to see if anyone is coming.'

With his hand compassionately resting on Myleesa's shoulder, he led her up a cobbled street to a tiny cottage. 'Claris, my trusty ol' gal' is out the back. She will see you well. Have you any food? It is two days ride to Glasgow.'

'No, Sir. I am alright without taking your food also. You have done enough, Sir.'

He shook his head, turned and entered the cottage. Moments later he returned with a cloth bag. There is enough food here. You will pass many a stream and the waters are good.' He then handed her an odd shaped cup. 'Climb up on my ol' gal. For my lost niece, I help you.'

Myleesa got on the horse as if she'd ridden all her life. 'Your niece will know you helped me. Thank you, my friend.' She then waved to the man and slowly steered the horse into a wooded area just to the back of the cottage. As soon as the man was out of sight, she stopped the horse and waited for Rebecca to catch up.

Joining her, and smiling, Rebecca said, 'I thought you were going without me. It appears you like horses.'

'I love horses. I have loved horses all my life. You can trust a horse. We will have no problem getting to Glasgow. I know the route. I travelled this route with my father before he died.' She then held her hand out to help Rebecca climb up.

As she did, a peculiar sensation came over Rebecca. She then watched as Myleesa's hand seemed to be disappearing. She leant forward to grasp her hand and as she made contact, Myleesa vanished. The last thing she saw was her wedding ring on Myleesa's finger glistening in the moon-light.

Before she had time to gather her thoughts, she could see bright lights coming towards her. Realising she was standing in the middle of a road she hurried to the side. Seconds later, a car hurtled past her, hooter blasting, missing her by inches. She was back home with a bang. The question was, where?

This sudden change, what with the car just missing her, sent her nerves jangling. Trying to compose herself, she looked around. She could see she was still close to a harbour, but it didn't look like the little fishing village she was in with Myleesa. Am I still in Carlisle, she wondered, trying to get her bearings? This place, wherever it was, had the feel of a city. She had been to Carlisle river side a few times and there was nothing here even remotely familiar. Remembering a Carlisle riverside restaurant that had so many lights outside, it looked like a Christmas tree, she looked around. There was no sign of it, but she did notice a ramshackle old building that looked oddly familiar.

Crossing the road, she went over for a closer inspection. As she got closer, she could see a sign outside this old building. Moving to see what the sign said, her inner voice had already answered that question. Sure enough, she was standing outside the Ship Inn, just two-hundred and fifty years later. With her emotions all over the place, she looked around trying to work out what the time was. With not a sign of anyone, she reckoned it was the early hours of the morning. Somewhat bemused, having never experienced anything like this before, she didn't know what to think or do. After a few deep breaths, she decided she had to focus on getting home. Her first thought, at this time of night, was a cab. The problem was, she didn't have any money. She then considered phoning Mary, but not having her phone and it being so late, that was a no-no.

Just then, she saw a cab heading towards her, so flagged it down. Infuriatingly, it slowed down and then sped off. Looking down at the state of her clothes, and knowing she was in Liverpool at silly o'clock, she wasn't at all surprised. Before she had time to think, the same cab came back.

The driver, a very elderly Asian gentleman who looked strangely familiar, wound the window down. 'Miss, it is you. I am sorry I didn't stop.'

This man's broad scouse accent made her feel oddly comfortable. She smiled. 'I need to get home but I don't have my money with me. Would it be okay if I paid you when we get there?'

'Miss, you saved our planet. Hop in, I'll have ya home before ya canna blink.'

Completely taken aback, having had no one recognise her for a good few year, she mumbled, 'err, Thank you so much. I still would like to pay you though.'

The man asked many questions about her stopping global warming and even called her Rebecca. It was clear he seemed to know her well. Happily answering his questions, something was telling her she knew this man, but she just couldn't place him.

'Can I ask if we know each other?' she asked as they pulled up outside the old manor house. 'I know you remember me, and I feel I know you, but I can't recall where from.'

The way he smiled, again seemed so familiar. 'Worry ya self not, me lovely. It will come to you.'

'Please let me pay you,' she said. Peering at him in his rear-view mirror triggered her memory. 'I know you; you took me to Liverpool years back. It was right around the time I was actually getting people to take my foresight about global warming seriously.' Then like a bolt of lightning, she realised he hadn't aged at all. She got out of the car and went around to his window.

'Rebecca, no payment. Give my regards to Meredith.' Then he was gone. The car didn't drive off or disappear, it just wasn't there anymore.

Chapter 21 – Back home

Standing by the front door to the main house, she didn't have a clue what just happened. Although it was the middle of the night, she felt oddly awake. Even so, with Duncan home the following day, she decided to head back to the summerhouse and get some sleep.

On the way down, her mind was jumping between what had just happened with the cab-driver and how he could possibly know Meredith. Mixed in with this was a need to know if Myleesa got to Canada, and if her intervention had brought the child abduction gang to a halt. Although she went straight up to bed, she lay there for ages, her thoughts going in circles. Before she knew it, she was once more woken by the sun shining through the open curtains. By the height of the sun, she reckoned it was mid-morning. After a much-needed shower, she headed downstairs. With a few hours before Duncan was due home, she decided to give Mary a call to see if anything had changed.

'I was just about to phone you,' Mary said. 'I am not one for guessing, but you've seen your girl I suspect.'

'I have indeed and what a bizarre sequence of events that was. More importantly, tell me more, obviously something has changed.'

'Well, change it has. I was sitting there reading through some old papers on that gang and I flipped back a page or three and the page I was looking for had vanished. Now, this is where it gets weird, I went back to the page I was just reading and that too was blank. In fact, every page was blank, and we're talking over a hundred pages.'

'You know how I feel now,' Rebecca said and chuckled.

'I do indeed. I must say, I found it rather exciting. So, I went on my laptop, a secure one I might add, and boom, everything had gone. There were no records of any incidents anywhere. I must say, when I picked up my phone, I was half-expecting your number to be missing again. It wasn't by the way.' She then laughed.

Feeling relieved, two of her questions had been answered in one go. She actually felt certain and satisfied Myleesa had gotten to Canada. Most importantly, her intervention had effectively put pay to this gang and their horrid exploits. 'Well, I was awake half the night wondering if my involvement had worked.'

'Your husband is due home today, so maybe we can catch up later in the week for a coffee. I've a couple of ideas I'd like to run past you.'

'You can't leave it there, a couple of ideas indeed. Tell me more.'

'Honestly, Rebecca, just a hunch notion. Nothing to concern yourself with. Enjoy seeing your hubby again. Oh, before I go, your wedding ring turned up. Did you lose it. We apprehended a well-known burglar and retrieved a lot of jewellery. I heard about it and went to congratulate the team and noticed your wedding ring among the retrieved articles. With it being so distinct, what with that peculiar shaped ruby, I knew instantly it was yours.'

Shaking her head with utter disbelief, she mumbled, 'err, umm. Heavens above. I gave that ring to Myleesa to trade it for her passage to Canada. And, and, that was two-hundred and fifty years ago. What is that all about?'

'I'll bring it with me when we meet up and you can tell me all about it.'

As she came off the phone, Rebecca was at a complete loss what to think. If Myleesa had traded it all those years ago, and even if she hadn't and instead decided to keep it, how did it end up in the hands of a burglar now. Over the years, many bizarre things had happened. Of late though, her journeys had gone in so many strange directions, the likes of which she'd never experienced before.

Pouring a coffee and sitting outside on the veranda, her thoughts returned to the cab driver. It was one thing him turning up in the middle of the night and knowing her, but knowing Meredith, having not aged, and then vanishing as if he'd never been there was weird. Mysterious for sure, she reckoned, but considering all that had happened, she realised this was now becoming par for the course. For a number of years, she'd thought there was some higher authority, if that's the right word, overseeing her movements. Somehow placing stepping stones in front of her every move, so as to smooth her way. Even the empathetic fisherman in Carlisle, all par for the course. What she couldn't get her head around was the cab being there and then not. Not vanishing, just it was there one second and the next it wasn't. For sure, there had been many incidents where people had seemingly evaporated, disappeared, vanished, whatever you wanted to call it, right in front of her. She'd known exactly what was happening though, unlike with the cab. With the cab driver knowing Meredith, and now her ring turning up were just two more incidents that were ambiguous at best. She could handle printed articles coming and going, she'd witnessed that many times in Meredith's painting. Even being in Carlisle one second and then without blinking her eye, she was in Liverpool two-hundred plus years later. That was how it worked, after all, she'd been to Mesopotamia and back, a round trip of eight-thousand years and ten-thousand miles. *I mean, really,* she thought.

Then just to compound her tangled emotions, the plaque on the bench suggesting Meredith saw her as a daughter came to mind. The one thing that had bothered her mostly though was how she'd reacted to finding out Duncan had died in a car crash. She was actually more disturbed by not being upset than she was about finding out about Duncan. *Yeah,* she thought, *I knew I could probably fix it, but even so.* Thinking about this made her consider how she'd reacted all those years ago when she discovered her mother had died in the gas explosion. At the time, she didn't have a clue she could fix it. For sure, she been beside herself with stress, but was her stress what it should have been. Would she have been any more or less stressed if it was someone like Mary. A dear friend, but her mother she wasn't.

She must have nodded off, because she awoke abruptly to the sound of Duncan's car pulling up. She apologised for not meeting him at the airport. As always though, Duncan was completely okay with this.

'When you didn't turn up, I knew there would be a good reason, When I saw you asleep as I pulled up it made me smile. I suspect you've been on one of your jaunts.'

'I am so sorry, Duncan. I have so much to tell you. That can wait though. How was your trip home?'

They continued to chat for a while longer, and although Rebecca briefly touched on her trips, she didn't feel it was the right time to talk at length.

With the girls home the following day, she focussed all her thoughts on Duncan and the girls. It helped that Mary cancelled their meet-up, because she urgently needed to go to Interpol in Paris. Being with the girls and Duncan was lovely and she soon forgot all about her detached emotions that had bothered her recently. A couple of weeks had passed and with Duncan in London for a couple of days, she decided to try and test how much of her gene Gabrielle had inherited. For some time, she'd wondered if Gab was somehow mimicking her, or if she was truly at the early stages of being another of her kind. A time-fixer as Mary had called her so delightfully.

'Gabrielle, come on. I want to show you something in Nanna's house. Faith, are you okay for a while?'

Yeah, Muvva. I'm gonna play footy out the back.'

'Mind the windows.'

'Bye, Muvva.'

Seeing Faith doing kick-ups with a small orange ball brought back a memory of an 11-year-old Tommy doing the exact same thing, except with a real orange, much to the dismay of Elizabeth. Rebecca shook her head, *Tommy to a tee*, she thought.

'Mum, what are we going to see?'

'I will show you when we get there.'

For a while, Rebecca had been wondering how Gab would react to the paintings of Meredith and Millicent. When she was on her own a couple of days ago, she'd got to thinking about the first time she saw the paintings. It was the day they moved in and even though it was over 25 years ago, she could recall her reaction as if it were yesterday. For sure, her senses had been overwhelmed by the size of the house and grounds. Her inner emotions though had focussed on the summerhouse. It made her smile when she remembered she had thought it was hiding behind the Christmas trees down by the lake. When she'd opened the front door to the house and spotted the two paintings, her feelings completely changed direction. It was as if her inner thoughts were reading a book. Gazing at the painting of Meredith, her innocent mind started making up stories about what had happened in the house. Looking back now, her imagination was right in every detail.

For sure, Gabrielle had seen the paintings several times in the past. Her focus though had always been on seeing her grandparents. Invariably, no sooner Rebecca had opened the door, Gab was past her and in the kitchen cuddling Nanna. She did once mention the painting to Faith. Her reaction reminded her of Tommy when he'd seen the key to the summerhouse. "Just a key," he'd grumbled without looking up. Faith was a tad more feminine. She'd glanced for a second and said, "nice dress I guess, not for me though."

Arriving by the front door to the main house, she turned to Gabrielle. 'Sweetie, before you dash in to see Nanna, I want to show you a couple of paintings in the hallway.'

'But, Mum, can't we look later? I want to see Nan and Granddad.'

She smiled, thinking this is going to be difficult getting her to focus. Even if she made her look at the painting first, her attention would be close to zero. *Right*, she thought, *let her see Nan first.* 'Okay, Sweetie, you can go see Nanna. I will show you the paintings after.' She then opened the door. Unusually, Gabrielle paused, albeit briefly, glanced at both paintings. She then hurried down the hallway.

Moments later, Elizabeth came into the hallway holding Gab's hand. 'Morning, Bex. Nice to see you both.'

'Hi, Mum. I wanted to show Gabri the painting to see how she reacted, and I thought I would have a cuppa with you.'

'I did wonder when you'd go down this road with Gabrielle. She mentioned Meredith several times while we were in Florida.'

Frowning with curiosity, she asked, 'what did she say exactly?'

'Nothing really. Sorry if that's a bit vague. Occasionally, she would say something like, Meredith would like it here. There was one thing though. We went to a show and one of the girls in the show was dressed in a green dress.' She nodded, 'yep, just like your one. So, madam here said, looks like the dress Meredith's daughter wears.' She shook her head. 'Have you ever shown her that dress?'

'No, Mum. Even if I had, how would Gabrielle know it was worn by Meredith's daughter?'

Pulling at Elizabeth's sleeve, Gabrielle said, 'because I saw her wearing it when we played on the swing in the woods.'

Both Elizabeth and Rebecca looked at each other, mouths open.

'What swing in the woods, Darling.'

'Mum, the one by the stream where the trout live.' She then pointed in an unexpected direction. Instead of towards the wood down near the summerhouse, she appeared to be pointing towards the back of the main house.

For years, Rebecca had intended on following the stream just to see where it led her. As always though, invariably, something had distracted her whenever she was near the stream. Most often, she'd ended up jumping somewhere, and knowing what she now knew about water, this was something she'd thought about recently. 'Gab, do you think you could show Nanna and I where the stream is?'

Shaking her head, Elizabeth said, 'you two go, I will come and look later.'

Rebecca smiled, still surprised her mother, after all these years, was still avoiding situations like this. 'Okay, Mum.' She turned to Gabrielle. So, Missy, do you think you could show me?'

'What about the painting you wanted to show me, Mother?'

With her curiosity bristling, Rebecca answered, 'Yes, Sweetie, we can look on the way out.'

'But, Mum, we need to go out the back. That is the way I always go with Roxanna.'

Completely thrown, Rebecca asked, 'who is Roxanna?'

She chuckled. 'It is Meredith's other daughter, Mother. You know her.'

I know her, she thought, her thoughts going in circles?

'Come on, Mum, I'll show you the secret place.' She then gripped Rebecca's hand and led her towards the kitchen. 'It is out the back in the yard.' She then took Rebecca out into the courtyard, and to the right along the 10-foot-high stone flint wall that ran at the back of the yard. 'It is just up here, Mum, through the hidden door.'

Rebecca was thinking *hidden door, I've never seen any hidden door.* Looking along the wall, she couldn't see anything other than a flint wall. She followed Gabrielle to the end of the wall. At the far end, Gabrielle led her through the old wrought iron gate and to the left. Beyond the gate, the flint wall ran for several feet and was covered top to bottom in dense ivy.

Pulling on Rebecca's hand, she said, 'it is up here.' After a few steps, she bent down a little and through a narrow gap in the Ivy.

At first glance, the gap appeared like a small break in the ivy and no more. Rebecca had walked around here a number of times in the past, normally taking a different route towards the summerhouse. Never had she considered there could be anything beyond the wall. She leaned down behind Gab. Seeing a tiny wooden door in the wall caused a sharp intake of breath. Instantly, her now child-like emotions jumped between youthful curiosity and excitement.

Gabrielle lifted up a round stone, picked up a heart shaped key and opened the door. 'This way, Mum,' she said, going through the door.

Rebecca had to get down on her knees to fit through. As she stood up the other side, the weirdest emotion surrounded her consciousness. In a breath, she felt like she'd been here before, even though she knew she hadn't. *Well, not in this life,* she thought. Just thinking that made her pulse surge, and instantly memories of her first time with Meredith flooded her thoughts. Trying to regain a tiny semblance of rational thinking, she heard Gabrielle speaking.

'Mum, Mum.'

'Sorry, Sweetie, I was away with the fairies.'

'Well, in this garden, you might see a fairy if you're quiet. Roxanna is not here today. We can still go and watch the fish and go on the swing. Come on, Mum,' she said, gripping Rebecca's hand.

As she followed Gab to the far side of the garden, she couldn't work out why she'd never seen this garden from one of the upstairs windows in the main house. Bizarrely, the grass was neatly cut, and around the edge was a myriad of climbing roses and clematis in every colour you could imagine and more. In the centre of the garden was a hexagonal pergola affair. Inexplicably, everything had a pristine appearance, as if it was regularly maintained. *How can this be*, she thought? *More importantly, who is maintaining it?*

On the far side of the walled garden was a delightful Victorian style swing, adorned in white flowers, resembling something you'd expect to see in some period drama on TV. Initially, with the flowers appearing so perfectly manicured, she thought they might be faux. On closer inspection, she could see they were real, again making her wonder who was tending this garden.

'Come and see the fish, Mum.'

Beyond the swing was a stunning crystal-clear pool. On the far side was a small waterfall where tiny fish seemed to be playing in the bubbles. At the back of the pool, where it seamlessly meandered out of sight, there were a number of bigger trout in the deeper water. They seemed, to Rebecca, to be guarding over their young.

'This is where you might see the water fairies, Mum. You have to be very quiet.'

'Have you seen them, Sweetie?'

'Not yet, Mum, but me and Roxanna can tell they are there. We can just sense them watching us.'

Listening to Gabrielle was like listening to herself talking to her own mother when she was this age. If she'd had any doubts about Gab's gene's she was now certain she was of her making. After pushing Gab on the swing for a few minutes, and having a go herself, it started to cloud over a little. 'Come along, Gab, we should be getting back.'

'But, Mum.'

'We can come back soon, Sweetheart,' she said, thinking, I've lived here 25 plus years and had no idea. 'How often do you come here with Roxy?'

'It's Roxanna, Mum, she dislikes being called Roxy. I see her most times I come to see Nanna.'

Narrow eyed, Rebecca was wondering how that could be, knowing her mum wouldn't let Gab out of her sight.

As they went back in to the kitchen, Elizabeth was pouring a coffee.

'Love one, Mum.'

'Crumbs, you two were quick. I put the coffee on as soon as you closed the door. Could you not find the doorway?'

Although she was used to this kind of outcome, her mother's comments still caught her by surprise. 'Err, well, we did find the garden and I thought we had been gone ages. Hey, Mum, you know how these things work. Gone for hours, or even days, back and it's only been a few seconds.' Just saying this, she realised how Gab could have gone to the garden without Elizabeth ever knowing.

Having told her mother all about the delightful garden, she said, 'right, I need to check upstairs. I can't believe we've never seen this garden from one of the windows. Not like it's small, must be sixty-foot square.' She then headed up to the second floor and peered through the window next to her bedroom. She could see where the garden should be, but there was no sign of it anywhere. After checking every view-point, she wasn't sure what to think. She actually did know what to think, her consciousness was just avoiding the realisation that her 10-year-old daughter was jumping back to the eighteen-fifties every time she came to see Nanna.

As she made her way downstairs, Gabrielle was standing looking at the Meredith painting.

'Hello, Sweetie.'

'I was just wondering why Roxanna is not in any of these pictures.'

'Well, there is only this painting of Meredith, so…'

'No, Mum, there are lots upstairs.'

'Really, can you show me.'

'Don't be silly, Mum. I can only see them when I am with Roxanna and her mum.'

Not that she was in any doubt, she knew for sure, Gabrielle was jumping, seemingly at will, between now and Meredith's time. 'How often do you see Roxanna?'

'Every time I am here with Nanna on our own. This is the first time I have been in the garden and Roxanna wasn't there.'

For some reason, the plaque on the bench came to mind. She wasn't sure why but it had triggered an odd thought. 'So, can you tell me what Roxanna looks like.'

'I can show you. There is a picture upstairs in your old bedroom of her and Meredith. Come on, I'll show you.'

As she followed Gabrielle upstairs, she was trying to think of the photos in her bedroom. As far as she could recall, there were only two. A large family photo and one of her and Tommy at one of his football matches. Then a penny dropped with a clang as she recalled the photo she'd found of Meredith and her daughter. At the time and ever since, she'd thought, by a bizarre quirk of this time jumping, it was a photo of her and Meredith. The fact that the girl not only looked identical, was also wearing her blinking cardigan, it had to be her with Meredith. Her mum had suggested it was a weird coincidence, but her mum was always like that in the early days. She was now wondering if perhaps her mother was right and in spite of the obvious coincidences, maybe it was actually Meredith with her daughter.

Following Gab into her old bedroom caused a surge of nostalgia.

'Here, Mum, this is Roxanna,' she said, holding up the photo. 'Roxanna is wearing the jumper she always has on. She says it reminds her of her other life.'

Completely thrown by Gab's comment, she wasn't at all sure what to say. She knew what she wanted to ask, just wasn't sure what words to use. 'What did she mean, her other life?'

'Oh, Mum, she means when she is here in this life. She has two worlds. One with Meredith and one here with us. You know this, Mum.'

Do I, she thought, at a complete loss what to think. There was something deep in the recess of her brain that was asking odd questions. The thing was, she wasn't quite ready to ask herself these questions out loud. Right now, though, she needed to speak with Gabrielle. 'I am not sure I know what you mean. Why do you think I know this, Sweetie?'

'Mum, don't be silly, you know because you do.'

After speaking with Gabrielle for a few more minutes, she realised, what with her innocent youthfulness and perspective, it was unlikely she'd get any conclusive answers. Also recognising Gab saw her time between here and Roxanna as a normal every day event, she decided to head downstairs and leave the questions for now. On the way down, she reckoned she'd just spend much more time with Gabrielle and see if that would shed some light on what was going on.

She had another coffee with her mum, unsure if she should tell her Gabrielle was jumping back and forth pretty much every time she came to visit. In the end, she reckoned her mother would be way too stressed if she knew. Because Gab always came back safely, she decided to say nothing.

'Mum, we need to get back to Faith and sort some supper out.'

On the way back, she quizzed Gab some more without being too pushy. The problem was, Gabrielle's answers were always understandably innocent. Gab simply believed there were two Roxanna's, one in Meredith's time and one in their time and importantly, she saw this as normal. The sticking point for Rebecca was why she'd never seen Roxanna, either in Meredith's time or in the here and now.

The things Gab had said gave Rebecca the impression Roxanna may be a little older. She wasn't sure why she thought this, it just occurred to her that Gab was speaking about her as if she were an older sister. 'How old is Roxanna?

'She will be fifteen on the same day as your birthday, Mum.'

This caught Rebecca a little by surprise. She wasn't sure if it was because Roxanna was fifteen, the age Rebecca was the first time she met Meredith, or simply because she had the same birthday. Once more, questions started knocking at her inner thoughts. 'So, when you see Roxanna, do you see Meredith at the same time?'

'Sometimes, Mum. Sometimes I only see Meredith. She always pushes me really high on the swing. Sometimes, Roxanna is away.'

'Away,' she asked, 'what do you mean, away?'

'She has jobs to do.'

'What do you mean, does she have to work in the fields,' she asked, recalling her first conversation with Meredith? One of the first things Meredith had said to her was they had to do their chores in the field.

'Don't be silly, Mum. There are men who work in the field. No, she has jobs to do with other people in our house. She always tells me she needs to fix the time. I think they need a new clock because she is always saying that.'

Once again, caught completely off guard by Gab's answer, she probed a little more. By the time they arrived by the summerhouse, it was clear she wasn't going to get an answer to her inner questions.

Seeing Faith still playing football changed her focus. While making supper, she kept going over Gab's comments in her head, but decided to leave it for now and focus on her family.

Waking up the following morning, again, she had odd questions rumbling around in her head. What with the plaque, Meredith treating her as a daughter the first time they met, the photo and everything Gab had said, she was wondering if her and Roxanna might be the same person? This was a daft notion, even with her open imagination, but everything was weirdly pointing in that direction. She stood by the shower door, thinking. *Surely, I'd know*, she thought, but also reckoned it would answer these horrid detachment questions she had rumbling around in her thoughts.

By the time she was out of the shower, she'd dismissed that notion out of hand.

Over the next few weeks, she went with Gabrielle to the hidden garden many times. Each time, it had been just her and Gab. Several times, she wondered why she'd never seen either Roxanna or Meredith, especially as Meredith showed herself freely, even from the other dimension. The thing was, she also felt certain if she had only seen Meredith, but not Roxanna, it would again point at her and Roxanna being the same person. On the flip side, she reckoned if she'd seen the two of them together, she'd know for sure her and Roxanna weren't the same person. Never seeing either of them pitched so many questions, questions that for now seemed unfathomable.

As summer faded into autumn and the girls returned to school, Rebecca wondered if there was any more for her. For some time, she'd felt desperate to speak with Meredith. If for no other reason than to answer some of her questions. It had now been four months since she had any notion of jumping anywhere and felt certain, what with her success with Myleesa her journeys were perhaps over. Although she still had so many outlandish questions rumbling around in the back of her thoughts, her focus had been on Gab. With the notion her time-fixing was perhaps over, she now found herself wondering if Gabrielle would step into her shoes and take over.

Sitting on the veranda, she mumbled, 'where is Meredith when I need her?'

'I am here.'

Finally, she thought. 'I have so many questions for you.' She asked about Myleesa first and then Evanora. Discovering, as she'd suspected, her efforts were successful, she asked, 'Your daughter…'

Before she had time to ask her question fully, Meredith held her hand up. 'The time is not right for you to know. In time, you will have your answer. Worry not, be strong, go forward and focus on Faith and Gabrielle.'

In a flash, she was gone again. Rebecca sat there for ages considering Meredith's words. Feeling oddly content, even though she didn't have an answer, for some reason, it no longer seemed to matter. It was a very odd feeling, having had this thought kicking the door down for months and now it didn't matter, as in really didn't matter.

Chapter 22 – A Football Twist

She shook her head and went inside to phone Mary. Every time she'd spoken to her or met up with her, she had forgotten to quiz Mary about her hunch, as she'd referred to it.

'Hello, Mary. I need to ask you about your hunch before we get side-tracked.'

'Oh gosh. I thought you preferred not to speak with me about it, what with your time-fixing being your thing. Retrospectively, I actually considered it rude of me even thinking I could get you to help me in some way. Look, I am in the car, hands free, and just around the corner. Coffee?'

'I'll get the beans going. How long?

'Five minutes.'

'Perfect, see you in a bit.'

By the time she'd ground the beans, Mary was ringing the doorbell. Opening the door, she invited her through to the kitchen.

Placing the coffee down, she asked, 'so, your hunch. Tell me more.'

'Well, having thought about it several times, I think it is a little inappropriate of me.'

Shaking her head, Rebecca smiled. 'Mary, we are a team. I have depended on you many times. Hit me with your hunch.'

'Well, I was going over some old unsolved cases. I got to wondering if you could help solve any of these. It actually occurred to me when I was with the New York Police. I may have mentioned, they use psychics to help solve crimes.'

'Funny you should ask. I have thought that a number of times myself. Meredith has always told me I can focus on any given event and it will happen. The thing is, although if I speak out loud, Meredith answers, or I know I am going somewhere, I kinda feel like I have some control. I've never been able to pick an event and go jump there. Although, I guess that would be unlikely to happen. By that, I mean in the past, I've always known what is ahead of me, like with Myleesa. What event would I pick? I would have to know before hand, not like I could make something up. Just speaking to you now, well, maybe this could work, especially if I had dates and places. All things considered, I'm still not sure though and I kind of feel a little hesitant, but I really don't know why.'

'That's okay, don't worry, it was just an idea.'

Thinking, she said, 'You know, I have never tried to force it. I've had no need really.' She narrowed her eyes a little. 'Maybe we could try something.'

'Well, I have a couple of files in my car. Bedtime reading,' she said and chuckled, 'I'll go fetch them.'

In an odd way, Rebecca felt rather animated by the idea she could help with an unsolved crime. Mary came back and placed down a huge pile of files. 'Bedtime reading indeed. Do you have a bed in your office,' she asked, grinning?

'Well, a lot of these are robberies and such like. There are a couple that relate to missing people though. I thought they were much more appropriate.' Lifting out one of the files, 'she said, 'this one in particular has haunted me. It is the tale of a fifteen-year-old girl who went missing. Sadly, social services had already been alerted to the life circumstances of this girl. Trust me when I say, my team and a crack team from social dug to china and back on this one. There was nothing. Not a jot of evidence anything was going on. The only thing we had to go on was one of her teachers at school alerting us several times to her regularly having bruised arms. We looked at all relatives, male and female, all close associates, neighbours, youth club workers, everyone who knew her or might have had contact with her, however insignificant. There was no evidence of anything untoward.'

'So, what happened?'

Mary looked down, appearing unusually upset. 'I was out walking my dog,' she said, wiping away a tear, 'and found her body.'

'Oh, my goodness,' Rebecca said, leaning over squeezing Mary's hand. 'That must have been so awful for you. No surprise you want my help. If in any way I can help, I will. I will even try and speak with Meredith, anyone who will listen. I will pour some more coffee,' she said taking the cups, really unsure how she felt. Without doubt, she was intrigued, there was however, something not sitting right with her. She returned with the coffee, convinced she had to at least give this a go, especially as it was still hanging over Mary.

'It has plagued me for months. I have gone over everything so many times, I can't tell you. Oddly, having found her pour soul, I feel responsible.'

'Well, I don't need to tell you, you shouldn't, but I understand. How old was this girl?'

Mary opened the file and as she did a photo fell out. 'Crumbs, she was a pretty little thing.' As the last word left her lips, she noticed the name. 'Roxanna, is that her name,' she asked, unable to believe what she was looking at.

'Yes, Roxanna Courtney, she was fifteen, bless her. Good at school, good upbringing, lots of friends. It is a sad, sad tale.'

Nodding she said, 'you did tell me her age.' She tried to get her focus away from the name, telling herself it was just a coincidence. Even so, part of her was wondering if she'd been given a message. 'Oh my. I know in your position you are supposed to remain unemotionally invested; it must be impossible with a case like this. Especially with you finding her body.'

Mary nodded and forced a half-smile.

Rebecca wasn't sure if she should mention Gabrielle's friend. In the end, she convinced herself it was an irrelevant coincidence. They continued to talk about that case and everything leading up to this girl's sad demise.

'So, where did this happen. Well, I know where you live, but did it happen there, and if so, did the girl live nearby?'

'No, she lived in Keswick, the posh part looking over Derwentwater. Her family and friends were all, shall we say, from the upper echelons of society. We don't know if she was murdered where we found her, or if her body was taken there.'

On a hunch, Rebecca asked, 'Can you take me to the area you found the girl and near to where she'd lived. Having never done anything like this before, I really don't know what I am hoping to find. It is just my intuition again.'

'Well, as I am working, and this is work, also if you have time, we could go now if you are up for it. At least then, I will feel like I am doing something.'

They finished their coffee and headed off in Mary's car. 'Where would you like to go first?'

'Where you found her.' On the way, Rebecca asked if they'd checked Roxanna's social media, even though she knew they would have.

'She didn't have Facebook, Twitter, Instagram or anything like that. We looked at her personal and school laptop, mobile, and tablet. There was absolutely nothing. We even did a search on all the dating sites, nothing. You know, after weeks, we reckoned it was as if this girl didn't exist, certainly from an electronic perspective.' She then seemed to think for a moment. 'I know it sounds an odd thing to say, but she must have used an identity to sign in to her online school work if nothing else. It was as if her identity had been erased. We questioned her friends and parents about her online activity and although they said she wasn't one for social media, she was always working on something on her laptop. We have had experts look to see if her identity had been removed somehow. They all agreed that if someone had done that, they would need to be a computer expert. As one of the guys said, the person with that skill would be working for Microsoft or Interpol.'

'Hmm, that tells me it is possible to remove someone's identity then.'

Nodding, Mary said, 'I hadn't considered it like that. Could be an avenue we haven't explored yet.'

'What do you mean?'

'Well, maybe we look at anyone who left the area soon after to take up a job working for one of the big internet players. Hmm.'

There was a question nagging at the back of Rebecca's thoughts. The thing was, it was a question she didn't want to ask, even though she needed to know. 'I don't want to know, but was the girl sexually abused?'

As if Mary could sense Rebecca's feeling on this, she just nodded, and looked down.

They soon arrived in the area where Mary had found the body. Rebecca stood there for a few moments, but directly she'd gotten out of the car, she knew there was nothing here for her. She really didn't know what she expected to see or feel, but was certain there would be some kind of something stirring her intuition. She drew a similar blank in and around the girl's home. After a light lunch in town, Mary drove Rebecca back home.

'Leave it with me. Something will come up, if it is meant to.'

'Thank you, Rebecca. I will go check the internet avenue we talked about earlier.'

No sooner she was indoors, Duncan came in with the girls. That evening after supper, she told Duncan all about her time with Mary. She also mentioned that Mary had asked if she could help in some way with old cases.

'Could you?' he asked.'

'I would love to, but I am not sure it works like that.'

'Well, if anyone can, you can, I suspect.'

As tempted as Rebecca was to talk to Duncan about her detachment issues and how she'd speculated about Meredith's daughter, she just didn't feel it was right. Something in the back of her thoughts kept telling her to say nothing every time she considered it, and as always, she was content to follow her inner voice.

Over the next few weeks, she spent a lot of time with the girls. Occasionally, she went with Gabrielle to the garden. Oddly though, she'd felt Gab wanted to go on her own and thinking about it, she knew she wanted to see her friend. Because it had only ever been her and Gab in the garden, Rebecca openly encouraged Gabrielle to go and see Grandma on her own. Faith had taken a knock in one of her games and was out of football for a couple of months. She was just like Tommy when he was out injured, a bear with a sore head. As hard as Rebecca tried, she couldn't fill the gap. After chatting to Tommy about it, he popped over to take Faith out for a football related day. Tommy made this a regular event and it had helped enormously, even more so, when she was ready to start light training again.

One day, as she was nearing fitness, Tommy came in with Faith. 'Sis, your daughter is better than most of the men she plays with. So, I was speaking to a friend of mine, someone I used to play with. Anyway, he is the manager of the Vancouver Whitecaps Ladies Team.'

Holding her palm up, Rebecca said, 'And?'

'Well, he would love her to go train with them. If she takes up the offer, I know they will make sure she gets all her exams and schooling. The thing is, she could earn ten times what she could earn here. Importantly, what an opportunity to live in an amazing city and play in front of sixty-thousand fans every week.'

With her emotions saying one thing and her common sense contradicting her emotions, Rebecca was at a complete loss what to say or think. She glanced at Faith, who had that look she gets when she wants new boots or something. Tommy had his 'twit' face on, the one she'd learnt to love. 'Well, Faith, we will need to speak with your father. I guess if he is happy, I don't see why not.' She considered Faith being ten-thousand miles away. Even so, she was adamant she wouldn't show any personal emotions because that wouldn't be fair. 'What a great chance for you, Faith.'

'Mum, I already asked Dad on the phone when TommyHawk told me all about this chance.'

'Oh, TommyHawk is it now?'

Grinning, Tommy said, 'you remember that name. It was during my last couple of years when I played for Stevenage FC. The fans gave me that nick-name. Still the best fans I've played in front of. Three thousand made more noise than thirty-thousand elsewhere. I loved it there.'

Just then Duncan walked in. 'I guess you know about Faith's possible move to Canada?'

'Yes indeed. What a fabulous opportunity.' He then patted Faith on the head, just the way mum used to pat Tommy on the head when he was a teenager. Unlike Tommy, who used to grumble, Faith squeezed her dad's hand nicely.

'So, what about Manchester City?' Rebecca asked.

Tommy rolled his eyes. 'Well, that was a week-to-week contract. More fool them I say, because they've missed out trying to save three quid.'

The four of them sat around chatting for a couple of hours. In the end, it was all settled. After Tommy had come off the phone to his friend in Vancouver, it was agreed Faith would fly out after Christmas, just after her 17th birthday.

Chapter 23 – Time Will Tell the Truth

The next few weeks passed in the blink of an eye as Rebecca focussed on helping Faith with her A-Level mocks. Before she knew it, it was mid-November. With the first signs of winter beautifully changing the appearance outdoors, she decided to go for a walk. She especially loved it when the sky was crystal blue and the grass white with frost. For her, the air just felt invigoratingly fresh. Rebecca had never lost sight of her youthful imagination and days like this stimulated her mood further. One of her favourite places on days like this was the spry wood, the place she first found the key. As she arrived by the fallen oak, her pad and pencil in hand, she sat down on the oak. With the grass crunchy under foot, the early morning sun glistening through the leaf-less willows, her mind drifted back to the day she first found the key. Even though it was 25 plus years ago, she could remember every detail.

Having decided to draw everyone a fairy Christmas card this year, she started doodling. Trying to focus her imagination, she felt someone's presence nearby. Although this kind of thing had happened to her so many times before, this feeling startled her today. In the past, she could always sense who it was. Oddly, today, it felt different.

She looked around, but there didn't seem to be anyone there. She turned back, reckoning she'd misread her feelings. No sooner she had, it was there again. There was someone there. She stood up and looked around, and still nothing. Then as she went to sit back down, she heard an unrecognisable woman's voice say, "speak to her."

Again startled, but not spooked, she said, 'who is there?'

With a soft, almost passive, clearly youthful female voice, someone said, 'my name is Roxanna. Can you help me?'

Rebecca's senses immediately went up ten-fold. She turned slowly, and seeing a slight, radiantly beautiful young girl standing behind her, she knew it was the young girl who had been murdered. Although this should have sent her emotions spiralling, she oddly felt calm. 'If I can help you, I will, Roxanna.'

'Thank you, Rebecca. The people I am with said you would help me.'

This caught Rebecca a little off guard, and with her thoughts now a little jumpy, she asked, 'who are you with?'

'I am with Bernice, Meredith, Matilda, Belisant and Ethernal. They have told me I am here with them to stay. I am here to help others like me.'

She understood from the girl's comments, she was probably in the other dimension to stay, and therefore wouldn't be able to save this girls life. This realisation made her wonder how she could help. No sooner she'd thought that, Mary came to mind. 'How did you end up in the place you are now? Did someone do something to you?'

'It was my school teacher, the one who told the police about the bruises on my arms. He made my arms bruised.' She then turned back as if she was looking at someone, and Rebecca guessed she was seeing the people in the other dimension. 'He has my underwear in his drawer at school. Bernice, who is from tomorrow, told me the police will have enough to convict him with…' she again turned as if she was speaking with someone, '…DNA.'

Before Rebecca could respond, the girl was gone and once more the spry wood fell silent. She sat there briefly digesting the last few moments. She then packed away her pad and pencils, and hurried back to the summerhouse to phone Mary.

Out of breath, and hurrying her words, she said, 'Mary, Mary, it was her school teacher. I have just been with

Roxanna. He has her underwear in his drawer at school and they carry enough DNA to convict him.'

'Officers on the way to the school now,' she said, her voice focussed. 'I will send a car to pick you up. I want you in the Police Station when we bring him in.'

She came off the phone feeling excited, exhilarated, but also there was a strong feeling of sadness for Roxanna's miserable passing. Considering her emotions, she sat twiddling her fingers waiting.

After around thirty minutes, the doorbell rang. Expecting it to be someone to pick her up, she was more than a little shocked to see Mary at the front door.

'I thought I would take you to the station myself. Come on.'

On the way, Mary said, 'as soon as the officers went into the school and opened his drawer, he admitted everything. I just thought it was only right you were there to see him charged.'

Rebecca wasn't quite sure how she felt about this, but was nonetheless delighted she'd been able to perhaps save another girl from this man's evil ways. She then thought about how she'd changed history, ridding it of Jack the Ripper and the evil gang of child abductors. Although she'd stopped them and halted this cold-hearted evil man today, realising the world was still full of evil people, hit home hard. 'I can't stop them all,' she said out-loud. 'Sorry, was thinking, words came out on their own.'

'I was thinking the same thing. As fantastic as it is, you solving this, plus the other things you've done, the world is littered with these evil people.'

'I know. Oddly, I don't know how I feel. Yeah, I am so pleased this man has been arrested and what with the other things I've done, but at the same time, I feel sadly frustrated. I just don't know what I am feeling right now. I think one thing that has thrown me is him being a school teacher. Someone we are expected to trust. It is a scary place if...' She then considered her feelings. 'What do we have to do, wrap our children up in a suit of armour? Do we tell them to trust no one, including those we are meant to trust?'

'It is a very unpleasant state of affairs. I will say though, a school teacher being of this making is a rare, rare thing. You know, on the way here I was thinking what next for us two. But I also thought we could be doing this forever. No sooner we rid the world of one, there is another right behind.'

'Yeah, kind of how I feel. It is like an endless fire we can never put out.' Rebecca was elated at stopping this man, but also frustrated knowing the two of them alone would only ever make a tiny impact on these horrifying scenarios.

When they arrived at the Police station, Rebecca didn't feel at all comfortable. As much as she was pleased her efforts had helped solve this horrid crime, she didn't want to see the man. Instead, she asked if she could listen in without seeing him. Even then as soon as she heard him speak, she wasn't relaxed.

'I am not sure I feel right being here. I can't tell you why, I just don't.'

Mary seemed to understand completely and took Rebecca back home. On the way, they chatted about Rebecca's brief interlude with Roxanna.

'I think, although I don't know, people who go to the other dimension are only those who have a strong soul, and perhaps a long way down the spiritual pathway. My understanding is it is a place for those who can change events positively. I am not sure I really understand it, but it seems to me it is a place I am destined for one day.' She thought for a moment about her own words. 'you call me a time-fixer and I like that. Although I have always believed there is only one of my kind for every generation, I now think there may be many.' She then told Mary about Gabrielle and how she was seemingly jumping back and forth between now and Meredith's world. 'I believe in time she will take over from me.'

'How do you feel about that?'

'I am actually excited for her. She seems to take to it like a fish to water. She sees it as a normal everyday occurrence. Whereas with me, as much as I dived in head first, I still always question what is going on, even to this day. I wouldn't say I get spooked, but it jangles my nerves without fail. Gabrielle, well, she just sees it as normal, as I said.'

They briefly talked about Rebecca possibly helping with another case, but what with Christmas around the corner and Faith's possible move to Canada soon after, Rebecca said she wanted to focus all her attention on the family. She suggested she didn't want anything that was going to distract her in any way.

'I get that completely,' Mary said as she pulled up outside the summerhouse.

'I will call you soon, Mary. Let me know how things go with the Roxanna case.'

'Will do and thank you once more. You've lifted a heavy weight from my shoulders.'

As Rebecca concentrated completely on her family, the days drifted into weeks and before she knew it the whole family were preparing for Christmas. Much to her delight, on Christmas eve, Amanda and Ruth, her mother's best friends, Roxy and Sam, the two closest to Rebecca, along with Tommy and Kaitlin were all coming over. She'd always loved these big Christmas events and delighted in helping her mother prepare everything.

It was two days before everyone was due to arrive. Duncan had taken the girls into town to do some Christmas shopping. Faith in particular was insistent she went with Duncan. Ever since she was around 10-years-old, she'd managed to get

Rebecca the best presents ever and importantly, always a delightful surprise.

With the afternoon to herself, she thought about heading into town to catch up with Mary. Something though was once more surfacing in her inner thoughts. It had been a couple of months since she'd felt the need to follow one of these gut feelings and wasn't about to ignore it now. Heading along the lake side, she was being drawn towards the woods. There was nothing obvious pulling her this way, but as always, she followed her intuition however insignificant it may have felt. She'd learnt over the years, that even the tiniest notion led to something big. She wandered around for ages and without realising it, ended up back in the spry wood.

It was unusually damp today and rather squidgy under foot. Reckoning there wasn't much here for her, she made her mind up to follow the stream and see if it led to the hidden garden. Just as she did, she heard a voice. It was the softly spoken Roxanna again. She turned around and could see this girl once more seemingly talking to someone Rebecca couldn't see. This intrigued her no end, but managed to make her feel a tad uneasy. She was sure she knew Roxanna was talking to those in this other world, but not being able to see them created a rather odd feeling. 'Who are you talking to, Roxanna?'

'Just my new friends. There is Michelle, Rosanna, Susan, and Rosemary, lots of us.'

A little taken aback, Rebecca asked, 'Are they all with you now?'

'Yes, we all left your world the same way. We need you to help us. We have a new friend from tomorrow and she needs you to help her stay with her mother. It is not her time yet. Can you help?'

Stunned by this girl's words and feeling unusually anxious, she uttered, 'yes, if I can I will.' Although she understood the notion of what Roxanna was saying, she needed to hear it exactly. 'Your friend from tomorrow. Is she still in my world?'

'She is, although she has come to visit us. We have seen the day when she joins us and cannot get back. This is because of her bad uncle. You must help our friend.'

'Tell me all you can, and I will try my best to stop whatever is about to happen.' This was a whole new concept for Rebecca and the notion of preventing something that hadn't yet happened left her reeling a little. Although she felt an instant need to help this poor girl, she didn't have a clue how this was going to pan out. *Well, let's see where this goes*, she thought.

'Meredith said you would help. The girl who is with us is Rochelle, and she is thirteen-years-old. She knows things that have happened in the past, but doesn't know why she knows. She is very upset and confused but she was able to tell us her uncle has done bad things to other girls before. He killed two girls and one was her friend. He hid the body of one girl in his garden, and another, her friend, in the woods near where he lives.'

Feeling both dismayed and angered, she tried to focus, and asked, 'Oh my goodness. Do you know any more details, like his name and where he lives?' She still felt unsure how this was going to work out, but could now see a possible route.

'We do know more and it is a horrid outcome, and that is why we need your help. She has also seen the future, but again does not know how. Her uncle will visit her in three days. He will do bad things to her and then take her life. It is not her time and you must help stop this.' She then went on to tell Rebecca the uncle's name, address, and exactly where he had buried the girls.

Before Rebecca had a chance to respond, she could feel she was on her own again. Perplexed and angry, but focussed, she started to write down all the details. As she did, she felt her phone vibrating in her pocket. She was a little surprised, because she never took her phone on any of her walks.

Looking at the screen and seeing it was Mary, she instantly knew everything was falling into place once more. 'Hello, Mary. Get a pen and paper. We can chat in a minute.' She then told Mary the girls name, where she lived, the uncles name and where he lived. She took a deep breath, relieved she was able to recall everything. She then explained all the horrid details. 'So, they told me the uncle will visit Rochelle in three days. He will then abuse and murder her. Importantly, I was also told the uncle had killed two other girls, one is buried in his garden and the other in the wood near where he lives. I know that wood well as my friend's house is nearby and I know the exact place where he has hidden the body. I don't understand how the girl would know what has happened in the past or will happen in the future unless she is of my making in some way.' Unwittingly, she'd just answered her own question, realising the girl was perhaps another of her making and this was the first time she'd had the need to use her ability. Aware she'd left Mary hanging, she said, 'Sorry I drifted there.'

'It is okay, Rebecca. This is a lot for you to take on board, so no wonder you have the need to think. That is one of the things I admire about you, you think before you speak.'

'Thank you, Mary. So, back to this issue. I suspect you have more than enough to go on and can stop the uncle getting anywhere near her. I must say, when Roxanna first started telling me this story, having never had to intervene with something that has not yet happened, I was a little unsure.'

'Oh my, we need to act quickly. I am guessing you've been somewhere to find all this out.'

'No, actually. Well, kind of. I'm in the woods now and Roxanna just came to see me. Evidently, and this bit is horrible, she was with lots of girls who have all fallen foul in the same way and by that I believe they were all abused and subsequently murdered by evil men. Anyways, Rochelle visited them from our time to tell them about her uncle. Presumably she is able to jump between here and there. As I said just now, perhaps another of my making. I am still trying to get my head around how this all works, but thank heavens it does.'

With her voice breaking a little, Mary said, 'we have three days to come up with a plan. I will pop over, should be there in around thirty.'

'See you then.'

By the time Rebecca had arrived back at the summerhouse, Mary was pulling up outside. She then followed Rebecca inside and placed her laptop down and opened up a detailed map of the area Rebecca had mentioned. Rebecca then pointed to the exact area on the map.

'Look, it will be better if I come with you and show you. I know this area well. I used to go to those woods with my friend and her dog.'

'I need to make a couple of calls.' Mary then got up and walked out onto the veranda. On the way out, she signalled for a coffee and smiled. Although Rebecca could see Mary's smile was fractious.

No sooner she had made the coffee, Mary came back in.

'Right, I have arranged for a squad to meet us by the woods. As much as I want to send someone to arrest the uncle, as it stands, we have no evidence.'

'Why can't we go to his house first and uncover the body in his garden? Both girls are dead, so surely that would be a better way around.'

Shaking her head, she said, 'I think I got so preoccupied with the map of the woods, I wasn't thinking.' Again, she shook her head and picked up her phone. Moments later, she came off the phone and said, 'Right all sorted, going to the house first. Do you still want to come with me?'

'Totally. I want to see this evil man and how he reacts. I nearly swore then.'

In the car on the way, Rebecca wondered how Mary described this scenario to her fellow officers.

'Mary, how did you explain that you knew about these bodies?'

'Well, I hope you are okay with this. When you first came to me, I had to speak to a couple of senior officers. As we know, all records of those events vanished. So, I had to speak to the same two senior officers again. Initially, my words were met with understandable scepticism. However, after the last situation, they are both totally on board. I have never mentioned your name, but most of the senior officers now know I am working with someone who can, let's say, see beyond the obvious.' She then seemed to think for a moment. 'One of the older officers asked me if it was you, what with him knowing your history. I didn't answer, but I could tell he knew.'

'I am absolutely fine with them knowing. How could they not. I mean, you phone them up and say, "on a hunch guys, go dig up this man's garden.'

It took them around an hour to get there, what with it being the other side of Liverpool. As they pulled up, Rebecca was a little surprised to see they were there on their own. 'So, where are the other officers?'

'I told them to wait until we were here before they entered the house. Time is on our side, so… Well, I just thought it was only right you get to see this man arrested, especially after what you said.' She then picked up her radio and made a call. Seconds later, several blue lights screeched to a halt outside. Mary got out of the car, and beckoned Rebecca out. They then stood behind the car on the other side of the road as a team approached the house.

Three armed police officers knocked on the door, but there was no response. Just as two officers with some kind a ram approached the door, the man opened the door brandishing a shotgun.

Rebecca stood opened mouth as all hell let loose. There was lots of shouting, followed by a single shot and then around ten shots. She turned to Mary, her emotions all over the place. From what she could see, the man had shot at one of the police officers and then was instantly shot dead himself.

'Wait here.' Mary then hurried across the road, and bent down to the female officer laying on the ground. She then stood up and spoke with another officer.

Moments later, she watched opened mouthed as the female officer stood up. This caught Rebecca completely off-guard. With her curiosity taking over, she headed across the road. Mary turned and met her half way.

'In situations like this where we know the criminal is potentially dangerous, we implement a sensible level of precaution. As such, we had several armed officers who were suitably protected. Fortunately, being at such close range, the female officers protective body armour took the full impact. She'll have a few heavy bruises, and will undoubtedly need time to come to terms with what just happened. Importantly, she is alive. We have a team of specialist who will deal with the outfall.'

Shaking, oddly feeling like she was in the middle of a TV news flash, Rebecca wasn't sure what to say. 'Err.' She was feeling really weird. For sure, she was horrified having just seen the man shot, strangely though, she wasn't feeling the way she thought she should. For her, it once again felt like a detachment issue.

'Don't speak yet, give yourself time to digest what just happened. Come on, we should go and have a coffee back at my office. We can leave the team here to sort everything out.

The media will be here imminently and I do not want to subject you to that ordeal with their absurd inane questions. Unbelievably we have a specialist team to deal with the media. I remember my first interview. I came away feeling as if I was being interrogated and they wanted to corner me, just for a story.'

Rebecca nodded. 'What is it they say, "why let the truth get in the way of a good story," or something like that. Trust me, I understand. The government had to put a ban on the press camping outside my house when I first went down the save the planet road.'

On the way to the station, they continued to chat about the media and in the end concluded for every bad reporter, there were ten good ones.

Mary said, 'that is the problem with society, it listens to the noisy minority and portray that voice, particularly when it's negative, as the opinion of everyone. It infuriates me.'

By the time they'd got to the station and had a coffee, Mary's phone rang. After she came off the phone, she said, 'well, they found the girl's body in the garden, sadly it appears she was around twelve-years-old.' She then seemed to go deep into thought. 'You know, that excuse for a human got off lightly being shot. I would have preferred him to rot in jail.'

Rebecca nodded. 'I get that totally.' She then paused to consider her feelings. 'Hey, we can work our way through these men, as long as Roxanna keeps coming to see me.'

'How do you feel about all this. Importantly, how do you feel about what just happened. I can't imagine it was very nice witnessing someone being shot to death like that.

'Do you know, I feel absolutely fine. I know I shouldn't but I do. Maybe it was because he was such a bad man.' Inside Rebecca was questioning why she again felt so detached from this reality.

'Well, although sadly we know two girls died, at least their parents will have closure. Horrid, but I believe it must be awful not knowing what happened. Left in a horrendous state of limbo. Importantly, your actions saved Rochelle. Perhaps that is why you feel the way you do.'

Mary's words were right, but even so, she still questioned why she felt so disconnected. Trying to focus on what just happened, she started wondering how long it would take her and Mary to make an impact on this seemingly endless list of bad people. 'You know that pile of unsolved cases you showed me the other day. How many of these child abuse incidents are there each year?'

'Well, far too many for my liking. The team I set up because of that gang didn't... Well, because you intervened and that gang disappeared, I had to set the team up again. As with all the records of that gang's movements, everything I had done around that gang disappeared. Hey, minor negative side.' She then seemed to think for a moment. 'There is no answer to your question. There are the incidents we know about but also, as with this case, there are ones we don't know of. We have a horribly long list of missing girls and boys. Unbelievably, and I had to double and triple check this, one-hundred thousand children go missing in the UK every year. The numbers are similar all over the world. Fortunately, over ninety percent return home. That still leaves around ten thousand a year unresolved. And that is just in the UK.'

Both horrified and angry, Rebecca again wondered how the two of them could make any serious inroads. Then an idea came to her. 'So, you know the psychic you spoke to in New York. I must say, I don't like the word psychic. Let's call them visionaries. Anyways, could we not draw up a list and get a number of us together to see if collectively we could have a bigger impact.' Again, she thought for a moment. 'For years, I believed I was the only one who had my ability, certainly in this generation. Because of Gabrielle, Rochelle, the girl we just saved and having Roxanna speaking from the other dimension,

I suspect there may be many. Perhaps, and this is just an idea, they all have different skills and all have different roles. Keeping history on track in their own special way.'

'Crumbs, that is, well, I'm not sure what to say. You might have opened a door there. Although we don't openly use psychics, sorry visionaries, we do have a list of trusted go to people. Heaven only knows what would happen if the British press found out, you can only imagine. Thinking about it though, they should, because of you saving the planet, have an open mind. Even so. Let me speak to a few trusted senior officers in other areas and see if we can set up a meeting of you visionaries.'

Chapter 24 – Visionaries, or not

What with seeing all her favourite people during the Christmas celebrations, Rebecca only thought about Rochelle in passing. It was now mid-January and the girls were back at school. No sooner she was on her own, Roxanna and Rochelle came to mind. Moments later her phone rang and it was Mary. The way this was all tying together over the last couple of months, she got the feeling this was a road to a new destiny. 'Hello, Mary. So weird, I was just thinking about Rochelle and co. Almost like this is meant to be.'

'Without doubt, especially because I was phoning to ask if you could meet up with some others of your making. I have made tentative arrangements for a meeting in Manchester on the twenty-fourth of January. How does that fit with you?'

Rebecca thought for a moment. 'That's next Wednesday. I can do that. Are you going to be there?'

'Wouldn't miss this one. Even if we only get two others on board, think of the in-roads we could make.'

The next week passed very quickly for Rebecca. She went in to the meeting full of enthusiasm. Within seconds though, there was a strong feeling of scepticism rumbling around in her head

Sitting down with nine women and one man, she glanced around the room. Oddly unable to make eye contact with any of the others, her suspicious feelings took a stronger hold. As everyone introduced themselves, she sat quietly, listening to their individual beliefs and standpoints. The more she listened, the more she felt increasingly uncomfortable. Within an hour, and still without saying much, she'd dismissed most of them as phoney. In an odd way, these people reminded her of the girl she'd met years before in Russia. She had no doubts they believed in what they were saying, but nothing so far had convinced her they were of her making. She didn't know what she was expecting to hear, but nothing so far had focussed her.

Almost as if Mary picked up on her mood, she suggested a coffee break. When they were outside, Mary said, 'you're not buying this are you.'

Rebecca shook her head. 'I had such high hopes, but… None of them have said anything that makes me think… Well, let's just say, my intuition would know one way or the other. I don't know why I know this, but I do.'

'I'll wrap it up and tell them I'll get back to them.'

Rebecca wasn't sure how she felt about this, being so dismissive and all, but didn't want to waste time. 'I would know if any of them could see beyond the obvious. I actually think one or two of them came across as arrogant.'

'I noticed that too and saw your reaction. There is a young girl in London who didn't want to come along to this meeting. Her reaction intrigued me. When I spoke to her about coming, she said she didn't want to be involved in something like this.'

Mary's words instantly caused Rebecca's gut to rumble. She wasn't sure if it was what Mary said, or the girl's response. 'That is intriguing.'

'That's why I mentioned it. Initially, I thought her response was a little negative. Now though, having sat through that meeting, I see her response differently. Shall I see if she is prepared to meet up with just us two?

Nodding, feeling unusually animated, Rebecca said, 'Yes, I feel I need to at least see this girl. You said young, what age is she?'

'She is seventeen.'

'How did she end up on your radar, if that's the right word?'

'Well, here is the thing. She went into a London suburb police station a couple of years ago and told of a crime that was going to happen. Sadly, the officer listened and then dismissed her nicely. Now, four weeks ago, the girl went into the same station with another tale. Because I'd already sent out a nationwide communication stating I wanted to hear from any officer who knew of events such as these, this time the officer made notes. So, the senior officer contacted me to say they'd investigated her previous claims and they'd proved to be completely accurate, albeit too late to do anything.'

Super intrigued, Rebecca said, 'well, it seems we potentially have the real deal here.'

'Absolutely. So, get this, the information she has given us leads to an incident in six days.'

'What did the first incident involve? Also, what is going to happen in six days and can we do anything with her information?'

'When she was fifteen, she told them about a boy being snatched in Norway and then taken to Scotland. You can see how the local officer thought it sounded far-fetched. So, it turns out she gave exact details. The Metropolitan Police have since involved the Scottish Police. They went to the address and found two bodies of young boys. The thing is, even if we had listened at the time, neither boys could have been saved. At least we've stopped this excuse for a man from any further evil deeds. So, the latest one involves a young teenager, but I don't know if it's a boy or girl at this stage.' She then explained what details she had and also said a crack team were now investigating the girl's information.

'I am assuming you have a London team on this.'

'We do. As the chief inspector said to me, the police world has changed forever. They are actively trying to recruit,' she shook her head, 'visionaries.'

Actively recruiting hit a nerve with Rebecca. Suddenly, she could see how she could make a huge impact. 'Now, this is where you and I can make a serious dent and make inroads towards stopping these obscene wrongdoings. We could be part of the team that interviews prospective candidates.'

Beaming with enthusiasm, Mary nodded. 'Perfect. I am not sure how I can help, but having watched you go through that group earlier, well…'

'You know me, and you read me, so your help will be just as important. Besides, I wouldn't want to do this alone. Remember, we are a team. There's no I in team.'

'Right, let me give this girl a call, see if she is up for meeting us two.' Moments later, she came off the phone. 'The girl, Melissa, said she would meet up with you alone first off.'

'Excellent, so, when am I going to London?'

'Oh, I want to come along, even if I don't get to meet the girl. I feel the need to be there with you. Besides, I want to introduce you to the chief superintendent of the Met. He is on board. Give me a few minutes and I'll arrange our journey down. I think going by train might be prudent, especially now we finally have the fast rail link running.'

Moments later, after checking dates with Rebecca while on the phone, Mary said, 'all sorted. We are on the train tomorrow morning and will be in London for an early lunch.'

'I am actually quite excited about meeting this girl, although, I've been down this road before.' She then told Mary all about her time in Moscow and meeting up with a girl of a similar age who claimed to have an ability to not only see, but travel into the past. 'Sadly, she was a fake. The difference is, this girl isn't waving her hands about. If you know what I mean.'

Soon after, Rebecca headed home. Once they'd finished supper and the girls were tucked up in bed, she told Duncan about today's events and what she was doing the following day.

'Well, that will be interesting. I was under the impression you thought you were the only one of your kind.'

'I was, although I now know for sure there are more like me.' She then told him all about Rochelle and how Roxanna visited her from that other place.

They spent the rest of the evening discussing Rebecca's potential role in all of this. When Duncan asked how she felt about the situation, although she assured him enthusiastically, nonetheless, something had been nagging her for a couple of days. More than once, she'd wondered how many girls there might be with this ability to see these crimes before they occur. She also considered her involvement and if it grew too big if she'd be able to take a back seat. Overall, as much as she loved the direction this might go, there was something niggling at her inner thoughts. She didn't know if it was good or bad, or what, it was just there. As she lay in bed that evening, she focussed on tomorrow. One thing she did know for sure was the whole notion could, as it had done previously, tumble down and fall flat. *We'll see*, she thought.

The following day, Mary sent a car to pick her up. As she got on the new super-fast train, she turned to Mary and said, 'Wow. In a word, this is so luxurious. To think, they once thought we'd suffocate traveling over twenty-five miles an hour and we are what, doing a million miles an hour?' She then giggled. 'You know what I mean.'

No sooner they sat down and had a coffee, it seemed they were arriving at Euston Station. Rebecca turned to Mary and said, 'Euston, we have landed.'

The two laughed so much, it made others on the carriage turn and look, including one or two who sneered.

'If only they knew who we were,' Mary said, mustering a serious face, then grinning. This again made them both laugh out loud.

Mary had agreed to meet up with Melissa, along with her mother, in the police station near to the girl's home. With a fair amount of traffic, it took them around an hour to get there.

Although they were early, Melissa was already waiting.

'Hello, Melissa and Mrs. Dantry. I am Mary and this is Rebecca.'

Mrs. Dantry said, 'I know we said Melissa and Rebecca could speak on their own. I have told Melissa I want to be there and I also want a senior police officer there too. I don't want any false information forced from her,' she said and pointed to Melissa in a somewhat indifferent way.

Mary explained her position within the police and it was agreed all four would speak. Although Rebecca was happy with this, there was an undertone from the mother that she couldn't put her finger on.

Sitting down and making eye contact with Melissa, Rebecca wasn't sure what she felt. The girl seemed a little sheepish and she wasn't sure if it was because she wasn't the real deal or because the girl was holding back, aware her mother was there watching. Oddly, it reminded her of the conversation she had with her own mother in the early days. Although they had a brilliant relationship, whenever the subject of time jumping came up, her mother always steered the conversation in a different direction. Over time, Rebecca realised it was because the whole concept frightened her mum. Still, though, this girl's relationship with her mother was different, almost starchy. She turned to the mother and asked, 'As a mother how do you feel about your daughter's ability?'

The way the woman narrowed her eyes before answering, Rebecca reckoned, irrespective of what this woman said, she was uncomfortably dismissive. 'Err, it is what it is, I guess.'

She then glanced at her daughter. 'I am not at all sure I am comfortable with her speaking to anyone other than me about this.'

'Why is that, may I ask?'

'Rebecca is it? Well, it is a daft notion to most people. The idea that my daughter can see what others cannot.'

As Rebecca listened to the woman speaking, she was picking up on an underlying tone of negativity. For sure, the words she was using were okay, but… 'Are you fearful of having your daughter evaluated and then potentially criticised?' Rebecca then smiled at Melissa and could see she appeared to be holding back in some way.

The woman kind of shook her head without answering. Picking up on this, Rebecca told the woman of her own journey and how people had reacted, including her mother and father. 'I think, overall, as long as your daughter has advocates around her, she will be fine. Ultimately, her power can help so many. That is partly how I drew my strength. Overall, though,' she said again turning to Melissa, mostly to see her reaction, 'my gut told me I was following my destiny. You know, in the seventeen-hundreds, I would have been tied to a post and burned for being a witch. Those same bigoted, narrow-minded men didn't value women, questioning if they had the right to be in the same room as them. Things have changed.'

Wide-eyed, Melissa said, 'You, Rebecca and women like you have changed them.' She then lowered her head again.

The way this girl reacted, Rebecca knew there and then, she needed to either change the mother's prospective, or speak to Melissa alone. They continued to chat for a while longer without really gaining any ground.

Mary, as if she had picked up on what was going on, suggested a break for lunch. On the way to the canteen, Mary pulled Rebecca to one side. 'We need to separate these two.'

'Totally. The mother cares, I think. It is not a bad thing, but the mother's own fears are supressing Melissa. That said, I am feeling something else from the mother. It is as if she is hiding something, or maybe stopping Melissa from speaking freely. I don't know what to think.'

'So, you think she is the real deal?'

'Undoubtedly.'

Mary seemed to think briefly. 'I get what you are saying about the mother. I have been trained to assess body language, eye contact and so on, whilst interviewing possible suspects. There is definitely something very peculiar with the mother's behaviour. It is as if she is hiding something. Also, I don't like the way she shuts Melissa down so quickly.'

After lunch, the four returned to the interview room.

'You know what,' Rebecca said, 'it's a bit starchy in here, interview room and all. It might have been better if we'd met outside, in a natural environment.' She glanced at the mother and then Melissa. 'It must almost feel like you are both being interrogated.' Knowing the mother had said earlier she had to be in work by 3pm, Rebecca had conjured up a plan during lunch. 'How about just Melissa and I go to the café around the corner. Then you, Mrs. Dantry can head off to work. I will look after your daughter, I assure you. After all, we are kindred spirits.' She then smiled at Melissa.

'Can I, Mother, please?'

The way this girl pleaded with her mother using the tone and manner of a six-year-old, compounded her suspicions this lass was being stifled by the mother.

Mrs. Dantry, appearing somewhat miffed, looked at everyone, and then, in a slightly irritated tone, said, 'I guess so.' She then got up and put her coat on. 'Right, be home by five in time to cook your father's dinner. Don't be late or else.' She then marched out of the room.

Rebecca took a deep breath, glanced at Mary who was looking peeved and then held Melissa's hand and said, 'You'll be fine with me. Would you like to go with just me to the canteen?'

'No, I am okay here with you two.' Although she spoke freely, she appeared a little uncomfortable.

'Are you okay, Melissa? You look a little anxious.'

'There will be hell to pay later when I get home.'

These few words bothered Rebecca and she knew there and then she had to dig a little deeper. 'Is it that strict at home?'

The girl suddenly appeared a little tearful. 'I can handle my mother; she is all bossy words and no more.' She looked down, glanced up at Rebecca and then looked down again.

Rebecca looked at Mary and raised her eyebrows. 'Melissa, you are with friends. Please feel free to speak openly. We will not judge you.' She then thought for a moment trying to find a few words that might encourage Melissa to open up. 'When I was fifteen and had my first journey into the past, I was frightened to speak out. I did though and aside from my mother, and even she was tentative… Well, I wouldn't say I was ridiculed or anything, but I was kind of dismissed. It took my father a long time to get on board. My mother, who I love endlessly, still struggles with the concept of me jumping through time. My Father is now totally on board.' Rebecca wanted to tell Melissa about her mother's own time jumping when she was young but had given her word, she wouldn't speak about this to anyone other than family.

Suddenly, Melissa appeared a little more animated. 'I never see into the past; it is only ever the future. As for my father,' she then looked down. 'He will never change. He treats me horribly every time I speak. I once got a report from school and…' She then recoiled inwardly again.

'Sorry to push you on this Melissa,' Mary said. 'Would you feel comfortable explaining how he treats you and what he does that frightens you so much?'

Melissa seemed to think for a moment. 'Please do not tell anyone.' She again paused, this time appearing a little tearful. 'A teacher sent home a questionnaire about my homelife because I was so sad in school. My father was so cross and slapped my backside so hard it started to bleed. He then took me out of the school and moved us to another area. He blamed me and said I needed to grow up or he will have to start locking me in the room under the stairs again.'

Absolutely fuming, Rebecca couldn't believe what she'd just heard. 'How old were you when this happened, and what room under the stairs, how big is this room?'

Melissa took a deep breath. I was eleven and had only just made friends. It was the fifth time we'd moved and it was always after someone had come to see us at home. When the man from social services came to our house, my father told him it was my mother who harmed me.' Then in silence, she stared aimlessly at the wall. 'I never saw my mother again. And the room under the stairs is the cupboard where the rubbish is stored.'

Dumfounded and breathing deeply, Rebecca again looked at Mary with raised eyebrows. Although she was furious this sad soul had been locked under the stairs, her focus was now on the mother who went missing. 'So, who is the woman who was with you this morning?'

'That is my father's sister. If I don't call her mother, I am either locked in the room under the stairs or the garden shed.'

'Hang on a minute,' Mary said, appearing utterly perplexed, 'that woman who was here this morning is your father's sister? So where is your mother?'

The girl took a deep breath and silently stared at the wall.

Rebecca was just about to speak, when Mary tapped her on the arm and put her finger to her lips. The two sat there allowing the girl the time she needed. After around five minutes, Mary asked, 'would you like a tea, coffee, or cold drink, Melissa?'

The girl looked up appearing focussed. Suddenly, her whole demeanour had taken on a different, slightly fixed stance. She took another deep breath, put her palms down on the table. 'She is in the garden.'

'What do you mean, she is in the garden? Mary asked, her eyes wide. She then turned to Rebecca, shook her head slightly and grimaced.

'I saw the police come to my house just now when I was quiet.'

Rebecca completely got what the girl was saying and was certain this girl had just travelled into the future within her head. 'When you see the future, do you go there, or do you just see it as if you were looking on from the outside, feeling as if you are invisible?'

Melissa's whole behaviour had completely changed and although still upset, she looked wide-eyed. She held Rebecca's hand and said, 'I am invisible. It is as if I am there but not. You have been there, haven't you, I can tell. My mother is buried behind the shed.'

'Right,' Mary said, 'I need to go and speak to the local chief inspector. Rebecca, take Melissa for a coffee.'

Rebecca took Melissa back to the canteen. 'It will be okay you know. I will look after you.'

'I know you will and I know I never have to see my father again. I am upset about my mother, but not as upset as I should be, which is odd. I have felt like this before though.'

This instantly resonated with Rebecca. She then spent the next few minutes talking to Melissa about her own detachment and objectivity issues. Now totally on the same page, the two agreed, having reckoned independently, that these detachment issues were part of the journey they both shared.

This kind of hit home with Rebecca. 'I think feeling so detached helps us stay focussed. Although our routes are different, we are both on the same journey.' Suddenly for Rebecca, she now had some answers. The brief, bizarre passing notion that Meredith might actually be her mother now felt border line illogical.

'I think you are right. Meeting you today, hearing your words, and seeing my dead mother has changed my world. I now know my destiny.' The girl then seemed to think for a moment. Open eyed, the child seemingly gone, this woman said, 'you live near a lake, is that right?'

Totally taken aback, Rebecca was now wondering just how insightful this girl's abilities could be. 'I do. I was going to ask how you know, but I suspect you saw it just a moment ago when you went quiet.'

Smiling, she said, 'you are right. I saw myself talking to you outside my new home, which was named Nadine. You and I were with your mother, Elizabeth.'

Over the years, Rebecca had been caught off-guard a number of times, but never like this before. Her emotions compounded because her father had recently employed an architect to draw plans for converting the old stables nearby the family's main house. The weird part was the name Nadine. Years before, while out exploring the grounds, she'd found an old name plaque in the derelict stables. The name plaque was Nadine. To compound her feelings, initially Tommy had considered moving in, but Kaitlin's job had taken them to London, leaving the stables empty.

'So, you said you saw yourself living there?'

'I did. It was weird because I have seen this before many times. The first time was soon after my mother left me.'

When Mary had left to speak with the local senior police officer, and reckoning it was to send a team to Melissa's house, she had wondered what would become of Melissa. Never in her wildest dreams did she imagine this young woman would end up living with her. 'Why not,' she mumbled.

'Yes, why not. I thought that too. In the past, not knowing you, none of it made sense, now though… As you said, why not.' She then seemed to think for a moment. 'That is if you are happy for me to live there. I don't know how I will pay to live there, but…'

'With your ability to see bad things, Mary will employ you to work with her team. I am sure Mary will arrange this.'

'I will arrange what?' Mary asked as she walked back into the room.

Rebecca and Melissa then told Mary everything they had just spoken about.

Appearing a little surprised, but focussed, she nodded. 'It is strange, because on my way back here, I was wondering about your future, Melissa. If you would like to come and work for me, I would love that. Rebecca, you, and I will make a great team. A team we would love to grow over time. So, if Rebecca is happy. Then let's do this.'

'I would love that. I will speak with my father, but I don't see why not. You will get on so well with my parents and two daughters. Let me speak with my father.' Rebecca called her father and then Duncan. 'All sorted. Both my husband and parents would be delighted to have you move into the Nadine stable.'

'By the way, Melissa, the incident you told the police about is in hand. We have a crack team on to it and I will let you know.'

'Can I come with you today, Rebecca? I don't want to stay around here anymore. I have already seen my mother's funeral in six days, so I will come back for that. Also, Mary, thank you for arranging the team to investigate my vision.' She then seemed to think for a moment. 'The outcome is good.'

'I suspect you have seen this, Melissa,' Rebecca said, glancing at Mary.

'Yes, the boy will be safe.'

Mary then made a couple of calls. After, she turned to Melissa. 'Okay, all sorted. Can I ask, do you drive?'

'I wanted to but he wouldn't let me.'

'I will arrange for you to have driving lessons. I would expect, mostly, you will work independently. By that, I mean you are free to work where you feel you need to and when you feel you need to.' Mary then seemed to consider her next words. 'There is no pressure for you to come up with anything. In your own time. The driving lessons are in case you need to go anywhere because Rebecca's home is a little off the beaten track.'

'Thank you, both. Mary, I have three things I have seen. One is us speaking with another lady who has the same vision as Rebecca and myself. She is strong and her name is Rosemary Doyle. The other two are a long way off yet. There is nothing we can do now.'

Mary glanced at Rebecca, then back to Melissa. 'In your own time. I am very intrigued to hear about this other woman though. Perhaps you can tell Rebecca and I all about her on the train. The first thing we need to do, is arrange for you to collect your belongings from your home.'

'It is not my home and there is nothing I need from there. I want to start afresh.'

'What did you mean, it is not your home?' Rebecca asked, intrigued by the girl's use of words.

'I lived there with my mother and father, but I was never meant to be there.' She then looked down for a moment. 'I believe I took the place of their daughter but I don't know what happened to her. I do not know how I got here, but I have always known this was not where I truly belong.'

Curious and intrigued rather than surprised by Melissa's comments, Rebecca wanted to dig a little deeper. She kind of had a handle on where the girl was coming from but needed to hear her own account. 'Where do you think you belong then?'

'I have come here from many years in the past. I do not know where from though. I know I am meant to be with you two, and although this is not my home, I feel at home with you both. I see my life with Nadine.'

Oddly, although this girl's words would scramble most brains, Rebecca knew exactly where she was coming from. 'I get that completely. I am like you. I know things and don't know why I know them. When I was your age it spooked me, now I just accept it.'

Mary, appearing a tad puzzled, said, 'I am following what you two are saying. It is, however, way beyond me. So, sorry if I do not add anything to the conversation.'

Simultaneously, both Rebecca and Melissa smiled towards Mary.

'You used the word spooked,' Melissa said, 'what does it mean? Although I understand many of your words, it is not my language.'

Melissa's comments about language caught Rebecca a little off guard. She immediately thought about her time with Matilda and Rebekah. Both had spoken in an unfamiliar language, somehow though, she was able to understand them both. 'Tell me more.'

The girl then started speaking in a language Rebecca oddly recognised.

'Hadhih kalamati wahadha lisani.'

Bizarrely, she'd understood what Melissa had just said.

'What did you say,' Mary asked, again appearing puzzled.

'I think she said, "These are my words and this is my tongue." I don't know why I know, but I do.' Seeing the girl nod in a particular way nudged at Rebecca's inner consciousness. She knew in a flash. 'That is Arabic. It is old Arabic though, the same as my friend Rebekah. She lived in Mesopotamia four-thousand years ago.

'I know that name but I do not know why,' Mary said.

'You may have read about her in the old testament, the book of Genesis. Rebekah is also the second Jewish Matriarch.'

Rebecca could see Melissa clearly thinking. Her face then seemed to go blank, almost as if she'd left the room. Rebecca watched, suspecting this girl was seeing some other world. Her and Mary once more sat observing this girl seemingly wander within her own thoughts.

'I can see the fringes of an arid world I feel I know. I also hear words I recognise. My emotions sense one day my destiny will take me to this place. The people are passionately led by a beautiful woman. The men freely advocate her compassion, strength and amiable charisma.'

For Rebecca, this girl's words could only mean one thing. She felt certain Melissa had seen Mesopotamia and was speaking of Rebekah. Adding in Melissa's ability to speak ancient Arabic just affirmed this notion. 'You spoke of a woman who leads her people. Do you know her name?'

Shaking her head, she said, 'I can only see the fringes of this existence. It is not my time to be with these people. One day, I feel I will return.'

Mary glanced at Rebecca and held up her palm.

Rebecca looked at Melissa, then back at Mary. 'I believe she is seeing the world she came from and one day will be back with her people.'

'You are right, Rebecca, although my time now is with you.'

Mary, Melissa and Rebecca had a brief, constructive meeting with the Metropolitan Police's chief superintendent.

Although he did more listening than speaking, he said, 'this meeting has been very insightful. Having met with you two, I know have a better understanding of how your visionary ability works, Melissa and Rebecca. I now feel better equipped to search for others who can help us further progress this bold adventure and new way of policing.'

Chapter 25 - The Move

Once home, Rebecca helped Melissa settle into her new home. Entering the stables was a weird scenario for Rebecca. The first time she clambered over the broken wall at the back of the stables and found the old Nadine plaque was many years before. Even though the building was unrecognisable, it still had the same peculiar feeling. In an odd way, it was so very familiar, and particularly more so now it had been renovated. This in itself created an odd emotion, because she'd only ever known it in its run-down state. For her, it was as if she knew this place way better than her one previous adventure inside.

'What are you thinking?' Melissa asked.

'I really don't know. It feels like I know this place way better than I should.' She considered her mood briefly, but didn't have an answer. Over the last few months, she'd had a number of remotely distant emotions. In an odd way, many of them felt as if they were pulling her in a familiar direction. The more she thought about it though, the further away she was from understanding these feelings.

'It will come to you in time. It is the same for me.' Melissa then smiled in a way that suggested she knew more.

Sensing Melissa had said as much as she wanted, Rebecca focussed on helping her arrange furniture. A couple of times, Rebecca wondered how Melissa, being so young and all, would settle in and deal with her new life. It did, however, quickly become clear this girl had a strength beyond her years. From the first moment she stepped through the door to the stable, it was as if she belonged.

Everyone loved having Melissa around. In particular, her and Faith formed a strong bond, what with being a similar age. Faith's move to Vancouver had been put off for a year, allowing her time to finish her A-Levels. This was a decision made by the family and facilitated by the football club, or soccer club as Faith kept pointing out.

Unsurprisingly for Rebecca, Melissa's kindred relationship with Gabrielle confirmed Gab was of their making.

Four days after Melissa had moved in, Mary phoned Rebecca. She was calling to say they had uncovered the body of a woman in her fifties exactly where Melissa had suggested. DNA identified the woman as Melissa's mother. She also went on to say they had found the body of a young girl next to the woman, but were unable to identify her. She suggested it was rather strange because although they were able to classify her genetics, DNA, and sample her teeth, there was absolutely no record of this girl having ever lived. 'Speak to Melissa and see if she has any ideas or insightful notions.' Mary then said the father and his sister had been charged with the murder of two females. 'Because we can't identify one of the bodies, there will be a delay in a funeral. Speak to Melissa and ask how she feels. I suspect, because of what she said about them not being her real family, something I am still getting my head around, she may not want to attend a funeral.'

'Leave it with me,' Rebecca said. 'I will do a little digging.'

After she came off the phone, she popped up to see Melissa. Over a cup of Mel's favourite tea, a spicy affair, which oddly reminded Rebecca of her time in Mesopotamia with Rebekah, she told her about Mary's call.

'I feel no need to attend any funeral. Although I am deeply saddened by the way these two women lost their lives, I feel it would serve no purpose.' She then seemed to think for a moment, although she wasn't as remote as she normally was when she thought. 'I do not know, but something is telling me the young body could be the daughter. I have always known I was there in place of their daughter. I was with that family for five years. Every day, I felt I didn't belong, and believed I had somehow replaced their real daughter. Of late, right up until you came into my life, I felt one day the daughter would return and I would go home to my world. I am now considering I may be here to stay; sent here to do the work the daughter should have done.'

'That did occur to me. I am, however, curious why you believe you are here to do the work the daughter was destined to do.'

'I never saw her. I am going on a conversation I heard the man and woman have. The ones who outwardly pretended to be my mother and father. One evening, I overheard him say, she had to go because she knew too much.' She shook her head. 'Never for one second did I think they had murdered her too. This is strange also because I am able to see such incidents. I knew, albeit only on the day I first spoke to you, of the death of the wife. I have seen many bad things, however... So, their comment about the daughter knowing too much suggested she was blessed with the same vision we have.'

Rebecca was at a loss what to think. 'Well, Mary said they are going to investigate further. Perhaps they will be able to shed some light. I must say, I do not have quite the same vision you have. My direction is more towards keeping history on track. Your route and destiny are to help stop harmful events in the here, now and tomorrow.'

'I do believe, although I am not sure.' She then paused again. 'If the other body turns out to be the daughter, my time here will be over. I do not know why I feel this, but I do. So, to this point, perhaps the power that controls my movement has hidden her identity.'

'I get that completely. Over the years many strange things have occurred to me. Inexplicable events and unbelievable sequences that would muddle most brains. Like you, I see how it could be and accept it as part of my journey. I too believe there is an overriding power.' Rebecca then thought for a moment. 'Do you know the name Ethernal?'

Narrow eyed, Melissa said, 'I do. I hear him speak with me when I feel lost. I never see him though. He is a guardian of my kind.'

'He is indeed a guardian, of all our kind, whether we are visionaries like you, or time fixers like me.' Just then a thought occurred to Rebecca. She now found herself wondering if Ethernal knew all the visionaries and if he did, could he help her find others. Thinking about this, she concluded if it was meant to be, he would visit.

The two girls sat chatting for a while longer. Mostly, the conversation was about their individual directions, stories and beliefs. A couple of weeks passed with no further news on the identity of the young female. Occasionally, Rebecca's compassion thought about this girl's stifled soul. In the end, she forced herself to believe it was part of a bigger plan and one day, her spirit will move on. Much of Rebecca's time was taken up with Gabrielle and Faith.

With the two of them back at school, she looked out of the window. Seeing the daffodils now in full bloom along the lake edge, she called up Melissa and asked if she fancied going for a walk. The two met outside the summerhouse and headed off towards the wood behind the stables. They had walked no more than fifty yards, when Rebecca's phone rang. It was Mary.

'Hello, Rebecca. I've spoken to the young lady Melissa saw in the vision. Only having her name, it took me a while to find the right Rosemary Doyle. Now, here is where it quickly became interesting. The woman answered the phone with, "hello, Mary, I was expecting your call." How weird is that? Importantly, having spoken to her for a few minutes and her knowing you and Melissa's names, tells me this woman is the real deal. So, with that in mind, I was calling to see if either of you have any issues with meeting her on the fifth of March. Could you speak to Mel for me?'

'She is with me, hang on.' She then turned and called out, 'Mel, anything planned on the fifth?'

Melissa walked towards her with raised eyebrows. 'Every day is free for me.'

Rebecca turned back to the phone. 'All good this end.'

Rebecca and Melissa continued their walk, chatting. 'Tell me, are you okay with Mary and I calling you Mel. It just occurred to me when I called out.'

'Feel free, my friend, to call me whatever you want.'

With it being a delightfully warm spring, Mel and Rebecca spent a lot of time walking and chatting. Much of their focus was on Rebecca's past journeys, although they also discussed what might lay ahead for the pair of them. Before they knew it, it was time to meet up with Rosemary. Although Rosemary was very open and clearly had shown all the right signs, there was something Rebecca wasn't sure about. The three of them, along with Mary chatted for a couple of hours.

'Well, it's been a pleasure meeting up with you Rosemary,' Mary said, 'I will talk with Melissa and Rebecca and we will speak with you soon.

After the meeting was finished, Mary, Mel and Rebecca went to a nearby café for a coffee.

'I am not sure,' Rebecca said.

'No, me neither. She said all the right things. What do you think, Mel?'

She shook her head. 'She can see, but she sees things differently to us.' She then seemed to think for a moment. 'I can't explain it, just not right. It is as if there is bad intent.'

Rebecca nodded. 'Yep, I got that too. I have known for a while now that for every one of our making, there is a malevolent counterpart.'

Mary, frowning asked, 'what do you mean, malevolent. Is she capable of doing anything bad?'

Rebecca shook her head. 'I don't think so, however…' She then paused, knowing what she wanted to say just had to make sure she used the right words. 'Okay, so you both now know about Evanora, and Belisant. We all know how that could have turned out had Belisant been forced into pregnancy, and well, we know the outcome. We also know of Evanora's ancestral destiny. So, what I am thinking is, even if Rosemary isn't capable of bad actions, her genes could pass to a child who would be capable of who knows what.'

'That is very interesting,' Mary said, 'we need to monitor her over the coming years.' She turned to Melissa who appeared to be going through one of her insights.

A couple of minutes passed, then she turned and said, 'She is bad, but is unable to carry child.'

'So, our search continues,' Mary said.

Melissa, with her eyes closed, held her hand up. Once more, Mary and Rebecca sat watching her eye lids flickering, almost as if she was in a dream like state.

Wide eyed, Melissa looked at them both, a look of shock on her face. 'Her brother, tomorrow. You must stop him. He is crowded with jealousy. He is the bad influencer and will stop Rosemary. She has goodness and he has forever stifled her spirit and enveloped her goodness with his evil intent.' She then shut her eyes for a second. 'Tomorrow, in the park, he will take her life.'

Mary asked frantically, 'which park, where and when?'

Shaking her head, Melissa answered, 'I cannot see. I am sorry. His evilness is strong and is blinding my vision as it is Rosemary's.'

'Right, I will put her under twenty-four-hour surveillance.' She then thought for a moment. 'I think we shouldn't tell her what is happening. Because it is her brother and she is under his power, she may tell him and he will back away.'

'You must not tell her. His strength is such it leaves her incapable of making the right choices. She is blinded by him. Follow her to the park. I cannot see if you will be successful.'

Mary nodded. 'I will put my best team on it around the clock. Let me make a call now.'

Moments later, she came off the phone. 'All sorted. Rosemary will not know she is under surveillance, if that is the right word. Then, if the brother strikes, we can stop him.'

'You must stop him. He is strong and his intent evil.' Again, she closed her eyes. After a few seconds, she looked up, and with tears in her eyes, said, 'you must stop this man. I've seen the day when he enters an infants' school with a gun.' She then shook her hands in the most peculiar way. 'I feel his sinful intent as if it were running through my veins.'

Rebecca looked at Mary, unsure what to say. The strangest feeling then came over her. It was as if she could sense Melissa reading her thoughts. 'Mel, how much can you actually see. I felt as if you were looking into my soul.'

'Your valiant courage and fearlessness are that of someone I once knew in a dream. When I feel your spirit, it reminds me of my home, although I do not know where my home is.' She then held Rebecca's hand. 'My home now is with you my beloved friend. My destiny is to follow the path I feel and see within my soul.'

The three continued to chat for a while longer. Just after midday, Mary explained she felt the need to go to speak with the team who were going to watch over Rosemary.

Rebecca drove Mel home. 'We make a great team us three. Let's hope we can change Rosemary's destiny and perhaps get her onboard once she is no longer burdened by her brother.'

'I am unable to see that day. That may be because her brother still influences her direction.' Melissa then shook her head appearing a little anxious. 'Normally, I see everything but I feel he is blocking me in some way.'

That evening, Melissa, along with Duncan, the girls, and Rebecca's parents went into town for a meal at Rebecca's favourite Italian restaurant. Watching Melissa interact with everyone, for Rebecca, it felt as if this girl belonged in her life.

The following morning, Mary called.

'Hello, Mary. I suspect you have some news. Hang on, I will put my phone on loud speaker so Mel can hear.'

'I do and sadly it is very unhappy news. Rosemary, along with her friend and two daughters went to the park near her home. They stood with the two young girls by the swing park. As you suggested, moments later Rosemary's brother appeared. Before we had time to move, even though my team was right there, her brother produced a gun, shot both Rosemary, her friend and the two girls. One of our officers shot him in the leg. He was then arrested. Wretchedly, both girls and Rosemary's friend were dead. Rosemary, although critical, survived but it is touch and go.'

'Oh, my goodness,' Rebecca said, 'will she survive?' In the back of her thoughts, she felt bothered, knowing even with all this information, they were still unable to stop this man taking three lives.

'She is in a bad way, but is showing signs of recovery.'

'She will survive, but you need to watch her brother. Do not turn away, or he will escape,' Mel said.

Rebecca turned to Melissa and shook her head. 'Have you seen all this?'

'Yes, and with him still alive, he still has a hold over Rosemary. He will use this to aid his escape. Watch both carefully.'

'Right,' Mary said, 'I will sort this now.'

Gradually, over the next few weeks, Rosemary made a full recovery, albeit, she was confined to a wheel chair. Mary had made sure both Rosemary and her brother were watched closely.

Mary called to say, unbelievably, the brother had been to court and the judge deemed him insane and unfit for trial. He had been sent to a prison hospital. 'I am so angry because he isn't insane. Somehow though, he convinced the judge otherwise.'

When Rebecca told Melissa about this, she shrugged her shoulders. 'He must be watched every minute of every day. His mental strength altered the judge's opinion. He can also alter the opinion of those who guard him.' She then thought for a moment. 'I have a blurred vision. In three days, Rosemary will drive to the prison. Her being in a wheel chair is a charade. There is no problem with her legs. This is again a sign of how strong her brothers hold is over her captured soul. One of the guards will open the doors allowing the brothers escape. I am unable to see a time, although it is during darkness. I will speak to Mary now.' She then called Mary and quickly explained the scenario. After she came off the phone, Melissa went very quiet.

'You said blurred vision. Is this as a result of him stopping you from seeing clearly?'

She nodded, 'it is,' she said, and then held her hand up. 'I am seeing something more, but cannot focus. All I know is it involves many gun shots between the brother, Rosemary and the police. I will phone Mary again.' After she came off the phone, she appeared a little more relaxed.

'How does it feel seeing all of this?' Rebecca asked, intrigued by Melissa's ability. In an odd way, her reaction to this girl's vision gave her an understanding of how people, including her mother and father must have felt when she first told them of her journeys. Although she'd always understood and accepted their initial doubts, this allowed her a clearer insight.

'I just accept it for what it is, I guess. Because I have always seen this other world, I know no different.'

The next three days passed quickly for both Melissa and Rebecca. They spoke often of Rosemary and her brother.

'I wish I could clearly see the outcome for Rosemary. I have seen it from a distance many times. Whenever I feel I am able to focus, I feel I am being pushed away. Although I previously only suspected this was because of the brother's strength, I am now certain. He has the ability to block all of our kind. Whenever I get close, I feel his bitter evilness. It is so strong. This man must be stopped. He can alter the opinion of all around him. His wickedness will alter this world.' She then thought for a moment. 'My destiny is to stop him and I feel with Mary's aid, this man will be no more. I have just seen a path where he no longer blocks my vision.' She went quiet, then smiling, but with tears, she looked directly at Rebecca. 'I feel my world is about to change, I can smell frankincense and it reminds me of home. I feel I am...' She then reached out her hand.

Before she had time to respond, Rebecca watched as Melissa started to fade. She stretched her hand out to Mel, but she was gone. With an instant surge of emotions and feeling unusually tearful, she tried to get a grip of what just happened. Having watched Meredith fade away in a similar way years earlier, she reconciled herself knowing Melissa was home and their paths may cross once more, just in another world. Breathing deeply, her emotions were interrupted by her phone ringing. It was Mary.

Rebecca responded to the call, but before she had time to say anything, Mary started speaking.

'They are both dead. Somehow, he got hold of the guard's gun and as he was escaping, our officers tried to apprehend him. He started firing. He was then shot dead by the officers. Rosemary made a grab for his gun and shot herself.'

Instantly, Melissa's words made complete sense. 'Seconds before you phoned, I was talking to Mel. She was telling me she felt her destiny was to stop this man. She was half way through her sentence and literally vanished in front of me. I think, with the death of that man, a man she said could alter our world with his evilness, her job here was done. I believe she is back home where she belongs, wherever that is. Much of what she has said recently, including speaking in Arabic, has offered me an insight to her true world. I am hopeful I will find out one day, somehow, someway.'

'Can it work like that? She lives in our world, but belongs in another? Has that happened to you?'

Rebecca explained to Mary all about her time with Etienne, including having two boys.

'I am not sure I could handle that. That must have been awful leaving a husband of thirty years and two boys behind.'

'Bizarrely, I felt no loss at all. I questioned this so many times, asking myself why I wasn't in pieces. My father suggested I wasn't actually there, just seeing that world through the eyes of another. As ludicrous as that sounds, it is the only explanation and it's one that sits comfortably with me and my emotions.'

'I do not think I will ever truly understand the way your world works. I am just thankful to be involved.'

Her and Mary chatted for a little while longer.

'So, our search starts once more for someone who can help us along this journey.'

On the way back to the summerhouse, although Rebecca felt sad not being able to see Mel, she was content this girl was home where she belonged.

Chapter 26 – The Door Opens

Often over the next few months, Rebecca thought of Melissa, and each time she did, she felt happy for her. When she tried to explain what had happened to Melissa, the only person who seemed to comprehend this notion was her father, James. With the girls, she'd decided to tell them Melissa had moved away. She did, however, get the feeling Gabrielle knew otherwise, even though she didn't say anything.

Her and Mary spent much time together speaking with various women and men who claimed they had visions. None of them proved beneficial to Mary and Rebecca's hopes.

It was late August and Faith had just received her A-Level results, having gained straight A's. Although, Faith, Duncan and Rebecca discussed university, they agreed Faith needed to follow her dream. After speaking with the Whitecap's manager, it was agreed Faith would fly out after Christmas.

The days drifted into weeks and often Rebecca wondered if there was any more for her. She also knew that if anything was meant to happen, as always it would do just that, happen. With Faith's eighteenth birthday this year and because of her excellent exam results, they all agreed a couple of weeks holiday wouldn't go amiss. With Gabrielle not due back at school until late September they decided on a week in Disney followed by a week on a cruise around the Caribbean.

At the last minute, James and Elizabeth decided to join them. As always with a holiday of this nature they had a fabulous time. Often, Rebecca reminded her father while waiting in line for the next Disney ride, that he so didn't want to go the first time all those years ago. He'd jokingly responded by suggesting he didn't know what she meant. This made everyone laugh and set a nice tone for more Mickey-Tee-Shirts.

In what seemed like the blink of an eye, they were back home and once more putting up Christmas decorations. Duncan had arranged a huge Christmas Tree on the lawn leading down to the lake. Even with everyone helping, it took them the best part of five days to decorate it fully. With it looking so fabulous, they all agreed it would become a permanent fixture in future years.

It was just a week before Christmas and although cold, Rebecca decided to go for a walk. Going outside, it was actually freezing, and even though she didn't much fancy it, something in her gut, something she hadn't felt for months, was telling her to head into the woods.

The further she walked, the stronger her feelings were. Arriving by the old fallen oak, and hearing a familiar voice from behind her, didn't come as a surprise.

'Ethernal. I have not heard your voice for a long time. I hope all is well.'

'Melissa is back where she belongs, although I believe you knew this. As you suspected, she is with Rebekah, her grandmother and her father, Esau.' He then paused unusually. 'Your journey is near completion. I have a list of names for you. People who will help you complete your final undertaking. There are many names. When I go, turn and you will find a scroll with said names. Take these and as always, be valiant, resourceful and with heart, follow your intuition.'

Knowing he was gone, Rebecca turned to see a scroll laying on the trunk of the oak. With it now becoming bitterly cold, she picked the scroll up and headed back to the summerhouse. Even though she was tempted to have a look, with the air a little damp, she decided to wait until she was indoors. On the way, she kept thinking about Ethernal suggesting her journey was near completion. This then made her consider Melissa. Once more, irregular questions nudged at her subconsciousness. Changing her focus completely, the name Esau suddenly rang a bell but she didn't know why.

Somewhere in the recesses of her brain, her intuitive side was telling her to look the name up in the bible. She'd meant to do this often, particularly for Rebekah. For some obscure reason, she always ended up distracted by something else. *No time like the present*, she thought.

She went in, put the coffee on and opened up her laptop. She then typed in Rebekah's granddaughter. After she'd scrolled through some fictional stories about a female vampire named Rebekah, she spotted an entry. Seeing the words, "Isaac's wife Rebekah could not have children," rang alarm bells. She opened the article up and started reading. Most of what she read wasn't really going anywhere. She did come across one section that suggested the Lord granted Rebekah twin boys named Esau and Jacob. After initially reading Rebekah couldn't have children, this left her a tad confused. Nodding, she mumbled, 'otherworldly intervention.' This in itself made her consider her own path, destiny and reinvigorated her belief there was someone or something overseeing her and all like her. Almost smoothly paving their every move.

After her coffee, she turned her attention to the scroll.

Unrolling it on the kitchen table, she was shocked to see a list of over one-hundred names. This extensive list included first and surnames, country of origin and residency, along with their age. Interestingly, all but three names were female.

Seeing a few were in Great Britain, she decided to type them all up on a spreadsheet. Her idea was to sort the names easily into a map of sorts. After a couple of hours, she had a list of 167 names, 38 of which were in the UK. *There's that number again*, she thought, wondering now about its significance. She'd considered this number a few times but it never seemed to point anywhere, other than always being there. She then turned back to the scroll, only to see all the names had vanished. 'Well, that's par for the course,' she mumbled. This wasn't the first time something like this had happened and it reaffirmed her beliefs, confirming there was an overriding power controlling all of this. *Just too many coincidences for them to all be a coincidence,* she thought.

Moments later, just as she was considering phoning Mary, Duncan walked in with the girls. Deciding to leave calling Mary until the morning, she focussed her attention on the family. After supper, they all sat going through their holiday photos.

'What I don't get, Bex, is how we manage to take hundreds of photos and the only time you're in them is at a distance.'

'I was thinking that, although it is mostly me using the camera.' She smiled, but it had made her think. In the end, she decided it was just one of those things. Still though, something was niggling her. The following day, she went through hundreds of family photos and it was the same. She was in them, but so distant, it could have actually been anyone. She zoomed in close on a couple, but oddly she appeared blurry, unlike those around her. She sat there trying to understand why this was and importantly if there was some kind of hidden message. The issue was, the more she thought about it, the underlying notions seemed increasingly ambiguous. *Right, let's call Mary,* she thought.

After a brief chat, Mary suggested she needed to pop over and see the list for herself. Being as they were now so close to Christmas, they agreed they would start contacting all those on the list sometime in January.

Christmas, as always was a fabulous family affair, the mood heightened by a good covering of snow. In what seemed like the blink of an eye, Faith was getting sorted for her big adventure. With her now being eighteen, Rebecca and Duncan felt a whole lot more comfortable.

'I guess we should look at it no differently than if she'd gone to university.' Although Rebecca was going to miss her, she was immensely proud and delighted Faith was following her destiny. The way Gabrielle, now thirteen, handled Faith going away came as a pleasant surprise. Rebecca heard her say a number of times how proud she was, often suggesting she was looking forward to coming over to see her big-sis play soccer.

Once Faith had left for Vancouver, Rebecca felt surprisingly okay. In fact, she was more concerned with Duncan, who seemed to miss her greatly. At one point, Rebecca felt the need to nicely suggest he didn't 'facetime' her every day and allowed her to grow her wings. Reluctantly, he agreed, only to have Faith call him every time he didn't call. One particular evening, it was lovely hearing her explain every last detail of her first game to Duncan and Tommy, a game they'd won three-nil.

It was mid-January and she was due to meet up with Mary at the police headquarters in Liverpool. Mary had put an extensive team together with the intent of contacting all those living in the UK. Also, she'd made plans with the Canadian, American, Australian and Israeli police departments. Disappointingly, this left seven names who they wouldn't be able to contact because their respective countries had declined the invitation to be involved. They had reckoned though, in time, these other countries may come on board. This initial set-up meeting took most of the day. If they'd hoped to get this up and running promptly, they were now in no doubts this was going to take months rather than weeks. They also agreed if they were going to give this new way of policing a chance, it had to be extensive and completed thoroughly.

Mary and Rebecca agreed to meet up once a week and speak on the phone as and when. In what seemed like a flash, it was early summer. Mary's team had made excellent in roads and with Rebecca's help, they had seventeen girls on the list. Brilliantly, within a couple of months, leads from three of these girls had led to the arrest of seven unscrupulous individuals. Two of them were believed to be part of a global gang and investigations were ongoing. Information from a young girl living on a remote farm in Wales had stopped an individual in her tracks. Not only was this the first female they'd identified, it was also the first time they had managed to prevent a wicked act from ever happening. The other three were historical, previously unsolved cases. Mary, Rebecca and the ever-growing team were delighted with their success. Their elation was further compounded when they received news of successes both from Israel and America. Now a global team, online meetings were scheduled every two days. Many members were stepping forward with their own initiatives.

On the way home, Rebecca felt extremely contented and proud of all Mary and her had achieved.

With Faith due home for a two-week break, Rebecca focussed all her attention on her family, leaving Mary to run things and contact her if need be. Just after Faith had headed back, Mary called and told Rebecca of further successes in all countries involved. She also said that the countries who had initially declined involvement were now fully on board. Further to this, two more countries had stepped forward, indicating they were searching for 'visionaries.' The elated emotions Rebecca was feeling reminded her of the way she felt when she'd finally got the world's governments working to one goal, bringing a halt to global warming.

After coming off the phone, Gabrielle asked Rebecca to go to the hidden garden with her. With her curiosity invigorated, having not been asked for a few months, she said. 'I'd love to, Sweetie.' Delighted, she followed Gab up to the main house, through the kitchen and into the yard. As she grew closer to the entrance, her senses were heightened even further by Gabrielle's silence. Gab had never been one for a lot of words, but even so. Oddly, it felt as if Gab was taking her somewhere for a reason.

As she clambered through the door into a beautifully sunny garden, blooming with a kaleidoscope of flowers, she felt really rather peculiar. It wasn't a negative emotion in any way, just weird. 'So, Gab, why are we here today?

'You'll see, Mum. Come over to the swing, someone wants to speak with you.'

Narrow eyed with curiosity, she followed Gabrielle to the swing.

'Sit on the swing, Mum and let someone special push you.'

Rebecca's intrigue was open to most things, but she wasn't expecting that. 'Okay, she said and sat on the swing. Gab was standing in front of her and Rebecca watched as she started smiling. Seconds later, Rebecca felt the swing being pushed. Without hearing a voice, or turning, she knew it was Meredith.

'Hello, my dear Meredith.'

She heard Meredith chuckle. 'Oh, it's Meredith today, not mum, or mother.' Again, she chuckled.

Recalling it as if it were yesterday, she remembered this as one of the first things Meredith had said to her twenty-seven years previously. Feeling Meredith's hand on the swing rope, Rebecca glanced to one side and put her hand over Meredith's hand.

'Your work in this time is almost complete. You will soon be ready to start again. Worry not about the when, why or how, all will become clear. Go with your usual courageous heart. We will be together again soon.'

'Come on, Mum, we can go back now. Meredith has gone home.'

Chapter 27 – The Door Back

Following Gabrielle back to the kitchen Rebecca's emotions were so topsy-turvy, she felt almost sea-sick. It was one thing Meredith's flippant comments about mum or mother, but her saying they would be together again, well... Also considering what else she'd said, left her perplexed, not knowing what to make of it all, and importantly, wondering where this was leading. Remembering everything that had happened over the last couple of years, once more the name plaque on the old bench came to mind. Suddenly the words, "for Rebecca, my daughter in another life," were more prevalent and could possibly signify more than a kind notion. She considered the idea that she could actually be the daughter of Meredith, but just as quickly, dismissed that idea, certain she'd know, or at least feel something.

There was though, another unpleasant concept rumbling around somewhere deep in her thoughts. As much as she didn't want to admit it to herself, everything was pointing in one direction. The thing was, she just wasn't ready to explore that direction yet. She was forcibly avoiding thinking about what could happen but it was still nagging at her thoughts. She stood looking at Gabrielle thinking I am not ready to leave this world yet. Over the last few weeks, she'd felt poorly a few times, to the point where she didn't feel like getting up in the morning, which was most unlike her. She'd meant to go and see the doctor, but what with her involvement with Mary, she'd just not gotten around to phoning the surgery.

Gabrielle turned to her and said, 'Mum, you are not going to join Meredith in her world of souls. It is not your time to leave this world. Do not be so fearful, Mother, you are not going to step from your life and join Matilda, Rebekah and Melissa in their world.'

Never had so few words had such an exhausting impact on her emotions. She forced herself to smile towards Gabrielle. 'Thank you. How did you know what I was thinking?'

'Don't be silly, Mum, I always know. I am sorry if Meredith's words and my comment worried you. Worry not, all will unfold as it always does. That is what you taught me.'

She knelt down and cuddled Gabrielle. 'My Sweetness, you have a great gift for life.'

Over the next few weeks, she often thought about Meredith's and Gab's comments. Heavily involved with so many new leads around the world, Rebecca's focus though was mostly towards working with Mary.

It was a rainy October morning and she was in an online meeting with Mary, plus three senior investigators. Two were in America, plus one new member in the middle east. Over the last couple of weeks, they'd been collectively investigating a vast global circle of child traffickers. They'd known of this team previously but had never been able to make any inroads. There had been a few arrests here and there for sure, but the key players had always slipped under the radar. Mary and Rebecca had discussed this group for some time now and both felt if they could stop this mob, it would significantly reduce the numbers of child abductions. With three visionaries working on this, who had all independently identified this gang, the team believed there could be as many as ten-thousand involved.

One of the American officers, Peter said, 'So, finally we have a landing spot. With the help of visionaries Julia, Christine and Sophia, we know the headquarters. As we speak, a crack team is on their trail.'

'That is brilliant news,' Mary said, 'When do you expect to have further news?' Wide eyed, she turned to Rebecca.

'This is the one,' Rebecca said. Oddly though, although she meant this is the one meaning a big win for the team, something in the back of her thoughts was telling her this could be her final mission and... She shook her head.

'Well, Ma'am, on my other screen, I am linked to the team leader directly. With the inroads we have made, we expect to have some kind of conclusion shortly. The headquarters is heavily armed and secure. We have our best squad there though. This specialist team have dealt with many unsavoury groups over the years, so I do not foresee any problems.'

'Okay, this call is due to finish shortly,' Mary said. 'I will, however, keep this channel open, so buzz me as soon as you have any news.'

She turned to Rebecca. 'This is the big one. It alone will make all our efforts worthwhile. I must say though, every team member around the world is in no doubts this would never have happened without you.'

'Well, I am not sure it is just down to me. With your thorough approach you were able to open all the doors.' She then considered her emotions as once more something was suggesting this could be an opportunity to step back and focus more on her family. Over the last few weeks, she'd felt she'd neglected Gabrielle and Duncan and actually couldn't remember the last time she spoke to her mum or dad. No sooner she'd thought that, Mary's online meeting screen opened back up. It was her American counterpart once more.

'Our mission was more than a success. Not only did we capture the key players, we uncovered an extensive list of associates. As we speak, teams around the world are moving in on more than ten-thousand unsavoury individuals. Importantly, we have released several young girls and boys who were being held captive. We expect this pattern to continue, hopefully reuniting many families.'

'Well done, Peter. That is excellent news and far greater than we could have imagined.'

'I must say here and now, on behalf of everyone involved, we want to thank you, Mary and Rebecca. Because of your tireless work, the world is a better place. I would also like to say a personal thank you from my family to you, Rebecca. Your industry with global warming means my children, their children and one day, grandchildren have a beautiful future.'

After the call finished, Rebecca and Mary sat around chatting.

'What next for you, Rebecca?'

Still coming to terms with the team's success, she had only briefly considered her next steps. 'I think some time at home with my family. I can't recall the last time I had a conversation with my mother or father. Similarly, I would love to spend some uninterrupted time with Duncan and Gabrielle as we have tentatively planned a trip to Vancouver to see Faith.'

'You deserve some time away and a well-earned break from proceedings. I will call you if anything significant turns up. With so many people working globally on this, I believe we can both take a little bit of a back seat. Go home now and enjoy this wonderful late summer we are having. Go enjoy some time with your family.'

On the way home, Rebecca once more considered what might be next for her. When she arrived back in the summerhouse, she was a little surprised to find it empty. She then noticed a note. "we are with Nan and Granddad."

She headed up looking forward to catching up with her mum and dad. On the way, she was feeling rather peculiar. She hadn't felt anything like this for some time and wasn't sure what to make of it. It certainly wasn't the feeling she got when she was about to go on another mission. This was a completely different feeling. As she arrived by the main house, she turned and looked back towards the summerhouse. She wasn't sure why she'd done this, just something stirred. She opened the front door and went through to the kitchen. 'hello, Mum, Dad, Duncan. Where is Gab?'

'Hello, Darling,' her mum said, 'She is out the back somewhere.'

Reckoning she would find Gab in the hidden garden, Rebecca said, 'I'll be back, just going to check on her.' For some reason, she gave all three a kiss and cuddle.

'To what do we owe this pleasure?' Her father asked, with slightly narrowed eyes. 'Are you going somewhere?'

Rebecca grinned. 'No, just to check on Gabrielle. See you in a minute.' Once more though, as had happened so many times in the past, her intuition was actually contradicting her. Walking out the back, something was questioning where she was going.

She looked around for Gab and felt certain she'd find her in the garden. She bent down to the secret door, and as she did, once more turned and looked back. She then went through the door and sure enough, Gabrielle was inside sitting on the swing. 'Hello, Sweetness.'

'Hello, Mum. Come and sit on the swing. It is your turn now.'

Although Gabrielle's words were clear enough, something was telling her she meant something else. She headed over and sat on the swing.

Gabrielle held her hand. 'Thank you for everything you've done for me and Faith. I love you, Mother. It is your time now.'

With every inch of her body tingling, her eyes filling with tears, Rebecca then watched as Gabrielle started to blur. She rubbed her eyes, and even though she'd been in a similar scenario so many times before, it had never happened with any of her own family. With tears running down her cheeks, she reached her hand out. Gabrielle had gone. Now with her eyes closed, she sat motionless on the swing trying to work out what had just happened. The reflexive silence was broken by a familiar voice.

'Hello, my dear Rebecca.'

Rebecca opened her eyes to see Meredith standing in front of her. Bizarrely, seeing this gracious woman, it felt as if she'd never been away. To compound these feelings further, not only was her beloved Meredith wearing the same dress she had worn the first time Rebecca met her, she appeared to be the same age she was all those years before. Trying to compose her thoughts, she glanced down. Instantly aware of her own youthful arms and seeing she was wearing the dandy green dress, sent her already tangled emotions spiralling.

'Fear not, my beautiful Daughter. Your journey in that other life is now complete. You are home where you belong. You are once more fifteen and your journey is about to follow new adventures. It is time for you to fulfil your heart with all the love you deserve.'

Author's comments.

Well, I didn't see that coming.

Printed in Great Britain
by Amazon